And tha she saw

"Tom?" she whispered.

At the sound of her voice it turned, twisting around on itself, quicker than a cat, to peer at her with berry-bright eyes. Leaves and thorns tangled where hair should have been. Bark and moss made up the body. Every part of it was composed of living things, of elements of the forest and the trees. It lurched forward, heading straight for the tree line, for her.

Jenny gasped and fell backward, the world tilting. Tom yelled her name and sprinted toward her. The trees surged after him. Vines lashed out, whispering, snapping, tangling around his arms. Roots burst from the ground to trip him. Tom fell with a crash, the air knocked out of him, his eyes wide. The ground heaved beneath them and the roots broke free of the earth, cracking, twining around him, reaching for Jenny.

"Run," her brother shouted, digging his fingers into the earth, trying to gain purchase. He tore up the grass and the dark earth beneath. "Jenny, run!"

With a sound like a million scratching leaves, the trees pulled him away from her and swallowed him in their embrace.

OTHER BOOKS YOU MAY ENJOY

The Treachery
of Beautiful Things

RUTH FRANCES LONG

The Treachery
of Beautiful Things

WITHDRAWN

speak

An Imprint of Penguin Group (USA) Inc.

SPEAK

Published by the Penguin Group

Penguin Group (USA) Inc.

375 Hudson Street

New York, New York 10014, U.S.A.

USA / Canada / UK / Ireland / Australia / New Zealand / India / South Africa / China

Penguin Books Ltd, Registered Offices: 80 Strand, London WC2R 0RL, England

For more information about the Penguin Group visit www.penguin.com

First published in the United States of America by Dial Books for Young Readers, 2012

Published by Speak, an imprint of Penguin Group (USA) Inc., 2013

THE LIBRARY OF CONGRESS HAS CATALOGED THE DIAL BOOKS EDITION AS FOLLOWS:

Long, Ruth Frances

The treachery of beautiful things / by Ruth Frances Long

p. cm.

Summary: Seven years after the forest seemingly swallowed her brother whole, seventeen-year-old Jenny, whose story about Tom's disappearance has never been believed, sets out to finally say goodbye, but instead she is pulled into a mysterious world of faeries and other creatures where nothing is what it seems.

ISBN 978-0-8037-3580-4 (hardcover)

[1. Fantasy. 2. Fairies—Fiction. 3. Kings, queens, rulers, etc. —Fiction. 4. Forests and forestry—Fiction. 5. Love—Fiction.] I. Title.

PZ7.L8578Tr 2012 [Fic]—dc23 2011027165

Speak ISBN 978-0-14-242606-7

Printed in the United States of America

Design by Nancy R. Leo-Kelly

1 3 5 7 9 10 8 6 4 2

For Pat, still my hero, always will be

prologue

The streetlights flickered on outside the window and Jenny looked up from her book. The artificial orange glow etched the silhouettes of leaves and branches against the glass.

In the other room, Tom's flute sang out, trilling through an arpeggio before breaking into "Haste to the Wedding." She heard Mrs. Whitlow laugh. Tom's music could bring delight to anyone, even the vinegar-faced music teacher who had, after two long years of lessons, declared Jenny unteachable. Mother wouldn't hear of that, naturally, so now Tom got a double lesson, and Jenny? More time to read. And their mother was none the wiser.

Jenny absently slid her locket across its chain and turned back to her novel. She liked it better lost in between the words, with Tom's melody filling her head like a musical score.

"All right, shrimp?" Tom was smiling down at her. It was already fully dark outside. She hadn't noticed the time pass. "Ready to go home?"

She looked up at her big brother, taking in his light, slightly rumpled hair, the smile that turned up one cheek, his eyes crinkled at the corners despite their grim, gray cast, and closed her book. Jenny didn't bother with a bookmark. She read like Tom played. Constantly. Hungrily. Her brother already had his backpack slung over his shoulder, the flute sticking carelessly out of it.

"Sure," she said, pretending not to notice his forced cheer. She slid her book into her schoolbag and followed him into the chilly evening. "We're going to be late for tea."

"We'll take the shortcut," he said, hopping down the steps two at a time.

Jenny opened her mouth to argue, but Tom crossed the road before she could say a word. In sunlight, she wouldn't think twice about taking the route past Branley Copse. It cut the trip home in half. But now, with the sun gone down behind the distant hills—

"Oh, come on, Jenny." Lately his laugh had developed a sharp, staccato edge. "Stop being so scared."

Jenny shifted her bag from one shoulder to the other. She couldn't hold it against him. No one could hold anything against Tom. His smile alone, the jokes that hung around his eyes, would soon persuade them to his side.

Tom strode ahead and Jenny ran to catch up before his long strides left her behind. At fourteen, he was already almost as tall as Dad. No wonder he called her shrimp.

"What did she say about the audition?" Jenny finally asked, careful to keep her eyes straight ahead.

Tom shrugged. "It'll be fine. Listen." He reached back and pulled out the flute like a musketeer drawing his sword. The notes floated out through the twilight, haunting and beautiful. For a moment the music beguiled even her. But not entirely. There was something about the stiffness of her brother's shoulders . . . She peered up at him in concern. Tom had a wildness about him tonight, something just a bit desperate, as if his music scared him and yet he needed it. His eyes slid closed, and for a moment she felt like she lost him, or maybe on hearing his music, lost a little part of herself.

They reached the tree line and turned to walk along its edge, leaving the streetlights behind them.

To her left, the ground rose to a mound where the trunks took root, forming a lattice of increasing darkness the deeper she stared into the woods. She and Tom were only cutting along the edge, Jenny reassured herself, not actually going through the trees. And Tom was there beside her, playing his music, just because he could.

Jenny paused, breathing deep for a moment, the notes clear and crisp as the air itself. They floated around her, soared and trilled, setting the hairs on the back of her neck shivering. They reverberated through her body, harmonizing with the rush of blood through her veins. The wind picked up, the trees moving almost in time to the music, the patch of woodland swelling in the darkness to embody something old and vast, the ancient forests that had once covered all the Weald. And all because of Tom's music, she thought distantly. Music that was more than half magic.

Tom broke off abruptly, sighing. The forest seemed to subside, his pied piper trick over. Jenny shook her head. Her imagination. That was all. Dad always said so.

She slid her locket back and forth along its chain nervously.

"You'll twist that right off one of these days," Tom teased. "Then where will you keep your secrets?"

Jenny let go of the empty locket and it fell back against her chest. "I don't have any secrets."

He tilted his head to one side. "Not yet. But you'll need somewhere to keep them when you do, won't you?"

Jenny shrugged. The silence stretched until she remembered her question. "Don't you want to do it?" she asked. "The audition?"

Tom glanced at her with a wry smile. "Mother wants me to do it." He picked up speed, the flute still clutched in his fist. "So that's that. You know what, though?" He only paused for a second, not giving her enough time to answer. "She hasn't thought it through. I mean, she'll have to back off a bit, won't she?"

"Well, maybe." *But doubtful.* Jenny didn't say that bit. His mood was fragile enough. Gifted, they called him, and Tom was, in so many ways. But while the world saw his musical abilities, Jenny saw only her brother. He loved his music, but not the pressure that came with it. From their parents most of all.

There was a sudden rustle of leaves beside her legs and Jenny jumped in alarm. "Did you hear that?" she asked.

"Hear what?" Tom walked on, but Jenny stopped, staring into the dark woods. No light reached inside. The streetlights were too far away, barely illuminating the edge. And the lights of the football field on the other side were still distant. She leaned forward.

There.

Something moved amid the trees, floating like a dream. Something made of leaves and bark, root and branch, but not.

"Tom?" she whispered.

At the sound of her voice it turned, twisting around on itself, quicker than a cat, to peer at her with berry-bright eyes. Leaves and thorns tangled where hair should have been. Bark and moss made up the body. Every part of it was composed of living things, of elements of the forest and the trees. It lurched forward, heading straight for the tree line, for her.

Jenny gasped and fell backward, the world tilting. Tom yelled her name and sprinted toward her. The trees surged after him. Vines lashed out, whispering, snapping, tangling around his arms. Roots burst from the ground to trip him. Tom fell with a crash, the air knocked out of him, his eyes wide. The ground heaved beneath them and the roots broke free of the earth, cracking, twining around him, reaching for Jenny.

"Run," her brother shouted, digging his fingers into the earth, trying to gain purchase. He tore up the grass and the dark earth beneath. "Jenny, run!"

With a sound like a million scratching leaves, the trees pulled him away from her and swallowed him in their embrace.

Jenny scrambled back as the ground beneath her began to buck and rupture. Before she could get her footing, they were on her again. Pulling, grabbing, tightening around her. Roots, vines, thorns tearing into her skin. She screamed. Something stepped right up to the edge of the trees then, gnarled and twisted as ancient bog oak, and everything fell still.

Jenny lifted her head. "Tom?" she whispered uselessly, too quiet to be heard. This was not Tom.

The ageless gaze trailed over her face, assessing, measuring. Then it turned away and was gone, back into the silent woods.

The Treachery
of Beautiful Things

chapter one

The trees had swallowed Tom whole.

How often had she worried at those words, turning them over and over in her mind until they shone like river-polished stones?

Jenny hesitated at the corner of the street, feeling the familiar lure of the trees. She could hear laughter. The sound of children playing in the distance maybe. Or perhaps it was in her head. She wasn't sure. She was never sure. And it never mattered where the trees were. They always called to her, whispered to her to find him. But here . . . here where it had happened . . . She couldn't believe how powerful the pull was here.

Tom had laughed as he strode ahead of her. *Oh, come on, Jenny. Stop being so scared.*

And the trees had swallowed him whole.

Her throat closed up as she remembered the frantic search, the disorienting horror of the woods at night. She'd only been ten, blind with tears and panic, tearing her way through undergrowth and brambles. Hours later when it seemed no time had passed at all, they'd found her with torn clothes, her skin scratched and bleeding, still calling his name. And no Tom.

Nightmares, endless psychiatrists, counselors, hypnotherapy, regression therapy, that face of leaves and wood in her head, and Tom's last, desperate order still ringing out. *Run, Jenny, run.*

For seven years.

Well, she was finished running.

Jenny drew in a breath and the world fell to silence as she stepped onto the grass of the football field. The traffic on Guildford Road and sounds of the village faded to vague echoes. She twisted the cuff of her cotton shirt around her fingers, pulling the fabric tight.

The trees whispered to her, murmuring. She found it easier than she had imagined to cross the playing field and walk up the slope, certainly easier than it had been in all her many nightmares. She was like an ordinary girl walking up an ordinary hill. Nothing unusual here, nothing to see.

She and Tom had come from the other direction that night, but she couldn't possibly have walked back down that path. Just the thought of approaching the trees that way made her stomach twist. And never in the dark. It had to be daytime, in sunlight. As she got close, a familiar ache bloomed in her chest, and cold broke over her body. She stopped. The world lurched around her, as if she were dragged in an instant to the top of a cliff and tumbled over the edge, plummeting.

Jenny focused on her breath, on calming its ragged edges.

They're only trees, she told herself, a well-worn mantra. *This is just in my mind. They're only trees, only trees. Who's afraid of—*

She'd tried this, any number of times, in a dozen or more places. And she'd always failed. The school trip to Sherwood Forest, the first time she actually made it beneath the canopy of leaves, had sent her into dizzy panic. Both breath and heartbeat spiraled rapidly out of control. She thought she'd seen it, just for a moment—that twisted face amid the trees. Just a brief moment and she'd screamed with all the air in her lungs. Loud enough that everyone came running. Loud enough that she'd never been allowed to forget it. How they'd laughed all the way home, a busload of mirth and mockery. And Jenny, sitting straight-backed and alone beside one of the scowling teachers, forcing herself to ignore them all.

They're only trees. Only trees.

Who's afraid of lonely trees?

She took comfort in the silly rhyme, running it through her head in a loop. It had started as a survival mechanism, a way of reminding herself that her fears couldn't be real. The frustrating thing was, it never quite worked.

But she was here now. If she didn't do this, she never would.

At the tree line, Jenny swung her bag around and took out the flowers. They were a bit crushed. She smoothed them out with shaking fingers.

On this, the seventh anniversary of her brother's disappearance, she had come home from the boarding school to which her parents had banished her and gone straight to Branley Copse to say good-bye at last.

Putting it behind her meant moving on. Moving on meant she wasn't going to be marked by something that couldn't have been real, not according to the rest of the world.

But she knew what she had seen.

She knew, didn't she?

Yes. Yes, she had to believe that, or she was indeed crazy.

She'd thought she would cry. Or at least feel something. Staring into the trees through the slanted sunlight, she felt nothing of the hoped-for release. Facing her nightmare, waiting for it to begin anew . . .

But nothing moved.

"Tom?" she whispered, her voice thin. "Can you hear me?"

Nothing, not even a rustle. Not even birdsong. The trees were silent.

"I wanted . . ." The words stuck in her throat. What did she want? To say good-bye and move on? It sounded so simple. "I finished my exams," she said instead. "And I'm done with that school. Thank God. I'm going away to university . . . to Scotland. Special scholarship. They don't want me to, Dad especially. But I can't stay here." With them. With their grief. With the constant, unspoken reminder that she had come home, and Tom had not. Wasn't it meant to get easier in time? But this last year had been worse than ever. The worst of seven terrible years. "Tom?" she whispered.

No answer. And there was never going to be. Tom was gone. Though photos still littered her parents' house, though everyone said she looked like him, Jenny could hardly remember his face sometimes. His real face, not the still image in picture frames. She could remember his laughter that last day, though. She could remember the tune he'd played as they walked here, the tune that had stirred up the trees. Jenny shook her head and was about to turn away when her eyes caught something glinting in the grass.

She spread back the long blades, parting them with fingers that had started to shake again, not from grief this time. Her hand flew to the heart-shaped locket around her neck, the one Tom had given her for her birthday only a couple of months before he'd vanished. He'd told her to put a picture inside, but she'd never been able to do that. Not after.

The breeze rustled the leaves over her head now, and she heard the sound of a flute, only faintly, a tentative invitation. But she couldn't tear her eyes off the thing in the grass—a gold locket, identical to her own.

For a moment, she couldn't move, could hardly force breath into her lungs. Then she reached for it. The air shimmered, a small, isolated heat-haze beneath her outstretched hand. As she disturbed the earth, something stirred underneath, the mud parting and closing as if it breathed. She jerked back her hand and the locket was sucked out of sight, into the dark warmth beneath the grass.

"What—"

A flute struck a cacophonous note.

A voice swore.

Jenny's eyes snapped up to the trees. Every hair stood on end. She scrambled to her feet, her bag spilling onto the ground as it slid off her shoulder. It lay there, forgotten, her phone, lip gloss, and Mother's pills she'd picked up from the doctor tumbling out of it.

It had been a joke between them, that while he played Tom kept tempo with curses, that every phrase was punctuated by a profanity. It used to drive their mother crazy. That was before Tom became so good he could practically charm the birds from the sky. When he played, her heart sang in counterpoint. It was Tom's voice now—Tom's music.

It was Tom.

Jenny didn't think, couldn't allow herself a moment of doubt. With her breath dammed up in her tightening throat, she swallowed her terror and plunged into the shade of the trees.

chapter two

Heat struck her in a wave.

Humidity sucked the air from her mouth. Jenny gasped as beads of sweat freckled her skin. It was hot, hotter than she could ever remember an English summer being. Her jeans and shirt seemed to contract around her body, suffocating her. The boiling breeze made her feel as if she stood before an open oven. It was like the wind that had surrounded her on the beach in the Fuerteventura last summer—the scorching wind that had raced across the Sahara and the sea as if to snatch her away from her parents' latest failed attempt to imitate a normal family.

Now the music of the flute came to life again, the same energetic jig she recognized as "Haste to the Wedding."

Her feet were already moving. She called his name again. Her heart beat the tune's quick rhythm in her chest, and before she knew what she was doing, she had broken into a run.

The path was narrow and twisted, treacherous with mud

and overgrown weeds. She pursued the music, but it was as devious as the trail, dancing on ahead of her and then— impossibly—behind her. Jenny tried to stop, skidded, and went down in a tangled heap. Her hands sank into the mud, cool and slick, sucking at her fingers like a greedy child.

She grunted her disgust and pushed herself back up, turning in a slow circle.

The tune continued merrily, beckoning her to the left, off the path and through the trees. She plunged through under- growth, forcing her way through bushes taller than she was, adding her own curses under her breath, and only pausing occasionally to shout her brother's name.

The piper struck a wrong note and spat out a word she didn't recognize. It didn't even sound like English, but something else, a language lyric and ancient. By its tone, though, unmistakably a curse. She pushed through two bushes, thorns scraping across her skin. It sounded as if he was on the other side, just a few feet away.

"Tom!" she shouted, and stopped just before the drop.

This time there was no music. The forest fell very still. No rustling of leaves, no fluttering of birds. Even the breeze had died down, and the heat had seeped away. She shivered. Beneath her feet, the ground fell away, a cliff of fifty feet that dropped into a depression, cut by a stream.

Where had he gone? Tom wouldn't just run off. Not her brother. He'd always been there for her. Right up until . . . until he wasn't anymore. She turned around, searching the bushes with her eyes. Her heel skidded at the edge, but she caught the branch of the nearest tree, steadying herself. Nothing moved. It was like he'd vanished into thin air.

Jenny shook her head as if trying to clear a fever. This was all wrong. Branley Copse wasn't big enough to contain all this, and certainly no stream went in or out of it. Branley Village wasn't even this big. The forest surrounding her now was ancient, and it showed no sign of having a far side. If she doubled back, she wondered, could she even find her way out?

Then another, more worrying thought struck her. Which way *was* the way back? She had no idea. Carefully, she skirted the edge of the hollow, where a path more suited to mountain goats led her down the steep incline. She was forced to cling to overhanging branches, leaning out perilously to avoid the tangles of briars. At last, the slope grew gentler and the tree cover began to thin. Slender birches replaced the cruder thorn trees, their bark like slivers of tissue paper curling away from the trunks. Green tones stained the sunlight as it fell through their pale leaves and the earth greeted it with a sea of bluebells.

Jenny wandered on, lost in the idyllic surroundings. Once she had watched a horror film someone had snuck into school, in which the main characters had gone astray in a forest, unable to find their way out. Along with the other girls, her sometimes friends, she had laughed at the simplicity of the solution the characters failed to see—to just find a stream and follow it out. She bowed to that advice now, picking her way along the bank. She tried to ignore the fact that she had been walking for much longer than it took to circle the copse, let alone cut through it. She tried to ignore the fact that the flora was different here, that overhead the sky was a clear and cloudless blue rather than the polluted slate-gray-striped-with-jet-trails she had left behind. There was no sign of airplanes, no traffic, no music. Nothing at all.

The silence gnawed at her, an unnatural, dangerous silence, but after a while birdsong slowly returned, and she heard the clamor of various insects she could not hope to identify beyond a grasshopper or a bee. The breeze rustled the trees once more. But the piper, it seemed, was not coming back.

"Looking for someone?" asked a voice.

Jenny stifled a shout and jumped back, but there was no one there, and no heavy undergrowth around her now—nowhere anyone could be hiding. She turned in a circle, searching for the source of the voice amid the birches, and looking, at the same time, for a stick with which to beat off any attacker.

The voice laughed, as surprised by her reaction as she was by its presence.

"Who are you?" Her words came out in a rush. "*Where* are you?"

"Look up once in a while." A boy was sitting in the tree above her head, perched amid the slender braches. His skin was as pale as the birch bark, his eyes unnaturally green. He had golden hair and could be no more than six years old. His legs swung back and forth, heels tapping against the trunk. He went barefoot, his soles stained green, and he wore some kind of tunic, almost the same color as the bark of the tree, like strips of it wrapped around him. She stared, trying to work out what it was. "Are you lost?" he asked.

Jenny blushed and looked up to his face. "I . . . I think I am," she admitted. "I'm looking for someone. Perhaps you've seen him. He was playing a flute. He must have come this way."

The boy raised pale eyebrows. "You're looking for the piper? He was here, yes. But . . . Why are you looking for the piper?"

The piper? It had to be Tom.

"He's my brother." Was it her imagination, or did he draw his dangling legs up out of her reach? "Are you lost too? Or stuck up there? Do you know the way out?"

"You only get one question," the boy said. "He's going back to her, to the castle. Like he always does. If he doesn't, he'll make her mad. And no one wants that. Now go away."

"What castle? What are you talking about?" The only castle nearby was the remains of Guildford Castle, and that was maybe ten miles away. Jenny strained her neck, trying to see the boy as he scrambled higher up his tree. "Come down here," she said, trying to be firm. "I need your help."

"Help? I don't give help. I shouldn't even be talking to you. If you need help, ask the others. Ask the Folletti—they're all over the place and see everything. Ask the air or the stream. Leave me alone."

"What are Folletti?" she called, but the boy was too high now. "Come down. Are you on your own? You shouldn't be in the woods alone." She tried to walk back, to get a better angle on the tree, but her foot snagged on something in the undergrowth and she went sprawling. The ground hit her heavily, driving the air from her lungs, and her head cracked off a stone hidden in the long grass.

Jenny's vision blurred and re-formed, leaving her stunned and aching. She shook her head, rolled onto her side awkwardly, and froze.

A small figure was hovering over a nearby clump of rough grass, bright light suffusing the air around it. The creature had delicate, childish features, set in a curious expression. Tiny wings beat as fast as a hummingbird's, a blur of blue behind its back. Even as she focused on it, it moved away, flitting back and forth, never staying still for more than a fractured moment.

Jenny found a prayer on her lips, one she couldn't quite voice.

"Help me," was all she managed to whisper.

The creature—the boy had said *Folletti*, hadn't he? Was that what these fairies were?—laughed, a trilling sound just on the edge of hearing that made her skin itch. From the corner of her eye, Jenny saw another one blink into existence, and then another. Bright and beautiful as butterflies made of light, they danced through the air around her, continually moving, their presence enchanting. Her fear melted into wonder.

"Fairies?" she whispered. "I must have hit my head harder than I thought."

They all laughed at that, holding their sides and somersaulting through the air. One came right up to her amazed face, looking back at the others to make sure they saw its bravery. Jenny thought it perfect, the features of a tiny child, from huge brown eyes and long lashes, to a rosebud mouth. It pursed its lips and, quicker than light, it planted a kiss on the end of her nose.

Then it twirled away from her, its companions cheering in the same musical tones.

Fairies. Jenny smiled in bewilderment as they darted about her. Their wings made different colored lights as they fluttered, no more than a smudge or a glow behind them to the human eye. The only sound was a faint, high-pitched hum—the sound of the wings themselves—and the trill of their laughter.

Crazy. The girls at school had always said she was crazy. She had half suspected as much for years. And here was proof—tiny, winged, glowing proof.

Ask the Foletti, the boy had said.

No going back now. Embrace the madness, Jenny.

"I need to find my brother," she said. "I heard him playing his flute in here. The boy said he'd gone to the castle. Called him the piper? Can you help me? Please?"

They rolled through the air around her and then one darted forward again, tugging at her shirt. Following its directions, Jenny clambered to her feet and the Folletti tugged again, leading her forward. The others reeled around her, their actions an invitation. Jenny smiled, unable to do anything but let them lead the way. It was like magic. And if this was merely a hallucination, at least it was a beautiful one.

⚜ ⚜ ⚜

The sense of magic didn't last long. The Folletti set a punishing pace from the start. Soon Jenny found herself stumbling in their wake, disorientated and exhausted until, when she rounded a turn in the path, they were gone and she stood alone, panting for breath. In less than an hour, or so it seemed, she felt more lost than ever. She wished she had a watch or a phone. But her phone was in her bag. She let out a groan. She'd left her bag back there at the edge of the copse, its contents spilled all over the grass. What if someone found it? What would they think had happened? Her stomach clenched in on itself and bile rose in her throat. What would her parents think?

Jenny stopped. The path twisted on ahead of her, back into the thicket of thorn trees. Where was she? Sure now that she had doubled back on herself, Jenny tried to get her bearings. What was she doing here? Dad would be sick with worry. Mother . . . Mother would freak. This was insane. The trees stooped over her, and she couldn't tell the sun's position through the dense foliage. Roots, thicker than her entire body, plunged in and out of the earth like a sea serpent's coils. Moss grew everywhere, as heavy as a coat of fur. Ferns clung like exotic parasites to the fallen trunks of lost trees, some dead, but some still living. Rocks and stones broke through the surface of the forest like the bones of an ancient creature. In the shifting, green-gold light, she could sense movement, always hidden, always out of sight, but there. Definitely there. The breeze hissed through the leaves.

Because of the sharp turns in the narrow dirt track, Jenny couldn't see more than a few feet ahead. And through the trees . . . through the breeze . . . she was sure she could hear laughter. And not a pleasant laughter this time. The bright trill of the Folletti vanished. This was a snickering, the sound of mockery, the laughter of people who enjoy the distress of others. She thought of the halls of St. Martha's School for Young Ladies, where Hazel Tully and her cronies held sway. The sounds reminded her of their voices, the way they'd followed her down the dreary corridors, their taunts echoing off the high walls, and something in her chest tightened. Day by day, they'd punctuated her existence with misery. She'd tried to ignore them, but in the end how could she? They'd made sure everyone knew she was different. That she'd lost her brother and told the world the trees had taken him.

But they *had* taken him. She knew for certain now that they had. That thing, it had been real. It was all real. The thought terrified her, and at the same time, it filled her with an unfamiliar rush, a surge of blood to her head, a pounding in her temples. How dare they? Whatever they were, how dare they?

"You're meant to help!" she shouted at the forest. "You're meant to show me the way!" Her voice cracked on the last word.

The snickering turned to tittering and Jenny started forward again. Brambles tore at her legs, tugging at her jeans, and her feet skidded in the mud. Her shoes were mud-slicked and saturated. She could hear her mother's voice even now—that barbed lemon-bitter tone, the implication that she didn't value anything, that she didn't think.

"This isn't fair." Her voice was a whisper. "Mother isn't like that. She's never been like that."

Not really. Not now. But then, Mother had never forgiven her either. Oh, she tried to make up for it with shopping expeditions and "girls' days out." But the memory of Tom, of Jenny coming home alone, it hung between them. That was the reason for St. Martha's. Because having Jenny at home—so like Tom in looks, so different from him in nature—meant their mother could never really move on. She could never forgive her daughter. How could she, when Jenny could never forgive herself?

Now Jenny forced a deep breath, ordered herself to be calm and still her racing thoughts. She'd seen the creature in the forest that evening seven years ago. She wondered suddenly if Tom's music had called it. She'd seen it first. But it had taken *him*. Why?

Something was messing with her thoughts, twisting her memories, pulling all her doubts to the fore and goading them into fury. Seven long years of whispers condensed to this—maybe she was mad, maybe she had imagined it, maybe it was all her fault—

The trees rustled and she was sure she could see movement behind the screening thicket. She could hear laughter, the same strange and sinister laughter, and through the leaves she saw the glow of the Foletti. As she started forward again, she heard a distinct and alien hiss. Turning toward the sound, though her instincts screamed at her to escape, she saw movement out of the corner of her eye.

"What's going—?"

Hiss. Sharp pain jabbed her in the hand.

"Ow!"

Hiss-hiss.

Something stabbed at her neck, her cheek, her ankle, all within a second. She raised her hand to see a trickle of blood from a small cut. Protruding from the tiny wound was a splinter no longer than her little fingernail. She pulled it out and brought her hand to her mouth, tasting a bitter tang mixed into the blood.

Small silver lines cut through the air around her, fissures in this unreal too-real world. Her consciousness lurched inside her skull and she dropped to her knees, all strength snatched from her legs.

Hiss-hiss-hiss.

Pain burst like raindrops over her exposed skin, little pinpricks that robbed her of her senses by heightening them beyond bearing.

The mud felt smooth and slick, marvelously cool. Her jeans and shirt grazed her skin, coarse as old sacking. Her throat scratched with each breath and her straining lungs filled with fire.

She stared at another dart in her hand. She could see it clearly. Too clearly. The end finished in feathers, tiny strands of thread tying them to the shaft in intricate knotwork. She reached out with her other hand—huge and fumbling—and tugged it out. It was topped with a tiny, perfectly formed flint arrowhead. Her own blood glistened on it, and on her skin a red pearl formed around the wound.

Her hand shook violently and went numb, the miniature arrow falling from her grip into the grass.

Hiss-hiss-hiss. Her body jerked convulsively with every tiny impact. She could do nothing to avoid them. One of the Foletti danced closer, its delicate wings a blur. It prodded her with the end of its miniature bow and laughed. Tears rolled from her eyes, fat and scalding on her cheeks and mouth.

"Enough," said a voice, a wonderfully human voice. "Be gone, you vicious little imps. Leave her be."

She felt herself lifted from the ground and a face merged from the blurs, a boy's face, or a man's, or someone just hovering between the two. In that moment he was the most beautiful thing she had ever seen, though his nose was not straight and his eyes were different colors—one green, one blue. Beautiful, but alien somehow. A fresh panic clutched her then. The Foletti had been beautiful and look where that had gotten her. Jenny struggled against his grip, but her body wouldn't obey.

"Hush," he said, sounding almost annoyed. Jenny felt an answering prickle of irritation and tried again to struggle free of him. She hit the ground with a sudden thump and lay there, stunned.

Had he *dropped* her?

She regarded the boy carefully through heavy-lidded eyes. His dark hair was too long, the cut ragged, the cast of his features sharp, and he wore . . . She started as her eyes focused on his clothes. They appeared to be made of leaves.

He smiled grimly at her, and in his mismatched eyes she could see wariness and hope and something else. Something she couldn't quite pin down. A strangeness in his gaze.

"You'll be right soon enough. You've been elfshot by the Foletti, but they're gone now." He glanced behind him.

"Who are you?" she tried to say, but her tongue was too large in her mouth, her lips swollen and dry. "Where . . . ?"

He leaned over her and she tensed. But he only moved her head so it was out of the mud, letting it down on soft moss instead and gingerly drawing back, as if loath to touch her at all. Then he sat back on his heels and studied her a moment, lifting a hand as if to lay it on her burning forehead, but pulling away when she flinched.

"I'm Jack."

Her eyes were growing heavy. They closed, but she forced them open again. Should she tell him her name? She searched his face, trying to make sense of him. "Jenny," she finally mumbled, still not entirely sure she should have.

"Hush then, Jenny." He smiled fully then, such a beautiful

smile. She scowled—or tried to. Beautiful boys didn't smile at her. She was too tall, too skinny, too *strange* for that. But this boy, this Jack, didn't seem to notice, and she was growing sleepier by the second. He leaned over her again. "You must sleep and let your body purge itself of their drugs. Hush now. I'll keep a watch, I swear it. When you wake I'll take you back to the Edge."

She frowned. "Can't . . ." she mumbled, finally dredging up enough strength to lift her arms and push him away. Well, push him, anyway. He didn't move. "Have to find Tom."

His smile melted into confusion. "Tom?"

"My brother. Have to . . ." Her voice shook and she tried to focus her vision. It defied her, swirling until her stomach threatened to empty itself.

Then a strange thing happened. Jack took her hand. Instinctively she wanted to pull away, but his grip was firm, and she'd used up the last ounce of energy left to her. Her muscles went limp, a tingling replacing any feeling in her fingertips.

"Later. Sleep now. It will be all right. I'll help you home, Jenny Wren. It's my duty to do so as Guardian of the Edge. No harm will befall you. I promise you this."

He sounded determined, as if she had no choice but to believe him, as if he was so used to being trusted that it didn't occur to him she'd find any of this odd.

And he'd called her Jenny Wren. A frown flickered over

her forehead. A strange name to use, like something Shakespeare would have written. If only she could recall it now. English classes were a very long way away and Mrs. Granger's droning voice had never made iambic pentameter flow like the poetry she claimed it was . . .

The ragged remains of her strength ran away from her like water through cupped hands. As darkness enveloped her, she caught sight of one more wonder, something else that had to be part of her fevered imagination. A man stood behind Jack, a little man, so small he would only come up to her hips. His lower body was covered in thick brown fur, like a dog's, and from his forehead two little horns projected. Goat's horns. He had goat's feet too. A name came to her, though rationality rejected it. But then, what was rational here? She was lying in a forest that didn't exist, watched over by a boy dressed in leaves with wildwood eyes who had dropped her on the ground.

As if sensing her discomfort, Jack's hand came up again. And this time he did brush her forehead, his cool fingers smoothing back her hair. She wanted to push his hand away, but couldn't find the strength. He murmured words she couldn't place.

"Never harm, nor spell, nor charm, come our lovely lady nigh . . ." He murmured rhymes that flowed over her like a lullaby, and she surrendered to sleep.

chapter three

"Be honest with yourself, Jack," said Puck. He rocked forward, chuckling to himself in that odd, infuriating way of his. "Can you look into her eyes and manage as much as a word that isn't a lie?"

Jack scowled and turned his back on the hobgoblin. He wasn't going to give the little devil the satisfaction of an answer.

Puck just broadened his smile and edged closer. "For one who claims to be friend to the lost, you don't act much like it."

"She doesn't need friends. She needs to get out of the Realm. Then she can make all the friends she wants. I'm just guarding the border, that's all. I'm just doing my job."

"Oh, aye. That's all you ever do, isn't it?" Puck slipped past him and knelt over the sleeping girl. His tail twitched, the coarse brown hair of his rump shivering in such close proximity to a mortal. "She's fair, though," he commented, and stretched out a hand toward her flushed skin. "Well, for a mortal."

It was true. A thin sheen of sweat glistened on her brow and the dampened hair at the edge of her face curled back, tiny curls, much darker than the chestnut tones of the rest. She had freckles too, a sprinkling of dapples across her nose and at the sides of her face.

Jack couldn't remember the last time he had seen freckles on a woman's flesh. The Sidhe were pale and flawless and all the fae were wont to imitate them, but this girl, this Jenny, was more perfect by far. She bristled like a hedgehog, though, and had a streak of stubbornness—the way she set her chin and glared . . . Jack hoped she wouldn't give him trouble.

"Shame she's elfshot, or there'd be some sport in her, I feel." Puck grinned up at him and twisted one of her curls around his dirt-soiled fingers.

With a snarl that surprised even himself, Jack seized the hobgoblin and hauled him back.

"Leave her be, you foul little thing."

Puck's laughter rang through the glade, answered by a dozen or more other voices gathered out of sight around them. So they were watching, the wee folk, watching and mocking. The Foletti loved their sport. Jack released him and moved back to crouch over Jenny, guarding her from them. If they could, they'd carry her off. And if they managed that . . .

Jack bared his teeth, and he drew his flint knife.

"Feeling protective, are you, Jack?" Puck asked, his

mocking tone more pronounced now. Friend and companion though he was, Puck could be a vindictive little toad, and he had no love of mortals beyond the poems they wove. "That's the lure of innocence you're feeling. Beware of it, lad, or she'll try to make you her own. Aye, and when the queen finds out . . ."

Jack's shoulders tensed at the mention of Titania.

The laughter surged again, trees and shrubs shaking with the Foletti's mirth. Oh, it was all too hilarious to them, all right.

"I don't belong to the queen."

"Try explaining that to her," Puck said, but there was no laughter this time. "Or to himself."

"Get gone, all of you," Jack ordered, to Puck, to those he could see amid the trees, and to those he could not. "I've watch of this place and I'll keep the peace. Go, Goodfellow, and take your folk with you. There will be no 'sport' here this day. Understand?"

"Elfshot is suggestible, Jack. Remember that when she wakes, and mayhap she can be made a threat to you no more."

He glanced at her sleeping face. "She's no threat." And yet he gripped the knife a little tighter.

"No threat?" Puck echoed, no longer visible, but his voice was as clear as if he stood at Jack's ear. "Woe to you Jack, if you deceive yourself so."

He laughed as he retreated. Jack looked up, an emptiness

opening inside him, a dark and cold place where his heart should be.

"Puck? We have to send her back."

The hobgoblin stopped and made himself visible again, looking back over his shoulder. "Are you asking for my help now?"

Jack scrubbed a hand over his face, shifting uncomfortably at the thought. He couldn't do this on his own. There was nighttime to consider. She would need a guardian in the Realm, and he could not do that come nightfall. He had duties that would not be ignored.

"Night will be falling soon enough. I—I'm asking for help. Please, Robin Goodfellow, help me and I will owe you a debt."

Puck turned back and gave a gracious bow. "I'll listen to your terms then, Jack o' the Forest."

"You'll help me watch her, tend her, and you'll not harm her. I'll have your word on that. When she wakes, we'll take her back to the Edge."

Puck sat down opposite him, his expression serious now. "But she won't go back. You heard her. She seeks her brother. She's on a quest."

A quest did complicate things. As honor-bound as he was to defend the borders and guide the lost, Jack was also oath-bound to aid all on a quest. Only his duty to the king outdid that. He pursed his lips. There was one way. A way of working around what his honor and oath said he should do. A way to get rid of her, and quickly, though to contemplate saying it was like a bone lodged in his throat. Puck was grinning, his mouth wide, all his teeth on display. He knew it too and knew how offensive Jack found the idea. Oh, hilarious indeed.

"As you said," Jack told him solemnly, "elfshot is suggestible." He hesitated and then plunged on, his words tumbling out of his mouth. If he paused again, he wouldn't have the stomach to finish. Honor be damned, the Realm was too dangerous for the likes of her. "We persuade her to go back, as soon as she wakes up. We get her out of the Realm as soon as possible."

"It's too late to get to the Edge before nightfall," Puck replied, eyeing Jack dubiously. "Far too late. She wouldn't be safe."

"Not alone. But we can get her to a guide, someone to take her the rest of the way this very night, someone who isn't bound as I am. The Woodsman could take her there."

Puck raised his eyebrows. "The Woodsman? Now there's a thought. You want me to find him and get a promise from him."

Jack nodded and his hand fell to almost brush Jenny's cheek again. He didn't touch her, though. Not quite. But he remembered. Her skin was as soft as the inside of flower petals, and so warm. He could feel the heat that rose from her. And her scent, like nothing he'd ever encountered. It was unnerving. More than unnerving. "And find out what the Foletti know. You can make them tell you anything. How did she get here? And where from?"

Puck scrambled to his feet, watching the pair unsurely. His tone gentled now, the mockery gone. "I wasn't joking about being wary of her, Jack. There's nothing so dangerous to us as her kind of innocence. Can't you see it in her? She shines."

Jack's hand recoiled from its place just above her cheek and he moved back, knotting his fingers in the grass. It felt real to him, a cool reminder of what was what. Puck was right, and that stirred more than doubt in Jack's mind. It stirred fear. "Just hurry. Be back well before dark."

᪥ ᪥ ᪥

Jenny's skin itched as if she'd rolled in nettles. She'd done that once. Tom had pushed her into a patch in the garden and spent weeks doing her chores to make up for it. That had just been her arms. This time she ached everywhere. Before she could wonder why, the memory jerked through her like electricity. She sucked in a breath and realized something else. She was being watched.

She knew it somehow, an unshakeable instinct. Knew it in the way an animal senses a hunter. A shiver crawled over the back of her neck on spindly legs. She tried to keep her breathing steady and at the same time open her eyes just a slit. Something betrayed her. She wasn't sure what, but the moment she saw his gaze fixed on her, she realized by the bitter quirk of his lips that Jack had seen through her pretense.

"How are you feeling?" he asked at length. "Often the elf-shot complain about headaches and pained breathing."

"No, I'm . . . I'm fine." Jenny pushed herself up, trying to ignore the sway of the world around her and the sickening lurch of her stomach. She wondered briefly if nausea was also a symptom of being . . . elfshot? She squinted up at him. "Who are you?" She knew, of course. But she wanted to hear him say it again, just to check.

He didn't seem fazed in the slightest. "I'm Jack."

"Jack. Right." A guardian, he'd called himself. Or something like that. She went to stand—she was fine; he didn't need to watch her like a hawk—but when she tried, her legs wobbled and she went down in a tangle of limbs.

He moved more quickly than she would have thought possible, not darting or rapid, not by any means overly eager to be closer to her, but as if he flew through the space between movements. He crouched suddenly at her side, his head cocked over toward his left shoulder, and caught her before her head could hit the ground. His was the swiftness of a wild animal.

She shook him off and rolled over, fighting the urge to scratch through her skin or, worse, vomit.

"Lie still and rest, Jenny Wren. We'll have you to safety and back home again in no time. I'll find you a guide to take you back to the borders."

Jenny rolled onto her back again and lay there, glaring at him.

"No," she said slowly. "I told you. I have to find my brother. I heard him playing." Jenny paused, squinting at him. "Why did you stay if you're so eager to be rid of me?"

Jack ignored this. "I think you must have been mistaken about your brother. The woods can play tricks with sound, you know."

She blinked her eyes and tried to focus on that thought. He was right, if you looked at it that way. The way the woods had been . . . the noises . . . the things she had seen . . . And yet, he was sitting in front of her wearing clothes made of leaves. She resisted the urge to pinch herself. Or, better yet, pinch him, hard enough to hurt.

But that would mean touching him. And if she touched him . . .

Jenny shook her head.

"You're real enough," she said. "And you aren't quite . . ." To say *normal* sounded so rude. *Human* would probably be worse. Her voice choked in her throat and she stared up at him. He had the most beautiful eyes she had ever seen. They caught the sunlight, the color so bright . . .

God, what was she thinking? She scowled at him.

If Jack noticed, it didn't seem to bother him.

"I'm as normal as you'll find around here." Was that amusement in his voice? Was he laughing at her?

Jenny held his gaze, trying to ignore the heat rising in her skin. He had so easily known what she wanted to say, as if he had plucked the thought out of her mind. God, what was *normal* about him?

"Look at you, at your clothes . . ." she said.

Jack laughed, and it was as if the birds in the trees joined in delightedly. "My clothes are normal too, aren't they?"

Even as he said it, she realized that he was wearing a green T-shirt with an abstract pattern like falling leaves and cargo pants, and nothing more exotic than that. Jenny's face burned hot and she felt tears sting her eyes. But it *had* been real. She'd heard Tom, she'd seen the Foletti, she'd been so sure. This time. It had been real.

"Don't lie to me. I was sure I heard Tom. And the things I saw . . ."

Jack got to his feet and helped her up, holding her hand long enough for her to feel the warmth of his skin. She pulled herself free as soon as she was standing.

"Maybe you hit your head when you fell, you know? Dreams can be so very vivid."

"A dream?" It made sense. Of course it made sense. She had fallen and hit her head and it was only after that she had seen all those strange things, wasn't it? After Tom had vanished, she had dreamed so many times that he was back. She searched for him in so many places. She'd thought she'd find him if she looked in enough of the woodland places of the world. If only she could make herself actually go in among the trees. She wished it. And so dreamed it. Dreams just as real, as vivid as this.

Jenny stared at Jack now, studying him for some sort of clue. The boys she'd known—and there weren't many— didn't look like him, didn't act like him. For all their bravado, they never seemed comfortable in their own skin. And that face. She frowned. No one was that good-looking and didn't know it. For all he appeared oblivious, he had to realize. His eyes hid far too much.

A rustling shook the bushes behind them and a figure pushed its way through, as tall as her waist and half covered in coarse hair—half man, half goat. Jenny screamed and crashed back into a shrub. Jack caught her again. She shook him off and he released her too quickly, as if he couldn't wait to be rid of her.

"It's only my dog," he said calmly. "Don't be afraid."

The world blurred, re-formed, remade itself into something . . . normal . . .

The brown mongrel wagged its tail, but seemed to glare at Jack with murder in its liquid brown eyes. Jenny glanced back just in time to see Jack's lips quirk into a smile and he knelt down to pet the dog. It bared its teeth at him and skulked off behind his legs. This wasn't right. She knew it wasn't. And yet there it was, playing out before her, perfectly normal. Jenny stepped back. Though not as hot as when she first stepped into the trees, the forest was still unseasonably warm. It stifled her breath. She didn't know where she was. If only it had been real. If only she could have truly found her brother.

A hallucination? Her heart thudded against her ribs and her stomach seemed to drop away inside her, leaving only emptiness. It hadn't been real. It had just been another . . . another *incident*.

She could imagine Dr. Griffin's face if she described this to him, right before he reached for the prescription pad.

She closed her hand tightly around the locket until it pressed its shape deeply into her palm. Not again. Never again.

Jack's voice was very soft as he talked to his dog, but the sudden breeze lifted the words and carried them to her. It was a strange conversation to be having with an animal.

"And what did he say?" He paused, ruffling the dog's hair. The creature all but snapped at him. "Good, good. We can be there before nightfall." The dog's eyes slid to hers, glaring, and she was sure she saw more intelligence in them than was possible. She stared at her muddy shoes, not really seeing them.

"It's all going to be fine. You'll see." Jack got to his feet and smiled at her brightly. The forest's hues seemed to fade when he smiled like that, all the wondrous color absorbed into his face alone. Jenny found herself returning it and felt strangely better. Jack held out a hand that folded around hers in a grip at once overpowering and comforting. "I'll take you to my friend's house. He'll see you home."

With her last hope of finding Tom fading, what could Jenny do but accept? She followed Jack, the smile slipping from her mouth as he released her hand.

chapter four

They must have walked for an hour or more, Jack leading the way along the narrow woodland paths. He never spoke, and Jenny had begun to wonder if he was ignoring her. The dog trailed behind them sullenly. Jenny glanced back at it from time to time, struck with the uncomfortable feeling that it was muttering under its breath. She had almost managed to ignore it and focus on the path ahead when Jack stopped abruptly, his body still. Jenny stumbled off the path to avoid walking into him, and she was sure the dog laughed. Almost sure. Because dogs didn't laugh.

Jack lifted his head as if he was smelling the air.

He was certainly odd.

"What is it?" she asked.

He held up his hand, like a soldier signaling for silence.

And he was certainly bossy.

Then his body twitched as a noise like distant thunder came from ahead of them. Muscles tensed all across his back. He cocked his head to one side, listening intently.

A figure stepped from between the trees ahead of them, a girl, dressed in a pale green sundress. She moved with quick, delicate movements, her sharply pointed face strangely beautiful and yet not—too thin, the features too narrow and long. She started and turned, stared at Jack and Jenny, her pale green eyes moist with fear. Her tiny mouth opened wide—too wide, as if her jaw detached. Jack jerked his head to the side urgently, an unmistakable signal to get out of the way, and she darted off, quicker than a rabbit, vanishing from sight. Before Jenny could say a word, Jack had grabbed her arm and was pulling her into the bushes, the dog darting ahead of them.

"Stay silent," he hissed. "Stay down."

Jenny opened her mouth to argue but thought better of it. Jack seemed . . . not scared, exactly. But his eyes had deepened to a hard green and blue, almost metallic. His pupils widened to deep black circles. She lay in the dirt under the bush and stared ahead, wondering what on earth was going on now. A smell filled the air then, the heavy aroma of flowers and overripe fruit, a thick stew of sweetness. It filled her nose and mouth, making her throat close with the need to gag, and then slowly faded to something perfumed and fragrant but bearable once again. Beautiful, in fact. Her head swam in it.

Just a few seconds later, horses galloped into the broad and airy clearing ahead, slowed and finally stopped, milling about as their riders chatted and laughed. Long-legged and elegant, the horses were the color of milk and cream. Their harnesses hung with bells that had been drowned in the noise of their hooves, but now made music as the creatures twitched and stamped.

And the riders.

Jenny stared, all thoughts of Jack and his strange mood forgotten. There were twelve of them, so beautiful they held her gaze like light glinting off the edge of a blade. They sat on their pale horses, almost human, almost angels, with a hint of something wicked shadowing every gesture. The men were all tall and broad-shouldered. The women laughed like birds and had eyes like hunting cats. They were all dressed in silks and velvets, flowing robes that could have graced the halls of Camelot.

In their center, a woman—more wondrous and terrifying than any of the rest—lifted her face to the sunlight and closed her eyes. She swayed slightly, like a snake scenting prey, but otherwise sat very still, as if listening to the air around her. Jenny felt an uncanny surety that the sounds of the forest were familiar to her as a childhood melody, that they told her far more than Jenny could ever decipher from them. The woman sat sidesaddle on her horse, her green-and-gold gown sewn with glistening threads in a pattern of flowers and vines. Her golden hair had been twisted in intricate braids and knotwork and studded with gleaming jewels. Her eyes glistened in the sunlight, two diamonds, harder and colder than any she wore. As she turned her gaze toward the bushes where Jenny and Jack hid, Jenny felt herself shrink back instinctively, a rising need to escape making her squirm in the dirt. Jack reached out silently and enfolded her hand in his. The gesture surprised her, and her instinct was to jerk out of his grasp. But she didn't. Instead her muscles turned sluggish and unresponsive. Why weren't they running? Why was Jack, so eager to get rid of her, preventing her now from fleeing?

Jack whispered something and glanced at the dog, who shrugged—*how could a dog shrug?* The thought shrank away from Jenny's mind as quickly as it came, and the air around them shimmered, as if sealing them off from the rest of the forest. Jack sighed, but he didn't let Jenny go. The warmth of his touch made her fingers feel even colder.

One of the men slid from his horse's back, moving with the grace and innate strength of a dancer or an assassin, and knelt down, pressing his hands to the soft earth. "He came through here, my queen, without a doubt. Probably less than an hour since. And others, more recently, something—"

"Which way did he go?" Despite the sharp interruption, the queen's voice sang rather than spoke. Jenny couldn't tear her eyes away. Her senses seemed to burn with an intensity so extreme it hurt. She was both attracted and repelled by this figure, wanting at once to escape and to throw herself at the queen's feet and beg the woman to look with pleasure on her.

"I—" The tracker faltered. "I know not, my queen."

"Fool," she sighed, as though his failure did not concern her, and yet, when the man turned away and Jenny could see his face, he looked stricken, terrified. "Maybe I should send you as tithe instead of the piper. You'd do just as well, if they'd deign to have you."

Jenny started at the words—*the piper*. Tom was the piper, wasn't he? Who else could it be? The boy in the tree had recoiled when she said he was her brother. She *remembered* the boy. Why did it feel like she'd forgotten him? And what was a tithe? She glanced at Jack, but he stared ahead, his eyes dark, burning with some strange emotion she couldn't place.

Then the queen began speaking again and all thoughts of Jack or Tom slid from Jenny's mind.

"No, not you," the queen told her tracker. Her tone was sharp as a needle. "No one but the dogs would have you." The man glanced back at her, his whole body stiffening, his eyes widening. And then he ran, sprinting from the clearing like something flung from a catapult.

The queen lifted her chin and let out a very high, undulating whistle. Jack's hand tightened on Jenny's and the urge to pull away flared again. But she couldn't move. Fear held her more firmly in place than Jack could.

For a moment there was nothing. Then, from the distance, Jenny heard a pack of dogs barking. They burst into the clearing and through it without pause, a host of white hounds, fleet as racing dogs but double their size. Jenny saw little more than a blur of white fur with patches of red, and their teeth. It was impossible to miss their teeth.

Beside her, Jack recoiled unexpectedly, his other hand clamping tight on her arm, and Jenny almost cried out. She bit back the sound just in time and turned to find herself face-to-face with the forest boy, clad once more in leaves, his blue and green eyes inches from her face. Her own gaze flicked back and forth from eye to eye, her mind scrambling to keep up, to process this new information in the face of something even more damning—the knowledge now rising up as if from the ground itself and filling her, the knowledge that somehow he'd tricked her. He'd lied to her. He'd wanted to get rid of her at any cost, even if it meant taking her hope and strangling it with a spell.

He'd made her believe she was crazy.

Black rage welled up inside her like a volcano about to blow, but before she could open her mouth or draw back her fist, one sound made her freeze with dread.

A scream rang out amid the snarls of the dogs, just beyond the clearing where the hunter had fled. And then silence.

Jenny looked back to the clearing where the horses and their riders still gathered. The queen sat, undisturbed by the sounds, and then gave a second whistle, less shrill this time. The sound of the white hounds faded until a single howl rang out in the still forest.

The queen smiled and Jenny caught a glimpse of her eyes, darkly shadowed and ancient. No longer beautiful. Something else lurked behind the stunning exterior. Something dark and hungry. Something not human.

But then, nothing here was human, was it? Jenny looked back at Jack, at his leaves and his wildwood eyes, at the stone blade strapped to his hip, at the odd cast to his features. He met her stare impassively. Nothing was human here but her. And anything to the contrary was a lie.

The queen's presence pulled Jenny's gaze back around. She didn't fight it this time. The sight of Jack filled her with a contempt and sorrow she couldn't explain.

"South," the queen declared. "My pets have him cornered, I believe. Soon my piper will be returned to our home. If he fears the blood tithe, he should think better of incurring my wrath. No amount of magic will draw another as well-suited as he is, no matter what he thinks. Follow me." She urged her own mount forward and the horse flattened its ears before tearing out of the clearing and along the forest path ahead of the others. Her companions, just ten of them now, were only a moment behind her. The horses thundered from the clearing, the earth beneath Jack and Jenny trembling with their passage. And then all was still.

They waited, their harsh breath the only sound around them.

"Come on," Jack said at last. "Let's get you to safety."

"*Really?*" Jenny burst out. "What— Who was she? Who are *you*?"

"You don't need to know. You just need to get home." He wriggled out from under the bushes and then bent to help her. She ignored him, struggling to her feet herself, cold and wet, her clothes streaked with mud.

"Come on, Puck. Get out and let's be going."

Puck.

Jenny stared.

The creature that emerged from the bushes was no dog. Jenny flinched at a sight that couldn't be true. Had to be a dream but wasn't. What was this place? She shifted her gaze to Jack, anger brewing again. He was clad not in cargo pants and a T-shirt, but in leaves. Leaves! Just as she had first believed. Her heart hammered. She swallowed. It was all real. All of it. No matter what they had tried to make her believe, all those psychiatrists she'd been paraded in front of. And even Jack himself. He had lied to her, tricked her, and now he told her she didn't need to know?

Jenny folded her arms across her body and planted her muddy feet on the ground.

"He isn't a dog," she said, making each word as sharp as glass.

The little man with goat's legs grinned at her. Jenny chose to ignore him. Ready as she was to face this reality, she wasn't sure about willingly speaking to a mythological creature just yet.

"Yes, he is," Jack replied, without so much as a glance at her.

Jenny had never taken well to being dismissed. Out of habit, she stood a little straighter, the muscles across her back and shoulders tightening. She twisted the end of her shirt-sleeve, knotting her fingers into the soft cotton.

"No," she replied, biting off the word. "He isn't." So, Jack was going to continue the lie, was he? Fine. She would address the creature itself. "What are you?"

The little man bowed, still grinning that filthy grin. "Robin Goodfellow at thy service, lass."

Something inside her balked, but she kept her stance. She had known, of course, had known all along. She had seen him before she'd blacked out, hadn't she? She balled her hands into fists until her nails bit into her palms. It would have been so much better if he was just a fever dream.

But would it?

If this was real, if it was truly real—

What had Jack done to her? She remembered the warmth

of his hand on hers, the way her doubts and protests had faded away when he touched her. How had he made her see things? Anger now warred with a fierce exhilaration. It was real!

She lifted her chin, waiting.

"Puck!" Jack exclaimed.

"It's worn off, lad. She knows it, and you should admit it too. You can't influence her when she's not elfshot."

Jack turned to Jenny now. She met his eyes.

His stubborn expression mirrored her own back at her. The urge to slap him made her grit her teeth until they ached.

"All right. Fine." He scowled at her even as he acquiesced. "But no one is going to believe you when you get home."

She met his words with silence at first. Then a sound punctured the air. It took Jenny a moment to realize it came from her. A laugh, brief and broken, almost like a bark. Another slipped from her lips. And another, growing and growing until she had no choice but to unwind and let it go free. The sound rang out across the forest and birds took flight. She couldn't stop. She ought to. There was every chance the hunters would hear and come back. But she couldn't. She threw back her head and let the laughter gasp out of her in waves, tears streaming down her face, her body hurting from the lack of air.

A furrow had formed between Jack's eyes. He put a hand

out, but Jenny slapped it away. Puck grinned, dancing from
foot to foot, reveling in this madness. And slowly, gradually,
Jenny regained herself. After the absurdity of it, reality swept
in on swift and heavy wings. The weight of it fell over her,
forcing her onto her knees. She gasped for breath, crippled
and bent double, the laughter fading as she struggled to
breathe. Oh God, she was going to have to go through it all
again. All the snide remarks, the sidelong glances, the psychiatrists, her mother's accusing eyes, her wringing hands,
Dad pacing back and forth for hours, the still face of Tom in
all those photographs—

But this time . . . this time at least she knew it was real.

"You think I don't know that?" She gulped, glaring up at
Jack, smothering her hysteria. "Of course no one will believe
me. They never did. They nod and smile and then talk
behind your back. And they laugh. There's nothing you can
do to stop them from laughing. Isn't even worth the effort.
Have you ever had people laugh behind your back?"

Of course he hadn't. Look at him.

His scowl, if possible, got even harder. "Then you understand," he said to her, "that there's no point in discussing
these events when you get home. And home you must get."
He glanced at the sun hovering just above the treetops, the
shadows of the leaves passing over his eyes. Jenny looked
away, afraid she would punch him otherwise. "If you stay
here any longer," he said, "your danger will deepen, Jenny

Wren. You saw the queen. You don't want to attract her attention, do you?"

For a moment Jenny almost said yes. It was a wild and reckless need, like standing on the edge of a tall building with the urge to jump coiling through her body. Now thoughts of the queen consumed her, greedily filling her mind.

"Why should I attract her attention at all?"

Jack approached her warily, animal-like again, and reached to take her hand. She snatched it away, putting both arms behind her back where he couldn't reach them. She wasn't making that mistake again. Jack's expression didn't change, but his outstretched hand fell back to his side.

"Because you're a mortal, and she sees any mortal in this Realm as hers to take, her prize, her prey. You're outside her power, independent of her. She has no hold over you and no way to bend you to her will unless you agree to it. And she hates that. She is Titania, the queen, who was once called Mab. They are one and the same, power upon power. Because somehow, and I don't know how, you can see through our illusions. You can see things in the Realm as they are. Which makes you a threat." Jenny opened her mouth to interrupt, but Jack continued. "Listen to me. I can get you to safety, but we need to go now."

"He speaks the truth, lass," said Puck, suddenly solemn. "Mab is old and hungry."

Jenny rolled back on her heels, the forest seeming to close around her. The Realm? Titania? *Mab?* She'd seen the darkness lurking beneath Titania's beauty, the flash of evil. Was that Mab? She shuddered, staring up at the trees around them.

And Jenny herself, a threat to someone—some*thing*—like that? The world seemed to twist around her. How was that even possible? Jack had deceived her, but for a reason. To get her home. Still, she didn't want to go home. She wanted to find Tom. As far as she was concerned, the *reason* Jack had lied was no better than the lie itself. No, she would not go home.

But then Jenny remembered the look in that woman's eyes . . . and she knew Jack and Puck were right. She did not want to encounter the queen again. The pull the woman seemed to exert over everything around her . . . Jenny had felt it. Like a drug in physical form.

"Who were they hunting?" she finally asked. "That girl?"

"No. She was just . . . she was just hiding, like us."

"What was she?" And how would she have looked without Jack's spell warping the world, Jenny wondered with a shiver.

"Only a Dame Verte. Simple souls, tree guardians, gentle and kind. She was just trying to avoid the hunt. The Dames are no threat to anyone."

"And the boy in the birch tree?"

Jack smiled, a gently amused expression. It suited him, but she wasn't particularly pleased to see it there. It irked her.

"Most likely a birch-boy," he said with a laugh. "They're all over the forest. A tree spirit, like her. Harmless."

"The Folletti weren't harmless," she muttered.

"No. Probably not. They like their tricks. But they aren't malicious." Jenny narrowed her eyes dubiously and Jack's face grew a little pained. "They're like children with a toy. They don't understand that sometimes it can break."

Jenny rolled her eyes. *Break.* Lovely. But now she was getting somewhere. At last. "And the piper?"

Jack ducked his head; the smile slid off his face and Puck shifted his feet. Did they exchange a glance? She wasn't sure.

"The court is forever playing games of the queen's invention," Jack said, his words a mask over something.

"She said the piper, Jack. Who's the piper?"

The need to know made her heart ache, and at the same time she dreaded finding out. It didn't matter, though; Jack wasn't going to give her a straight answer.

"Her servant, Jenny Wren. That's all. A servant in her castle. And it doesn't do to get in the way of the Wild Hunt. Come, Jenny, please. I'll take you to the Woodsman and his Goodwife. He knows the forest, serves as a guide too. He will take you home before the moon has even risen. They are our friends. You can trust them."

⚶ ⚶ ⚶

They reached another, much bigger clearing as the sun slid low. Jack glanced behind them with every other step and looked often at the fading light in the sky. His answers, those he would give anyway, were curt.

Jenny stamped along behind him, struggling to keep her features expressionless. She'd have to bide her time. And then find Tom herself. Maybe she could persuade Jack's friends to help her instead. Maybe they'd set her on her way to find Tom. No matter what, she'd be better off free of Jack and his constant insistence that she go home.

The ground began to slope down to a narrow stream, and on the nearest bank there was a cottage and stables. Jenny frowned, the fleeting thought that it should be made of gingerbread brushing across her mind. The door opened and a plump woman wearing a shapeless brown dress and starched white apron came out.

"Go on." With a firm but gentle hand, Jack pushed Jenny clear of the last trees. The Woodsman's wife laid a bowl of cream down at the doorstep and straightened up, smiling. Her sharp eyes snagged on Jenny at once, standing bedraggled and miserable at the tree line.

The woman studied her for a second and then her gaze moved onward, behind her to where Jack still stood.

"Jack? Who've you brought to us?"

"A friend in need. Thought your good husband could

guide her back to the Edge this evening." He stepped back and the forest seemed to draw in around him, shielding him from her.

"Come here, love," said the Goodwife. "You don't want to be among the trees come nightfall. And you look half starved."

"She'll help you," said Jack, glancing up at the sky's fading light once more. "Keep you safe. Get you—" He broke off with a curse, a sharp-edged and violent word in a language she didn't know. When he next looked at her, he was frowning. "Wait, I should have said. Don't eat their food. They're good people, generous, but you can't accept a meal they prepare. Fruit, milk, anything grown naturally is fine, but food prepared by fae hands has a way of trapping you here." He looked at her, mismatched eyes searching her face. "Do you understand?"

This just got better and better. First he wanted to get rid of her, then palm her off on someone else, and now—

"No food. Right." She was already ravenous, couldn't remember the last time she had eaten, and now she wasn't allowed to eat at all? *Had he said fae hands?* The woman looked human. But then again, she'd already discovered looks could be deceptive here.

"No pies, no porridge, anything like that. They know it, so you'll be safe with them. But, just in case you're tempted. Faerie food stays with you, it changes you—"

"*Faerie* food?" Jenny said, frowning back at him. This seemed to exasperate him more.

"If you take some willingly," Jack rushed on, "you're tied to the Realm forever, even if you manage to leave. If it's forced on you, then the spell doesn't work. But if you accept what is offered— Just remember."

"What about you?" The words slipped out before she could stop them. She didn't care what he did, or what became of him.

"Me?" Jack laughed, a brittle sound now, not the sweet music of earlier, when she'd first pointed out that he was dressed in leaves . . . and he had deceived her with a trick. "I'm Jack o' the Forest, Jenny Wren. I'm the guardian. My place is here. Go on. The Goodwife's husband can guide you back to the Edge, to the gateway, and home." He glanced toward the sky. "And don't delay. It's late enough already."

"Why can't you do it?"

A smile tightened his lips, but he didn't meet her eyes. "I have other duties."

Jenny made no reply. Just looked at him and pursed her lips.

She heard him sigh, and the sound almost made her smile. Almost.

"Stubborn," he said quietly, and smiled at her, nearly laughed again. Just for a moment. But then all kindness bled from his words. "And foolish. Go home, Jenny. You don't understand the common dangers of our world. How can you expect to stand against the greatest danger of them all? Your Tom is gone, seven long years ago. Leave him be and go home."

And then Jack was gone too, as if he had never been there. She couldn't say how she knew he'd left. It was just that the forest was suddenly still and she could tell. It took on another air now, in the deepening twilight. Cold, silent. She should be glad to be leaving it, but it clung to her, enticing her back. With a curious reluctance she didn't understand, she started toward the house.

chapter five

"Head to the Edge tonight?" the Woodsman muttered as he dropped the logs beside the hearth.

His wife looked up from the laundry she was folding. "That's what he said. Seems foolish though, doesn't it?" She smiled at Jenny, who sat in one of the armchairs, her feet curled under her. "It's late. And there's a storm rising."

"Well, there you go then." The Woodsman gave a snort and sat down opposite Jenny. "You don't want to be out there in a storm, do you?"

She didn't want to be out there at all, not heading back toward the Edge anyway. "Maybe . . . maybe we don't need to go right away," she said as if she was only conceding to logic. A flash of guilt rose in her. She'd been gone all day. What could they be thinking at home? Or maybe they hadn't noticed she was missing. No, they'd notice. They'd have to. They might not believe it just yet. And when they did . . .

Jenny pushed her parents from her mind before the guilt could rise so high it would tumble and crush her. She looked up at the Woodsman, hoping for some sort of validation. A way out.

He smiled, a warm and pleasant expression. "Morning's early enough, eh?"

"You must be exhausted, dear," his wife added. "Let's get you something to eat and a bed for the night."

Jenny shifted uncomfortably. "Jack said not to eat anything."

The Goodwife laughed. "Of course he did. No, you'll have to prepare it yourself of course, but there's no harm in some warm milk, is there? Shame though. I've bread and scones in the oven."

The scent of her baking was everywhere, and Jenny's stomach growled. Warm milk seemed like a sorry substitute, but it was better than nothing. The fire was working on her now, making her eyes heavy. She was tired, bone tired. She'd never understood what that meant before. A bed sounded like the finest luxury in the world.

Outside, the wind was rising, buffeting against the house, making the trees roar. The Goodwife crossed to the window, pulled the curtains. "He really whistled up the wind this time."

"Every time the queen turns her back, that piper of hers is off causing mayhem," the Woodsman replied.

Jenny jerked herself awake, staring at the woman. "The piper?"

"Yes, the queen's piper. You look like you've seen a ghost. Are you quite well?"

Jenny pushed herself out of the chair. She couldn't go back without him. Not now, not if there was a chance they thought— She couldn't do that again. "He's my brother. I think. I heard him playing. I came here looking for him. It has to be him."

They both stared at her, their eyes intently studying her, their faces grim.

"Are you certain?" the Woodsman asked. "There's a resemblance, to be sure, but—"

"It has to be him. No one could play like Tom. I heard him, in the trees. I followed him. That's how I got here. But Jack just kept insisting I had to go back."

"Hush now," the Goodwife murmured. "All's well. We won't send you back if you don't want to go, my dear. If it's your brother you're seeking, he'll be with the queen. Always goes back to her in the end."

Jenny's legs wobbled beneath her. She sat down abruptly, the air rushing from her lungs. "Then he's here. It's Tom."

They glanced at each other, a brief exchange of looks that could have meant anything.

The Goodwife stepped closer, reached out to stroke Jenny's hair. "You need food and sleep, my dear. The rest can wait till morning."

❦ ❦ ❦

Jenny pulled the patterned quilt up to her chin and tried to get to sleep once more. The nightgown they'd given her was unfamiliar, old-fashioned, and either tangled around her legs or crept up far too high. Outside the little cottage, the wind hurled itself at the diamond-patterned windows and rain splattered heavily against the glass. Had Tom really caused this? Whistling up the wind, they'd called it. If anyone could do it, she'd believe it of Tom.

And they knew him. Or knew of him. They saw him in her, and that gave her a slim, tenuous hope. She and Tom had looked alike as kids—Jenny, Tom's miniature. Everyone said so. Same eyes, same freckles, same bones beneath their skin. They'd laughed about it, threatened to switch places, as if that would have fooled anyone. Jenny smiled at the memory, and at last, with an ache in her chest, she dozed.

The storm woke her some hours later to complete darkness, wind and rain warring with each other outside. She could hear something moving through the wild night. It slouched through the darkness, circling the house. She was sure it was her imagination at first, a combination of dreams and exhaustion. Twice, she got up and pulled back the curtains, which had been brightly colored in the candlelight but were black as pitch now. Sheets of gray rain obscured almost everything from view. She was about to turn away the second time when she caught a glimpse of something in the night. It slid between the trees on the edge of the forest, part storm, part animal, part natural world. A thin sweat broke over her skin, and trembling fingers clenched around the locket at her throat.

The creature slid through the shadows, flowed like water down the windowpane. The impact of the raindrops on its outline was almost all that defined it against the black night. Abruptly, it was gone, but she stood transfixed, knowing that it circled the house and could reappear at any moment.

Sure enough, it was back within a few minutes. This time she caught a sense of something ancient, powerful, covered in leaves and vines, and an aching panic ballooned in her lungs. But she stood, unable to move away, watching, as it circled closer. She couldn't take her eyes off it.

Even with a brief glimpse, she knew it. Remembered it. Its berry-bright eyes. The way it had twisted around on itself quicker than a cat. The way it had vanished into the trees, and Tom with it.

Your Tom is gone, seven long years ago. Leave him be and go home.

Jenny's heart knotted as she remembered Jack's words. *Seven years.* And her breath caught. She tugged at her locket, winding it around on the chain until it tightened and she let it go again so it could unravel. Had she told him the amount of time? In fact, had she said anything at all about it?

"Is she asleep?" The voice came as an insistent whisper outside the door. Jenny turned from the window. Her bedclothes were a tangled heap on the bed, almost as if someone still lay beneath them. She dropped the curtain and was about to go to the door when she heard the Woodsman speak.

"She must be—has to be. She won't be missed, not if she's meant to have gone home already. They're hungry. We have no choice, unless you would appease them yourself."

"I can't. You know I can't, not anymore." The Goodwife paused, and when she spoke again, doubt infected her voice. "She's not much older than our Hannah was."

He choked at the mention of the name. "Hannah—Hannah's gone. They won't stay content with pig meat, and I can't lose you. She's here now and if she *is* the piper's kin, maybe she'll be as special as him. They like that. You heard how restless they are. They've scented her. They know she's here. Her blood will stir them up to a frenzy if we don't do something."

Jenny shrank back into the shadows around the window, crouching to make her body and breath as small and undetectable as possible.

The door creaked open, light coming from the lamp the Goodwife held. She saw the Woodsman approach the bed, his mouth set in a grim line, while his partner fidgeted by the door. The Woodsman held a cloth and, with a hand too practiced, he threw back the sheet and brought the cloth down where Jenny's mouth should have been.

Unable to help herself, Jenny sucked in a breath. They both turned toward her hiding place in shadows.

"Now, now," said the Goodwife, "you shouldn't be awake." The lamp swung lazily from side to side as the woman stalked toward her. Her husband advanced too, his movements more furtive, more like a rat than the hulking man he was.

Jenny's heart thundered inside her. The ache in her chest expanded, slicing at her lungs. What were they doing? What on earth—

"Stay still now, my darlin' girl," the Goodwife cooed. "It'll be all right. The little fellas need to be fed, and on nights like this, milk alone won't do. Now, I can't help them all, but you can. I'd swear you'll be sweet as honey to them." She reached out, open-palmed, beckoning the girl to her, and Jenny saw the length of her arm exposed. The expanse of white skin was covered in puncture wounds, bite marks, some almost healed, others raw and fresh. The skin around them was mottled, hard and almost . . . almost like the chitin of an insect's shell.

Jenny's fingers scrabbled behind her, trying to find the catch on the window, to prize it open before they could reach her. She felt her nails tear as she dug them into the wood, straining to lift the window. She wrenched it up and the storm enveloped her, invading the room like a vortex of wind, rain, and whirling leaves, like the forest itself enraged. The lamp gutted and went out. The Goodwife gave a cry. At the same moment, the Woodsman's hand closed on Jenny's arm. Her scream joined with the wind's shriek and she wrenched herself free. Before she knew what she was doing, she had hurled herself out of the window.

She landed heavily, the hard earth slamming the air from her body. The lamp was quickly relit inside. Its light through the window framed her on the ground, and the rain pelted against her skin. Mud slicked through her hair, oozed against her skin. She struggled to get up, and sharp pain lanced down her spine. Jenny cried out, sinking back.

She heard the Goodwife snarl. "She was meant to last. If they take her now, out there, they'll gorge!"

"It's too late," said her husband. "Call them. It isn't long till dawn."

The woman stuck her head out of the window, her eyes bright with malice, and opened her mouth to emit a high-pitched trill that was almost snatched away by the storm. Under other circumstances, she might have been calling her chickens. Jenny recoiled and tried to force her body to move, to get up, to run. A fierce chittering filled the air, drowning out the rain and wind. Jenny tried once more to get up. She gasped as her body spiked with pain. At the sound of her distress, something sprang into the light, a spider-like thing about the size of her hand. The black torso rose from splayed legs. The skin shone, as if covered in molten tar. Its eyes gleamed yellow and its crested head was a bright scarlet. Fangs glistened in its open mouth.

A crooning sound came from deep inside its vibrating chest as it tilted its head to one side, examining her. Jenny stared back, the rain drenching her, running icy fingers over her skin beneath the sodden nightgown. She sucked in a breath and pain sliced through her until it turned into a sob. Shock, terror, pain all conspired to pin her there. She couldn't move, transfixed by this tiny horror.

It darted forward, straddling her outstretched arm. Jenny made to pull back, but the creature latched on to her, wrapping its legs around her limb. Involuntary spasms racked her body. She tried to roll away. But another leaped out of the night, latching on to her other arm. The lead creature snarled, bared its teeth, and bit into the exposed flesh of her arm.

Jenny screamed and, as if summoned by the sound, more of the monsters swarmed over her, their teeth like hypodermic needles, piercing clothes and skin. A thousand points of white pain twisted her scream to a higher note. She could feel them drawing on her blood, draining it, drinking it down. Something else surged into her, numbing and terrible, a poison robbing her of senses and strength.

Her voice fell to a moan as two large shadows fell over

her. The Goodwife and the Woodsman lifted her between them, careful not to disturb the creatures' feeding, and, without a word, carried her back inside.

The door slammed shut, locking out the storm, and any hope Jenny had for escape.

chapter six

Jenny woke to brilliant sunlight and blinding pain. She was aware of it before she was fully aware of her own consciousness. Her skin burned everywhere, pinpricks of fire. Her back and shoulders were raw agony. Tentatively, she tried to move her arms and legs, but coarse ropes grated against the bite marks at her wrists and ankles. A gag cut against the corners of her mouth, filling it with the taste of dust and mildew. As she opened her eyes, she saw the bedroom from the night before. The window was roughly boarded up, the gaps between the wood no bigger than her hand, and the door was firmly closed. Dried blood flecked her skin and the surface of the night-dress, blood from so many tiny wounds that she couldn't hope to count them all. It wasn't like being elfshot. She'd thought that had been bad, but it was an itch and discomfort compared to this. This was pain, a thousand times over, everywhere.

She collapsed back into the damp sheets and closed her

eyes. The familiar weight of her locket rested against her chest, one single comfort, one last shred of normality. All she had left. The thought made tears sting her eyes.

Jack had brought her here, promised her safety and rest, sworn blind they'd take her home even if it was against her will.

He'd deceived her once. Had made her believe the worst of her fears was true. Why had she trusted him again? Should she be surprised to find herself here, tied up like a sacrifice?

She'd followed along behind him, bleating about finding Tom, about changing things, and all the time he'd been bringing her here. For this.

Had he known what would happen? Or was it possible he had he been deceived by his "friends" too? A small hope, less than a prayer, but all she had.

Jenny struggled once more against the ropes, gritting her teeth, trying to get free and failing.

He had to have known. These were people he trusted to do his will. She should have known better than to believe him. She screamed in frustration, her voice smothered by the gag in her mouth. He'd deceived her, tricked her, lied to her. Why had she been such an idiot?

Sunlight leaked through the gaps between the boards on the window, slanting across the room and falling across her face and the floor in uneven bands. Dust motes danced in the columns of light and fled with the breeze when the door opened.

The Goodwife bustled in with a tray heavy with food. Thick slabs of bread were spread with creamy yellow butter, and a huge bowl of fragrant soup cast tendrils of steam up to surround the woman's smiling face. There was a red apple and a jug of water beside the wooden mug. She might have been a kindly nurse bringing a wholesome meal to her patient. Jenny's stomach churned.

The Goodwife set the tray down beside the bed and pulled over a chair. Then she unhooked the gag from the girl's mouth, gingerly, as if Jenny might bite her.

"Time for food. We'll soon get you fed, my lovely. I've a fine beef broth here. It's good for building up the blood. Come now. You must have a fierce hunger."

"Let . . ." Jenny's voice was harsh in her throat. She coughed, swallowed and tried again, letting her anger boil over. "Let me *go!*" Her voice broke against the ceiling. "You can't do this to me. What were those things?"

The Goodwife's eyes shied away from her.

"Just Redcaps, little one. They're helpful souls really, but they do have their hungers. They liked you. You're blessed. They haven't liked anyone so much since my little girl came to womanhood. They came, they nested, and before we knew it . . . well . . . They help really, around the house, on the land and in the forest. But we have to take care of them too. If we don't feed them . . . well . . . Now . . ."

Jenny stared at her like she was mad. "You're farming them?"

The Goodwife gave a nervous and uncomfortable laugh. "No, lass. Not at all. They help us, you see. Protect us."

"From what?"

The woman's gaze slid away. "Many things stalk the forest hereabouts, love. Many things it doesn't do to cross. The Redcaps keep us safe in the night. Just about all we can rely on for that."

"And you feed them blood?" Jenny cringed inwardly, but kept her face like stone. "I'm wrong. They're farming *you*."

With an impatient tut, the Goodwife lifted Jenny's upper torso, pushing a plump pillow behind her. She didn't untie the ropes, so Jenny's arms strained and she let out an involuntary gasp. The Goodwife hushed her like a fond nursemaid and lifted up a spoonful of the broth. In spite of all she knew, in spite of the reasons behind this apparent kindness, Jenny found the aroma working on her senses. Her mouth watered. But Jack had warned her not to eat. With some effort, she forced her lips tightly together and turned her face aside.

The thought of Jack sent a thousand questions scattering through her mind. Would he have told her not to eat if it wasn't important? Why bother? If he'd meant for her to be a prisoner and food for the little monsters, why would he tell her how to avoid being trapped in the Realm by eating the wrong thing? That aside, they could be trying to drug her, to make her weak and unable to fight them. Not that she could, not really. Jenny turned her head the other way, trying again to avoid the spoon.

A shout came from outside the window.

"Anyone there?"

A burst of emotion lanced through her—anger and relief and something else.

It was Jack.

Jenny drew in a breath to cry out, but the Goodwife was too quick, her meaty hand closing over the girl's mouth, pushing her down. Her skin smelled of onions and blood and Jenny gagged.

The Woodsman's voice had a note of surprise, but no alarm.

"Jack? What are you doing here?"

Jenny thrashed, desperately trying to make a noise, any noise that Jack could hear, but the Redcaps had left her too weak and the woman was much stronger. Her foot caught the corner of the tray, sending it clattering all over the floor. The Goodwife slapped her hard across the face.

"Lie still," she hissed. "Be silent or I'll call them to silence you. He won't help you. He wouldn't if he could. He isn't like you. He's of the forest, a servant of the Realm, always has been and always will be. He brought you to us, didn't he?"

Jenny fell back as if doused in freezing water.

". . . just wanted to find out if it went all right." Jack's voice sounded apologetic. She could picture him, standing there, hands casually behind his back. He was a liar, and a consummate performer. Tears stung her eyes and she blinked them back. Had it all been an act? Was that why he'd stopped the Folletti? Why he'd brought her here? To be food for the creatures of his precious Realm?

"Oh, I took her to the Edge last night and she went through no bother."

"No bother?"

Jenny fixed on the words, on the tone of Jack's voice. He sounded surprised.

"Aye, lad. Good as gold, she was, as meek as a lamb." When Jack didn't reply at once, the man went on. "Said her thanks, polite as any lady of the Sidhe, relieved to be going home."

"Jenny?" Jack sounded amused. He gave a wry chuckle and her heart jerked inside her. He believed the Woodsman? He believed that lying sack of—

"Just as well, really," Jack said. "She had no place here. She belongs back in her own world. Well, my thanks for all your help."

No! She wanted to scream, but the Goodwife's hand

remained firm over her mouth. He couldn't believe that. He couldn't.

She thought he had gone. But a moment later he spoke again, his tone speculative. "Had some bother last night, though?"

"The—ah—the storm took out the window is all." The Woodsman sounded uncertain now.

Listen to him, Jack, Jenny thought. *Listen to him and hear that he's lying.*

But after a brief pause, Jack's voice was as calm and unaffected as ever. "Hannah's room? That's a loss. Do you want a hand mending it?"

"No, lad, but the Elders bless you for the thought. It'll wait until later. I've a store of work lined up for the day. There's a herd of pixies holed up by the river and I'll have to move them on or the trees will riot. You know how they are."

Another pause.

Don't believe him. She squirmed in the ropes holding her. *Even if you do want me out of your hair, don't let it be like this. Don't you dare believe him.*

"Farewell then," Jack said. Firm and certain, the tone so light Jenny's heart twisted inside her, and her voice choked up in her throat. How could he believe that? How could he believe any of that? He wasn't just a liar, he was an idiot as well. It should have made her fight, but despair leeched what little remained of her strength, swelling up around her like a black wave and swallowing her whole.

Jack was gone. Jenny's eyes met those of the Goodwife. The older woman pasted her smile back on her face and nodded.

"Well, you've wasted the food. Nothing for it now, though. Can't wait any longer." She took a box from her apron pocket and opened it. "We need to get started. Let's take things slowly this time." A small, spindly Redcap crawled onto her hand. Immediately, it made to bite into her palm, but the Goodwife chuckled and lifted it clear. "They swarmed last night, out of control. We're just lucky they didn't kill you. Just a baby, this one. She won't take much. We'll build you up over time, get you used to them and them to you until you can feed the lot."

Jenny shrank back into the bed, but there was nowhere to go. "Get that thing away from me."

"Look, my dearie, last night should never have happened. Too many, all at once like that, but you're strong, thank the Elders. That makes you special to us. Aye, and to them."

She laid the black creature reverently on Jenny's flesh. It nuzzled into the hollow between neck and shoulder. The claws felt cold as they scratched her skin. Then it bit deeply.

Jenny whimpered in pain but strangled her scream. She wouldn't give the woman the satisfaction. She closed her eyes, wishing she could block out the sucking sound as easily as she could the Goodwife's satisfied expression.

※ ※ ※

The day stretched to evening and as it did another storm rolled in across the forest. The Goodwife had closed the curtains, sealing off the room, though with the window boarded up, Jenny couldn't see the point. The wind still came through the gaps, making the curtains billow out like ghosts. It seemed more like ritual or habit, tucking in the bedclothes around her, wiping the beads of sweat from Jenny's forehead and puffing up the pillow for her. Like a mother who cared.

A candle burned at the bedside, though again Jenny was sure this was not for her benefit. She slipped in and out of consciousness, but not into anything resembling sleep. Tears chilled the sides of her face, wetting the pillows on either side of her. She shivered constantly. Blood loss and the poison secreted by the Redcaps left her weak and listless. She'd lost count of how many had been brought in, one after the other, a stream of hungry little monsters to feed on her. Her empty stomach churned.

Only when she'd passed out did they stop.

And when she woke it started again, until night fell.

The wind was rising again. Outside, she could hear the forest, and the same sensation swept over her of something unseen circling the house. She caught her breath. Could it be the whole swarm of the Redcaps again? A sticky, metallic taste filled her mouth. Maybe they wouldn't wait for the Goodwife's agenda, but were coming en mass to feed from her again.

No. This was something else. As dark and insidious as those creatures were, this was bigger, darker—

A thundering pulse of panic rose in her now. A shivering sweat spread over her skin. She strained at the ropes. They slid across her slick wrists, biting deeper. Her breath clattered in her chest like a scrabbling animal.

She knew it. Remembered. It lived in her nightmares.

A scratching at the window jolted her. The boards rattled, as if a tree scraped its branches against them. But as Jenny could clearly recall, there was no tree in the yard outside. The sound continued, now with an ominous creaking. Jenny knew that sound. It came from the ancient oak in her grandmother's garden when the wind had worried at it on dark nights like this. Rhythmic, strangely soothing and yet threatening, the sound of rocking, the sound of her gran cradling her when she woke from a nightmare, creaking, whispering, a low rumble.

This is just in my mind. They're only trees. Only trees. Who's afraid of lonely tr—

The candle flickered, guttered in a sudden draft. Then it went out, plunging Jenny into darkness. She cried out. Bound, straining, a sacrifice to whatever came in the dark.

With a crash that shook the world, something tore

through the roof and wall, scything to the left above her and collapsing the main part of the house. Timber shrieked and glass shattered all around. The cold night's air engulfed her and something else, small and hairy, smelling of animal musk and wet fur, touched her face. A gnarled, leathery hand stilled her mouth and she saw the horned silhouette.

Puck!

He grinned in the broken moonlight, his teeth very white. He didn't say a word, lifted a finger to his lips, and quickly set to work freeing her.

A tree lay across the debris beside her, the house and the stables beyond crushed beneath it. Outside, leaves, branches, flailing roots, whipping rain, and the wild wind— it tore through the rubble like a demon.

"There was no tree," she whispered as Puck pulled her to her feet. She wobbled unsteadily, forcing herself to stand. "No trees nearby big enough to do that." Despite the fact that one had crushed the house. But she thought of the yard, the outbuildings, the river. There had been no tree near enough.

"No," he agreed. "But the forest looks after its own. And exacts terrible vengeance on those who betray it. Always has. Come on now, blossom. Let's get back to the safety of the trees."

Safety of the trees? There was no such thing. She of

all people knew that. The memory of her brother sliced through her then like a knife. She lunged for her clothes, scooping them up, the jeans and shirt still folded on a nearby chair, and hugged them to her like a protective charm, a single element of the reality that had been stolen from her.

"Wait. Where's Jack?"

Puck eyed her warily, though he wasn't rushed, wasn't afraid. "He'll follow with the sun. Come on, lass. Those cursed Redcaps may not be dead, and without their keepers they'll run riot unless they're taken care of."

Jenny opened her mouth to argue, but Puck tugged at her arm, his strength surprising. In the night, the wind screamed and the forest gave a roar like a monstrous animal woken and enraged. The great tree heaved and Jenny saw something move within its broken branches.

A figure. A figure formed of bark and moss, of leaves and thorns, a figure made of the stuff of the forest itself.

Jenny staggered back, would have fallen if Puck had not been pulling at her. Panic exploded through her chest. Her lungs ached. She couldn't let it see her, couldn't give herself away. She scrambled back, away from the gaping hole in the house, back toward the bed.

The creature flowed from shadow to shadow, coiling like ivy, springing like holly, its lined and cracked face caught in a snarl or a smile. It reached the place where the Woodsman struggled beneath the mess of branches and rubble, and crouched low, its head cocked to one side. When it reached out its hands, tendrils shot from the fingers, sprouting like new roots. They plunged through the man's body as if he was nothing more than freshly turned earth. The Woodsman gave a terrible scream. Shoots exploded out of his mouth and nose. He convulsed, kicking out his useless legs as leaves unfurled against his skin. Jenny remembered the ancient carvings in the school chapel, the way she'd shuddered every time she lay eyes on one. Greenmen bedecked the pews of England's oldest churches, and the walls of its stately homes, men who were only half man, and half some ancient god born of the forest itself. The thing she had seen, all those years ago. The thing no one else believed in. This was it.

The Woodsman would have looked like it too if not for the blood. And crouching over him, watching its work patiently, feeding on the agony of its victim, a greenman. The same thing that had taken Tom. Her own personal nightmare. As if aware of the girl's wide eyes on it, the creature turned slowly, and moonlight showed her its face.

Leaf and tree it was, moss-encrusted bark and the gloss of a newly unfurled leaf. Berries tangled in the undergrowth of its hair. Even at this distance, it reeked of earth and bark. Its body twisted like age-old roots. Two eyes gazed at her, bright fires like marsh-lights. They ran with sap, the substance glistening as it tumbled down the barked cheeks. There was no thought behind the eyes. None she could discern. The expression was alien to her, to anyone. Its mouth stretched—a grimace or a smile, bearing thorns instead of teeth.

Jenny closed her hand over the locket and pulled so tightly it dug into her palm, the chain dragging on the back of her neck. She sucked in a breath, then another. *Only trees* didn't help right now. *This is just in my mind* wasn't comforting at all. Her ribs tightened and she couldn't catch her breath. Her heart stuttered.

Puck hauled her back, jumped onto the bed, and pushed her against the remaining wall.

"Jenny, we must go! Now! Before it finishes them and looks to us. It has no love of anything not directly of the earth—humans least of all. Run!"

"But the Redcaps—"

"It'll take care of them."

"What is it, Puck? What could—"

He kicked her shin hard enough to make her yelp. "Come now!"

Before Jenny could protest again, the hobgoblin's surprising strength had overpowered her and he dragged her into the night and the safety of the forest. And it felt safe now. Anywhere would feel safe so long as she was running away from that thing. Rain hammered into her face, drenched her to the skin, but she didn't care. She stumbled after Puck until her legs gave out from exhaustion and she tumbled onto the wet ground and beneath the clinging undergrowth. Puck was at her side a moment later.

"Jenny? Jenny, can you hear me, lass?"

She tried to answer, but her voice was just a croak. She swallowed. "I can hear you. I'm okay."

It felt like a lie, though. She was exhausted, her heart still racing, and every nerve sparking with terror. But she was alive. She was here. And she was safe.

She hadn't imagined it was still possible to feel safe. Certainly not here, in the forest at night.

They're only trees. Only trees. This is just in my—

But it isn't.

Puck lifted his face to the brambles and bushes hanging over her and she heard him whistling, a curious, inhuman tune. All around her the plants shuddered, not from the wind and the rain, but with sudden life. They moved, drawing closer together, closing up the gaps until the rain no longer reached her and the wind was locked outside. She huddled in the center, arms wrapped tight and shivering. Her teeth hammered against each other, and though her muscles ached from tension, she could not make them relax. Terror had turned them into hard, unyielding wires.

"Puck," she managed to ask at last, "where's Jack?"

"He's coming, lass. He'll be here. You'll see."

"Why didn't he come back?"

Puck eyed her curiously, studying her face, and compassion flooded his gimlet eyes. "He won't desert you. No, little Wren, he won't make that mistake again."

chapter seven

Jenny jerked awake, the itch of the Redcaps lingering, the leering faces of the Goodwife and her husband filling her groggy mind. Light stained green and gold as it filtered through the undergrowth that twisted around her like a cocoon. Her hair was tangled and filthy. Scabs of dirt and dried blood clung to her. Her body ached everywhere, every pinprick bite still burning on her skin. The nightdress clung to her in a twist, a mud- and bloodstained rag.

She was still alive. It didn't seem possible. Though she hurt everywhere, though she was filthy and exhausted, she was still alive.

She reached out and pushed back the bushes surrounding her, unfolding them like an unlikely moth emerging from a chrysalis. Sunlight warmed her skin. Its touch helped. She could almost believe it had just been a nightmare . . .

Almost.

Jack appeared at her side in an instant, crouching near enough to be attentive, far enough away to remain nonthreatening. He raked his dark hair back from his forehead, his bright, mismatched eyes fixed on her, as if he was trying to see inside her and solve a riddle.

"Are you . . ." he began carefully and reached out a hand. He tried to smile, but faltered when she didn't return it. "Are you all right?"

"I need to wash," she told him stiffly. Jack just frowned for a moment, as if he didn't quite understand. She tried again. "Those things were all over me. I need to wash."

"There's a river nearby, and a pool. I'll show you."

Jenny nodded and ignored his offered hand, pulling herself to her feet.

Jack had sent her to that house. And left her there.

"I need my clothes. I need to change . . ." She picked them up and then realized they weren't in much better shape than the muddy nightdress that hung from her.

"This way," he said, apparently unaffected by her mood, though he kept his eyes from lingering on her for too long. She caught Puck's attempt at a reassuring nod, but could find little solace in that. Jack had tricked her. Just to be rid of her. And it had almost worked too well. He could have at least said he was sorry. He could at least say *something*.

But as they walked, he was as silent as a stone.

He hadn't even come back for her in the night. No, he'd left Puck to do that. Anything might have happened. Jenny tightened her fists, knotting them on the material. It didn't help. If he *did* turn around now, if he *dared* to say anything to her, she . . . Well, she didn't know what she would do, but it would be bad.

Jack didn't say a word. She hugged her clothes against her chest. They were filthy, but it didn't really matter. She just wanted to get rid of the nightdress and pull on some semblance of normality again.

Normality, sure. She snorted a bitter laugh. Jack stiffened and glanced back at her, frowning, but he still didn't speak. Instead he led her to the most beautiful stream Jenny had ever seen outside of a picture book and all thoughts fled her mind. The amber-tinged water danced over the rocks to fill the pool.

Lights drifted on the air, over the surface of the water, little dots of brightness that spun on the breeze and against it. As Jenny stopped at the water's edge, they flew away, like luminous thistledown on the breeze, one moment there, the next gone. Jenny hesitated—they reminded her too much of the Folletti—but they didn't return.

"They won't hurt you," said Jack. "They're just sprites. They're gone now anyway."

Hopefully. She frowned, and switched her attention to the river instead. Anything but look at him.

If she knelt in the water, she would be able to wash comfortably enough, though it would only come up to her waist. It was cold to the touch, but that was just the chill of freshness, and Jenny could not resist its lure right now. The thought of being clean again . . .

Sunlight fell dappled through the forest canopy, warm and relaxing. She reached for the hem of the nightdress and was about to shed it when she realized Jack still stood there, watching her with a curiosity she found both unnerving and amusing, as if he wasn't sure what she was doing.

"Go away," she told him.

He shook his head. "It's too dangerous. I made a terrible mistake when I sent you down to the cottage because I thought you could not come to harm there. I was wrong. I won't let you walk into such danger again. Jenny, I'm sorry."

Sorry. Right.

She kept her gaze hard as the shining river stones scattered around her. But Jack didn't say any more. Silence wrapped its web around her, around them both, and eventually forced her to look up. The moment her gaze locked on him, much to her surprise, he blushed. It wasn't embarrassment, she saw, but shame. Then she realized, the apology wasn't for not leaving her alone now, but for sending her to the Woodsman and his wife in the first place. Perhaps for not seeing what was happening, or for not coming to her aid.

Shame. She could hardly believe it.

"They were my friends." He stumbled over the words, knitting his fingers together as he struggled to explain. His eyes looked so very young. A boy's eyes, not a man's, shining but downcast, his long lashes casting shadows on his cheekbones. She almost wanted to believe him. "At least I thought they were. I didn't know . . ."

Friends. The word made her stiffen. Maybe he was telling the truth. Maybe he meant that. The spark of anger flared up again, burning away the bit of sympathy that had been growing there. Well, lucky him to have such *friends.* Or perhaps lucky her to never have to deal with *friends* like that. Better no friends at all. Certainly safer.

"They *fed* me to those things! I don't know how many there were. They were going to let them drain me dry. You said they'd help, but they *tried to kill me.* You left me there!"

Jack looked shocked at first and then, suddenly, unrepentant. "They tried to use you only to save themselves. It was misguided, but— It doesn't matter now. They're dead." The bitterness in his voice soured his features.

"That's insane," she growled at him. "They're monsters. Both of them. They're—"

"They're dead!" he shouted, his voice so loud it startled her into silence.

Her anger boiled over then, scalding through her chest and throat. Two steps brought her close enough to shove him as hard as she could. He barely reacted, which made her even angrier. It was like shoving one of the trees standing witness around them.

"Leave me alone, Jack."

Jack answered quietly, with the patience of stones. "I can't. I'm Guardian of the Edge. It's my duty to keep you safe. And it isn't safe here."

The problem was, he could be right. She probably wasn't even safe from Jack himself. His motives were unclear. His alliances always shifting, his moods unnerving . . . He stood so close now she could feel the warmth from his body, his scent like the forest itself. A deep, beguiling fragrance that curled around her. Jenny shifted her gaze so she was looking over his shoulder. She couldn't think straight with him that near. She took a measured step back. A deep breath. She glanced at the trees around them shushing faintly in the breeze, and the image of the greenman rose up once more in her mind.

Inside her, everything twisted. She drew in a single constricted breath.

"That thing in the night, that creature . . ."

"Creature?" He took his own step back, his eyes flicking over her face, blue and green points. "You saw a wood spirit, that's all. They're dangerous when raised, worse when crossed. All natural spirits are. Just stay out of its way."

Dangerous enough that Jack was nowhere near when Puck came to her aid. *Puck,* of all people. But not Jack.

"I saw what it did. What kind of *natural spirit* would do that?"

Jack crept a little closer again, his voice softening to a gentle hum, a balm on her jagged nerves. "Nature is harsh, unforgiving. It can destroy as much as it can create. That's—that's its *nature*." He cast her a nervous smile, as if trying to cheer her but unsure of her reaction, and reached out toward her.

"Don't touch me," she said, stepping out of reach. "I don't know how you influenced me before, but—"

"I had to. You shouldn't be here. And being elfshot meant you were easily swayed. A touch is sometimes all it takes."

She glared at him. "Don't touch me," she said again. "Ever."

He looked at her steadily. "The influence is gone now and it won't return. But that's not to say something else won't snare you. You have to be careful in the Realm. The sooner you realize its dangers, the better."

"I thought Faerie was meant to be beautiful," she said bitterly.

And then he did laugh, a fantastic sound, full and vibrant, infectious the way it rolled through her.

"Look around you." He spread his arms wide, indicating the little river, the forest with its bright colors and cool shadows, the sea of golden daffodils through which they had waded. She hadn't noticed at the time. Now that he pointed it out, she was almost ashamed that she had passed it by. "Is this not beautiful?"

She smiled, but it was short-lived.

Yes, beautiful, but too beautiful. Hiding dangers behind that beauty, like its queen, the woman she had seen hunting. Dangers like its greenman.

The stream flowed on, murmuring its song. Sunlight glinted on the surface, tinged with green as it filtered through the leaves. The forest whispered when the breeze shifted through it. She stood on the riverbank, shivering slightly.

"And what was the thing I saw last night?" she asked again, a powerful shudder running through her at the thought. That wasn't beautiful, but terrible. Terrifying. And worse. It had been there, watching her in the trees that night Tom was taken. She wrapped her arms around her body. "This place isn't beautiful. It's two-faced and treacherous, and so is everything here, in this . . . this . . . whatever this place is! I saw that creature before—the night I lost Tom. That thing was there. It sent the trees after him. It took him."

"No." Jack closed his eyes.

Jenny paused, her mouth still open, and shut it with a click, startled by this sudden show of empathy.

She pulled the sleeves of the nightdress down over the tops of her hands and said, "Well, the sooner I can find Tom and get back home, the better. And I will find him. I have to. Knowing what I know about this place now, I have to."

Jack drew back with a ragged breath and shook his head.

"I fear you will be disappointed, Jenny."

"Let me worry about that. Just turn around, if you must stay. Turn around and don't look at me."

To her surprise, Jack obeyed. He settled himself on the ground, his back to her, and took out his stone-bladed knife. He picked up a piece of deadwood and began to carve. She watched his hunched shoulders, the way the shavings fell like curls of apple peel on the ground beside him.

Nervous, but sure he would not turn around, Jenny slipped out of the nightdress and threw it, with force, toward the trees. Jack tensed sharply at the sound it made as it hit. It fluttered to the ground beside him and he reached out to pick it up.

"What would you do with this?"

"Burn it."

He bowed his head but said nothing, laying the white cloth aside next to her own clothes.

The curious urge to trust him rose up again. She shouldn't, she knew that. He was a guardian, and he'd said the word as if it really meant something to him. But at the same time, something about him scared her more than she could say. Somehow it felt as if his will was the only thing that controlled him, and that if he lost that restraint, things could be very bad indeed. How could he be the guardian of a place as wild as the forests of Faerie without

being infected by the same wildness? The way he looked
at her, studied her, as if trying to see beneath her exterior
and into her soul . . .

She shook the thought aside. Everything here unnerved
her. She'd been shot at by tiny fairies; she'd been kidnapped
by people who served a swarm of monsters; she'd been rescued by Puck while something just as monstrous murdered
her captors. No doubt it would have come after her and
Puck next.

Anyone sane would give in and go home.

But she wouldn't, not without finding Tom.

She'd thought she was ready to put it all behind her, that
she was finally prepared to forget and move on. And maybe
she had been, back there in her own world, when she had no
hope of ever seeing him again. Now she knew different. She
couldn't just throw it aside. Every moment she had spent
searching for him, wishing for him, turning over her memories of that night . . . She could not give up now.

The water was blissfully cold. Her skin tingled and the
bite marks stung with its touch, but it felt so good to clean
off the grime and blood, to run water through her hair and
feel it trickle down her back. To scrub herself clean. To feel
human again. She closed her eyes.

The rustling of leaves startled her out of the reverie. Jack!

He moved forward, his eyes clamped shut, his leaf cloak
draped across his hands. On his knees, he eased his way to

the bank, and yet each movement was filled with studied grace, as if he felt the earth beneath him as a guide. He crouched at the water's edge, still without looking at her, and offered the cloak.

"If you'll let me, I'll wash your clothes. Your own clothes, I mean. You can use this until they're dry."

Jenny wasn't sure which image struck her as more comical—Jack kneeling there with his eyes closed for fear of embarrassing her by seeing her naked, or that of him doing her laundry.

"You'll wash them with your eyes closed?"

Confusion flickered over Jack's face and she realized he had been in earnest. Resignation replaced confusion and she felt a stab of guilt when he frowned.

"If you really think I ought . . ."

Her own laugh took her by surprise. She wasn't in any mood to laugh and yet there it was.

"I'm sorry," she sighed. "I was joking. Just . . . just give me a minute."

Jenny took the cloak and rose from the pool, quickly wrapping the strange fabric around her as she stepped onto the bank beside him. Warm and surprisingly soft, the cloak carried the scent of spring mornings, like blossoms and new growth. She'd expected it to be scratchy and harsh, but it wasn't. Leaves wrapped around her like an embrace. She lifted the fabric to her face, inhaling. When she opened her eyes, Jack watched her again, his eyes like two jewels. There was no expression she could discern on his features now. The silence stretched.

"Thank you," she said stiffly.

He nodded once and gathered up the clothes, as quietly formal as a hotel bellboy.

He paused for a moment, his head cocked to one side as he studied her jeans. Or rather the pockets of her jeans.

"What is it?" she asked, bemused by his confusion.

"These . . . things in your clothes." He pushed his fingers inside and pulled the pocket inside out.

"They're pockets." She smiled, then laughter broke her voice again. He looked up at her sharply, so quickly, and the look silenced her. He expected her to mock him. It was a look she knew too well, having worn it herself too many times. She forced her voice to be gentle, softened its edges with kindness. "You put things in them, things you want to carry with you. Like that pouch on your belt. See?"

Jack nodded and bent his head, concentrating on gathering her clothes together instead of looking at her.

The sun passed behind a cloud and in the shadows, she saw something else. Jack crouched low, like the creature had crouched over the Woodsman's body. Jenny drew back and shivered. It haunted her, the thing she had seen. Like a bad dream dogging her all day.

"Jack? Why didn't you come with Puck? Didn't you . . ."

She paused, finding herself unable to ask the question she really wanted to ask.

He looked up. Was it a flash of concern in his eyes? Or just surprise? Jenny couldn't tell. She had a hard time reading him.

"There are many things in the Realm that are dangerous while appearing wholesome, and many that are quite the opposite. No one knows the real motivations and drives of another." His shoulders sagged. "I thought they could be trusted. They were my friends. I had no idea the Redcaps had claimed them. Please, believe me. I would never have sent you there if I had."

Pain wormed its way through his voice and Jenny felt a pang of unexpected sympathy. For him. For them. She didn't like it much, but she couldn't deny it either. There it was. "What killed them?"

"The forest. Nature itself. As a Woodsman, he had an agreement with the trees, which—by serving the Redcaps, by threatening you when he promised to aid you—he broke. There are things that—that— Leave it at that, Jenny Wren. Any more, you don't want to know. Come now, Puck has gathered some food for you and I will take care of these." He cradled the clothes against his chest. She looked away from the dirty white fabric of the nightdress.

As they left the river, the water stirred, the ripples changing. They shifted direction, moving. Jenny glanced back and for a moment, the light on the surface looked like eyes watching her.

She blinked and reached out to stop Jack, to show him. But in that instant the breeze changed again and the curious alignment vanished. Just light on the surface of the water. That was all. She shook her head and hurried after Jack.

❧ ❧ ❧

Jenny ate sparingly of the berries Puck had gathered while she had washed. They tasted sweet and tart all at once, but she didn't feel like food any longer. The day had slid onward to afternoon while she hadn't noticed. Jack had gone back to the river to wash her clothes, taking that filthy nightdress with him. And now Puck dozed in the sunlight, stretched out like a satisfied dog, belly up, snoring.

Time to herself meant time to think, to plan. Jack was determined to see her go back home. He wasn't terribly forthcoming with information. He wasn't likely to lead her to Tom. And right now she had no idea where her brother might be other than the queen's castle. But she could find out, couldn't she? If she asked the right questions. How hard could it be to find a castle when almost everything else in this world seemed to be trees?

Jenny got to her feet, stretching her sore limbs. The pain had mostly gone now, the touch of the water having soothed the bites and hastened the healing process. She almost felt herself again.

Except for the fact she was wearing Jack's cloak of leaves. And was completely naked underneath.

She wondered where Jack was. The river, she supposed, still washing her clothes as he had promised. Which meant only Puck was there to keep an eye on her. Puck, who snorted, muttered something, and rolled over, smacking his lips together.

How far would she get before he noticed? Neither of them was even bothered to keep an eye on her.

Jenny walked out of the camp. Moving through the forest, her instincts sharpened, the old fear reasserting itself. Forests were dangerous. Leaves and twigs crunched beneath her bare feet. She'd forgotten her mud-clogged shoes. Backtracking, she found them on the edge of their hiding place. The mud had dried, so she scraped it off and slipped the shoes onto her feet. If only she had the rest of her own clothes. Maybe Jack had finished and they were already dry in this warm air. She set off again, picking her way through the forest, back toward the river.

She hadn't gone far when she saw the tree. Not as big or as impressive as many of the others around her. It was a small, twisted hawthorn, gnarled and ancient. Its branches carried both white clumps of sweetly scented flowers, and sharp thorns. And tied amid the branches, from the lowest to the highest, were scraps of white cloth. They fluttered in the breeze. Jenny reached up to touch the nearest rag and shied away again as she recognized it. The remains of the nightdress.

She recoiled, her breath caught like a lump in her throat.

"There you are," Puck said sleepily, his voice emerging from the undergrowth a moment before him. "Don't wander off. It's dangerous." She glanced down, irritated that he'd appeared. "Don't scowl at me, lass. Jack said I was to keep you safe when he's not here. He doesn't trust anyone else to do it, barely trusts me. Made me swear binding oaths. My life wouldn't be worth dirt if anything happened to you."

A rustling in the bushes ahead made them both stop, frozen on the narrow path, fixed in place by a jolt of sudden fear. There was something in the bushes, something small and furtive, coming closer.

"Down," Puck barked. "Use the cloak to hide. Stay still."

Jenny drew in a breath and dropped to her knees, the leaf cloak camouflaging her against anything that might come out. She made herself small and still. Waited.

Then she realized, Puck was gone. Completely gone.

So much for her fearless oath-bound protector.

A tiny figure, like something a child might make from clay, lichen, and fungus, tumbled out from under the bush, dragging a sycamore leaf twice its size after it. Jenny made a surprised sound and it twisted around in front of her, baring its teeth and a tiny knife. The obsidian blade flashed in the late afternoon light and they both froze, staring at each other.

The little creature took in the cloak she wore and slowly lowered the knife. Jenny allowed herself to breathe again. The thing retreated, dragging the leaf after itself, then stopped suddenly and tried to jump up at the tree, the lowest branches far out of its reach.

Jenny followed its frustrated gaze to a spiderweb spun between the branches of the rag-strewn tree.

"It's a pixie," said Puck's voice from behind her. "It just wants the gossamer. Silly thing. It's too high. Let it be, let's go back."

But Jenny didn't move. She rose slowly, taking care not to startle the pixie, not to move too fast. She pulled the web free carefully, trying not to break too many strands, and bent, offering the web. The pixie stared at her, jerking forward suddenly to snatch it from her hand, grabbed hold of its leaf again, and took off into the darkness of the undergrowth.

"You shouldn't have done that," Puck muttered. "Taken it off the tree. May Tree's magic. It's dangerous."

"Right, dangerous. It's a tree." She was careful to say it casually, but a chill passed through her. Who was she kidding?

"The Realm is dangerous," Puck said. "Especially to those who would be kind, like you. Especially when the queen is out and about. Mind you, she'll follow the river home soon enough and we'll all breathe more easily."

chapter eight

It started like a warm summer breeze moving through the trees in late afternoon, a whispering voice in the forest itself. Jack lifted his face to greet it, closed his eyes and inhaled. Sweet summer flowers, all things in the fullness of life . . . and beneath it, decay, the moment where everything began to eat itself away.

Titania.

It could only be Titania. He shifted, looking around for Jenny and Puck, but they were back at the camp. The river sang on, the clothes hanging to dry in the sunlight. It would be evening soon. But he could not ignore such a summons. Nor did he want to. He only wished he did.

"Your Majesty." The words stuck in his throat, bitter, but her pleasure broke over him in a wave of sweet fragrance. A series of notes rang out in the air, a trill of magic in the music. Light exploded inside his mind and he cried out wordlessly at the shock of pain.

And then he was gone from the forest.

"What's a May Tree?" she asked, ignoring his admonition. He couldn't know what she was planning. The idea itself was only germinating, and she'd need to pick her moment.

"That is." He yawned and scratched his rump, referring to the tree tied all over with scraps from the white nightgown.

"The rags, Puck. What are the rags? Did Jack do this?"

Puck froze and then his face fell. "Ah . . ." he sighed. "Yes, probably. He would do that."

"Why?" She folded her arms across her chest, the effect of which was lost inside the cloak. But her expression seemed to do the trick.

Puck rolled his eyes to the heavens. "They're wishes. Each and every one. They're his wishes."

"So many?"

"No. Jack only has one wish. But he wishes it a thousand times a day." Puck turned aside, gazing off through the trees where the song of the river came from. "He dreams of it, dreams of a future. Few creatures in the Realm are so cursed as to live in hope. Poor Jack o' the Forest, Jack in Green. He only longs to be free."

He stood instead on her marble floor, its surface shining, inlaid with intricate patterns of roses and thorns made of many shades of stone. This was her audience chamber, the great mirrors lining the walls reflecting everything a thousand times, capturing light from the high windows overhead, multiplying it until it filled every corner. It was like standing in the center of a cut diamond. Countless Jacks, with the same blue and green eyes, gazed back at him. He shivered. But held his ground. To show weakness before Titania was suicide.

Beautiful as the sun itself, she stood before him in a gown of pale green that hugged her neck, her arms, her torso, but fell away in a sweep of silk from her slender hips. Her golden hair was arranged to emphasize the elegant curve of her neck and the porcelain smoothness of her heart-shaped face. Everything artfully prepared to show her beauty, and it worked. He couldn't take his eyes off her. The queen. His queen. His heart sped up, hammering against his rib cage. She smiled to see him, a smile that didn't reach her eyes, and opened her arms in welcome.

"It has been a very long time, Jack."

Not long enough. The thought sprang up. But he couldn't speak the words even if he'd dared. Even if he'd wanted to. Here, in her domain, her power held sway—over him, over everyone. He was only a creature of Faerie. She was its queen.

He struggled to clear his head, forced his shoulders to relax, his hands to loosen, though he kept his weight on the balls of his feet.

They weren't alone, of course. The queen was never alone. With effort, he dragged his eyes away from her. Two blank-eyed servants in their dove-gray clothes stood at either side of her throne in the great mirrored room, awaiting her command. Jack didn't need to look in the mirror to know that behind him, three shallow steps fell away to the vast lower part of the chamber. He could hear the drone of her courtiers, elegantly beautiful Sidhe lords and ladies, standing where the queen's balls and entertainments took place, perfectly positioned so she could look down on them all. They hovered in their fine clothes, perfect hands covering perfect mouths, sharp smiles reflected a million times over as they laughed at him, at his freakish apparel and wild appearance.

In the mirror, Jack's eyes picked out another figure. Beyond the queen's courtiers, alone in a corner and watching everything with flat and passionless eyes, stood her piper. Of course Titania had retrieved him. She always got what she wanted. So now he waited on her. Waited to be called upon, waited to be of service. His silver flute in hand, he gazed at the queen in rapt adoration. And there was no mistaking him.

Jenny's brother.

He looked like her—the same coloring, the same brown eyes—and yet not like her at all. Aloof, cold. Familiar, though. Jack had seen the piper often enough. He'd grown to manhood in the Realm, and that left its mark in the coolness of his gaze, in the disdain that clung to his every expression. A far cry from the boy Jack had found in the forest seven years ago, this man. He should have noticed the resemblance in Jenny when he first saw her, but he hadn't been looking for it. He'd only been trying to get rid of the girl. And now within reach was the one thing that might make her leave the Realm. Not that he could bring her brother to her. The queen would not stand for that, and neither, Jack suspected, would the piper.

Jack studied the young man's reflection, trying to work out how he could use this knowledge to his advantage, before he realized, too late, that he had taken his eyes off Titania. Never wise.

She stood too close. Far too close, the scent of roses that clung to her encircling him as well. Her fingertips brushed his cheek and she laughed when he flinched away.

"I'd forgotten how handsome you are, Jack."

He took an involuntary pace backward and Titania followed him, matching him step for step. Theirs was an old dance. He knew it well and it never failed to seduce him into thinking things might end differently this time.

"Nothing to say?"

His voice finally found a way of escape, even if it was at her implied command. "Why did you bring me here?"

"I want to talk," she said lightly. Her hand caught his wrist, closing on it like a vise. His pulse thundered beneath her touch. The pressure was both intimate and threatening. "Are you guarding her, Jack? Keeping her safe? Taking her to *him*?"

Venom dripped from the final word and he saw the flash of sharp teeth behind those full and luscious lips.

"I'm doing my duty, Your Majesty. The one with which I was charged."

"Ah yes, your duty." She glanced down the great mirrored hall to where the piper stood, now staring blankly into the fire. He seemed to sense the queen's eyes on him and turned; his gaze, though without passion, lit at the sight of her. "You're remarkably good at that, Jack o' the Forest. No one better." She didn't release him. Instead, she leaned in closer, peering into his eyes as if to see all his secrets. "You never call me 'my queen.' Everyone else does. Why would that be, Jack?"

Her lips were too close to his. Her presence stole his breath. Even though he was aware she was throwing every glamour she had against him, even though he knew the being beneath this charade and all that she was capable of, he still wanted to kiss her. He licked his lips, his face turning toward hers—

Wires of pain shot through him, breaking the creeping tendrils of her enchantments, and he felt suddenly sick with himself. His curse protected him, and damned him. It kept him from Titania, and kept him free of her.

Still Titania didn't release him. Her grip only tightened. "Do you remember what it was like, Jack? Before, I mean. When you weren't"—she brushed her silken fingertips against his cheekbones, underlining each eye—"as you are now?"

Remember? Of course he remembered. It was seared into his mind. The power, the strength, the pure wonder of freedom. She must have seen it in his eyes, on his face, in the tight line of his mouth.

Titania tilted her head. "I can give that back to you, Jack."

The hall grew quiet with expectation. The light through the high windows cast crimson-gold bands around the room. Outside, the sky would be turning red.

Chains of iron seemed to be crushing his ribs, and Jack realized he had stopped breathing. It wasn't possible. She couldn't. He belonged to Oberon. They both knew that. Unless she and Oberon had worked out a deal . . . But Titania never bartered. It had always been orders, or threats, or simply torment. Never cajoling. Titania didn't need to offer honey when her sting was so vicious.

She turned away, luring him after her as she swept up the steps to her Rose Throne and to the mirror beyond it. He staggered to a halt at her side and tried not to look into the mirrored glass, staring at his feet instead. He couldn't listen to her. What she implied, what she could be promising— it was too much. The thought of it dangling so close and yet still out of reach. Freedom. His mouth was dry. Oberon would never allow it, would unleash all his fury if he even thought she was suggesting it. And Titania would never make such an offer, veiled or not, unless Jack had something she wanted.

For the queen surely wanted something in return.

Jack forced his mind to calmness. He stood straight, spread his feet on the cold marble floor, and made himself look up.

Titania stood just behind him, facing the mirror. Her free hand shook as she smoothed back her golden hair from her face. She hid it through sheer force of will and an expertise gained from centuries of being watched. But Jack could feel it when he stood so close to her, when he forced himself to be detached and wary. She pressed her body to his back, snaked her hand across his chest and rested her cheek against his upper arm. He shuddered.

His eyes followed her every move. He couldn't stop watching her.

And neither could her reflection.

She lifted her eyes to meet those opposite her and Jack had to bite the inside of his cheek to keep from crying out.

They weren't Titania's eyes staring back. Mab, dwelling within her like a malignant spider at the center of a web, peered out at him. Not a trace of Titania's seduction now. Her gimlet gaze made him quake inside as ancient half-remembered nightmares surged to the edge of his mind. Titania's heart beat so hard he could feel it through his own body. She drew a breath, trying to calm herself. Even after so many centuries, the terror never died. He knew it as well as she did. It bonded them together, the fear. Mab ate at their shared past like a cancer.

And the old queen was hungry again.

"What do you want?" Jack said steadily.

A smile flickered over the mouth inside the mirror, a movement that did not originate in Titania's smooth face.

"A May Queen has come. I sense her in the forest, in the water, changing things as she journeys toward us. Jack knows. Oh yes, he knows it too well."

Mab's voice snaked around them both, a voice like old nails scratching on dry skin. It reeked of malice, of hatred and bloodlust. Mab was old, older than any of them. She kept to the old ways, forcing Titania to do the same when she willed it. And the old ways cried for blood.

Titania's voice was music in comparison. "Then we must get rid of her."

"She's too precious to kill. We need her. She will make us young and whole again."

"We *are* young." Titania ran her hands down her body. It should have been seductive, a demonstration of her beauty. But it wasn't. Jack shivered, his skin contracting around a frame that was suddenly too large for it. "And whole. Beautiful. What more do you want?"

Mab laughed, mocking laughter that rang around the room, bouncing off the mirrored walls. Jack wanted to recoil, but didn't dare show any weakness. He stood as still as a tree with deep roots before the storm. Titania's grip crushed him. She was afraid. Very afraid. As well she might be. He pitied her, but that didn't make him want to help her, or make him loathe her any less. He had made that mistake before.

"And are we innocent? She's fresh blood. Her heart is so full, so ripe. She knows not what she is, what power she could wield. Her innocence, her heart, her will. Her choice. She knows not what it could mean. And she's ours. She must be. Quickly, before Oberon claims her. Time is short."

The mirror image lifted a small casket, rosewood inlayed with gold, carved with filigree designs. The catch was a golden heart pierced with a knife. Behind him, Titania's arms jerked up like those of a puppet, mirroring Mab's movements perfectly. Her hands slid up the sides of Jack's body. And came to rest on either side of his torso. In the mirror, the casket glimmered in the center of his chest.

The metal heart gleamed red in the reflected light.

"You were a hunter, before you were a guardian." Titania's breath played against his ear, stirring his hair. She had
pushed her fear of Mab aside to be all seduction once more.
He longed to give in. It would be so much easier. But he
couldn't. It was just a glamour, just her magic working on
him. It would beguile him, trick him, use him. "To be free,
you just have to hunt again, Jack."

Jack swallowed. "I can't," he said, straining to keep his
voice even. "You promise more than you can deliver."

"Do we?" Mab laughed, the sound clawing at him. *"I think
you forget my power, Jack o' the Forest. Oberon certainly does.
Underestimating your foe is certain defeat."*

Mab held the casket out to them, an offering. Jack stared,
hypnotized by horror and need as it moved closer to the
glass and then, with only the slightest resistance of reality, pushed through. The mirror bulged, distorting their
images. The hag who appeared in Titania's place grinned,
revealing needle-like teeth. Titania released him and he
almost sagged to his knees but struggled to stay upright.
At the first show of weakness, Mab would slash his throat
before his heart could beat again. She'd drink down his
blood and his strength. She'd promised it, so long ago, and
Jack knew she was only biding her time. She used Titania as
her agent in the world because it suited her, because despite
her strength the current queen would never be as powerful
as the old one. Strength and power were different things.

But the moment Titania failed her, or fought too hard. The moment Titania was no longer of use . . .

Mab's eyes flashed when Titania reached out to take the casket. The glass wobbled like the surface of a bubble about to burst, rippling with a rainbow sheen. Nails scraped over the queen's hands, leaving a raw trail as they pulled back into the far side of the mirror, tearing skin, but leaving the glass intact once more.

"Nothing can replace you, my Titania. Not if you make it ours. Part of us."

And then she was gone. Titania gazed at her own perfect reflection, the casket weighing heavily in her bleeding hands.

She turned slowly and offered it to Jack. But her voice reached out to the whole room. Jack remembered suddenly that they were far from alone. Her courtiers gathered at the center of the chamber, at the foot of the steps leading up to the throne, hovering, humming, waiting. Every moment, every movement, watched. Every word heard.

Titania could never show weakness. In that way, she and Jack were alike.

"A mortal girl is loose in our forest. Whosoever brings her to me will be rewarded. Beyond measure." She dropped her voice and suddenly she was speaking to him alone. Intimate, like a lover's whisper. "I can give you your desires, Jack. Your freedom and your hope."

She knew him too well. She knew him better than he knew himself. His dreams, his wishes, all the things he had given up on. She knew each and every one.

"I can't."

But he knew his duty.

"Because of your oath?" She laughed. "And where has your oath brought you, Jack?" She said his name like a curse, like a slur. "And what value can we place on an oath you were forced to make?"

Jack stared her in the eye.

She was right. He hated it, but couldn't deny it. He dropped his gaze to the marbled floor.

"She'll bring ruin to the forest. Oberon will take her, make her his, refuse to let her go, and winter will sweep back over us. And what will become of the forest fae then? We all know he hates them. Nothing will stay his hand if he takes her."

Titania placed the casket on the table beneath the mirror and turned back to him, smiling again. A predatory smile. Jack knew it of old. It was more like Mab's than she would care to admit.

He needed to get out. He needed to get away from her. And he longed to stay. To let go. To obey.

The casket pulled his attention back. Did he hear a beat from inside, an incessant rhythm, like the pounding of a pulse? It called to him, and he wanted to answer. But if he brought the girl here, what would it still take to win his heart from that box? Her own in return?

Titania's hand clutched his. "Bring her to me, Jack. Or I'll see you suffer more than anyone has suffered in the Realm."

Jack met her eyes, a challenge rising in him. "Why not just bring her here yourself, as you did me?"

Titania's upper lip lifted. "That's against the rules of this game. If you still had an ounce of what you were inside you, you would know that. I can't snatch her from the forest. She doesn't belong there, and she isn't mine. Yet. You, on the other hand, promised to serve faithfully. You gave a vow both to me and to my husband. And to her. A dreadful mistake, my Jack. No one can serve two masters. Let alone three." Her patience had fled now. The game of seduction had failed. "If you don't cooperate with me, you will regret it for eternity. Believe that."

"She must come to you willingly," Jack said. "Those are the rules. Offer all the rewards you want to anyone here, but they can't force her, any more than you can."

Let them all hear it. Let them know that despite her offer of rewards, the task was impossible. And remind himself of the same thing.

"Then *make* her come willingly," Titania snarled. "Persuade her. You were charming once. Or don't, if you're that obstinate." She flicked her wrist as if to wave away an insect.

"There are ways and means around it. It's her heart and soul together that make her strong. Break her heart, strip away her soul, and I can take her as I will. You, Jack . . ." She turned and slapped him hard, the flare of humiliation more a shock than the pain. "You know full well what to do."

Titania pushed past him and stalked down the steps from the Rose Throne to the receiving area, then down the three steps to the intricately patterned main floor of the chamber. The light from the high windows overhead filtered down, turning reddish purple as the day neared its end.

"My queen?" said a nervous voice. Jenny's brother. One who soon enough would know all about the blood required from the Realm. Jack shook his head. The poor fool didn't realize that come the time of the blood tithe, he'd be the forfeit. Jack paused in his thoughts.

Or maybe he did. Was it a coincidence the piper was at the Edge playing his music? Or did he have a purpose of his own?

"Does he know what he did?" Jack called after Titania. "Does he know who he summoned?" She scowled at him, and he knew he wasn't going to get an answer.

Instead, she turned to Tom, her touch possessive. "You had a sister, piper. Tell me about her. Tell me what she loved, what tunes you played just for her . . ." She curled her fingers through Tom's hair, caressing him.

"My . . . my sister?" Memories struggled through his eyes.

"Titania?" Jack asked warily. "What are you planning?"

But Titania ignored him, that cruel smile playing across her lips.

"Yes, your sister. Tell me everything. But first, my piper . . ." Her voice transformed to a purr of satisfaction, one with an edge. "Play for me. Something soothing. Drive the wild from our home."

The flute struck a series of notes, music that made magic in the air. Magic that had once, years ago, roused the forest and brought Tom here. Finding the boy lost on this side of the Edge that morning, terrified, raving about the trees, Jack hadn't known what to do. What could one do with a fool who could wield such magic? Jack couldn't leave him loose in the forest, not with such power, nor send him back to do it again. And so he had brought him here, to Titania.

So who was the fool?

The music rose high and the world blurred around Jack, twisting, the ground falling away beneath his feet. The last thing he saw was the casket, the gold trims gleaming, waiting, as hungry as Mab herself. Neither of them gave up anything willingly. His heart . . . or Jenny's. And if he did what the queen asked, Titania would do with it as Mab had done with all her rivals' hearts. She would eat it.

Jack slammed into the forest floor, his breath driven from his body, pain lancing through him. He was back by the river. Jenny's voice drifted from the trees, coming closer, laughing at something Puck had said. Jack scrambled to his feet. The last light of day was vanishing. He was running out of time. Titania was weaving more than one web. And now he had a decision to make.

One girl. That was all she was. A mortal. Not even one of the fae. And all he had to do was take her where she already wanted to go.

Jack set his jaw and glared at the forest surrounding him, as if it challenged his intent.

He didn't have to like it. He just had to do it. A chance of freedom was within his grasp. And she was only one girl.

The sun slid out of sight and Jack cursed it as it vanished.

chapter nine

Night fell on the forest, the evening song of birds settling amid the trees, the red-gold light of sunset fading to purple darkness. Jack made no reappearance, though Puck had gone to investigate and had returned with her clothes, clean and dry, perfectly folded.

Jenny pulled them on gratefully, but kept the cloak too. She wasn't sure why—a protection against the forest, perhaps, to be clothed as part of it. She lifted the cloak to her face and breathed it in. Its scent made her feel safer. Jenny smiled grimly. She knew how that sounded. She also knew she was only looking out for herself now. She had a plan.

"Where is he?" she asked Puck yet again.

But Puck just shrugged, continued scratching his back on a tree trunk, and answered in the same vague way. "Something must have called him away, that's all. He'll be back with the dawn. Get some sleep."

Back with the dawn. Back with the dawn with some

other way to be rid of her, no doubt. And what sort of monster would he deliver her to next? Okay, maybe that was unfair. On the riverbank, she'd felt sorry for him, yes. For a moment. And for a moment, he seemed to have understood her when she said Tom had been . . . had been taken. But now Jack had vanished again without explanation. He wanted her to trust him. He'd washed her *clothes* even. But could she truly trust anyone who called the Woodsman and his wife friends? And even if she could get past that, she knew he only intended to return her to the Edge.

The crawling, pinprick sensation of Redcaps raced up her arms again and she rubbed them, trying to scour the memory away. It was no good. They'd come in the darkness. They would come again, them or something like them.

Jenny felt for the locket and held the metal against her fingers. She ran it along its chain, listening to the faint series of clicks it made.

The boy in the tree had told her the piper would go back to the castle, to the queen; the Woodsman and his wife had said he always went back to her in the end. But the queen had hunted the piper when he ran. It seemed less like he went back to her and more like she took him back. So if Tom was the piper and he was running away, he clearly wanted to get home. Had he tried all these years to escape? To get back to them? Had he been trying all along?

"*. . . she'll follow the river home soon enough . . .*" Puck had said.

The locket clicked along the chain, and Jenny tightened her grip.

Puck was sound asleep, and all around them the forest was still. Not even a breeze to disturb the trees.

Jenny swallowed. Jack had called himself a guardian. Of the Realm. The Edge. His job was to keep people out. She couldn't begrudge him that. In fact, she could make it easier on him.

Jenny rose silently, her eyes fixed on Puck's sleeping form. Boarding school dorms had taught her to be quiet at night, to make that dark trip from bed to bathroom without disturbing anyone. Of course, boarding school dorms didn't include dried branches underfoot or crunchy leaves and undergrowth. They didn't feature low-hanging brambles or the hooks of exposed roots or rocks. But she managed. Moonlight helped her, a moon much bigger and brighter than anything she had seen at home. It silvered the world and drove the shadows back.

Jenny crept through the forest, back toward the stream, which would lead her to the river. Which would lead her to the queen and Tom.

Once she moved away from their camp, the forest at night wasn't as silent as she had thought. The shadowy form of an owl swooped from tree to tree, its large moonlit eyes studying her as she passed, following her for a time before taking off after prey. The undergrowth shook and trembled as something hurried past her. Jenny jumped, stifled a cry, but it was gone as suddenly as it had come. She must have startled some nocturnal animal or woken something that slept. Above her, the treetops swayed slightly in the moonlight. The leaves whispered to each other.

They're only trees, she reminded herself, and she almost believed it, perhaps for the first time ever. The thought should have been comforting. Instead it suddenly occurred to her that this was a terrible idea. Alone, in the forest, in the dark. She pulled the cloak around her throat, burying her fingers in its leaves.

She couldn't go home without Tom. Not again. She thought of her mother. The dark circles under her eyes. Her sad smile. The nightstand cluttered with orange prescription bottles.

No, without Tom, better to never go home at all.

The stream glittered in the moonlight and Jenny picked her way along the bank, almost enjoying the music it made as it tumbled over the rocks and sang its way downstream. But the rest of the forest had fallen silent. A different quiet from that around the place where she and Puck had settled for the night. That had been comfortable, safe, a shield against the night. Here it was watchful, poised. She stopped and crouched low to the ground, breathing as quietly as possible.

Nothing moved. Not a rustle in the undergrowth, not a

movement among the leaves. Nothing. She moved forward again, scanning the darkness around her. The silence deepened. Even the river seemed hushed. Something crawled from her wrists up her arms and she realized it was her own flesh, the tiny hairs on her arms rising. A creature slid through the trees, just out of sight, shadowing her. It kept pace with her, part of the forest, part of the darkness. Jenny stopped, balanced on a rocky outcrop that jutted from the undergrowth like bare bones. She stared into the inky places between the trees.

It was there. Impossible to actually see it, not clearly. But she knew.

Berry-bright eyes, leaf-tangled hair, bark and vines . . .

Jenny swallowed down the fear that rose in her throat. She balled her fists so tightly her nails dug into her palms. The bite of pain made her temper burn more brightly.

"I'm not afraid of you," she whispered, as if daring it to come closer.

It didn't, though. It faded back into the trees, out of sight, but still there. She was sure it was still there—hostile, alien. Then realization slipped silently into her mind. She was the alien in this world, not something formed of it, part of it. She was the other.

The forest heaved as if a sudden gale rampaged through it, leaves and branches roaring like a thunderous sea. A mournful cry, carried on the wind, eerie and unnatural, reached her and she froze. The night pressed close all around her. She shifted to the balls of her feet, but before she could run, everything went still and quiet again. Only the shimmering river danced on, still murmuring its quiet song. Through the trees, the moonlight picked out a leaf here, a thorn there.

There was no sign of the creature in the forest. No sign of anything at all. This was a new kind of silence, born of terror so great that nothing dared move.

Another cry rang out, a weird and plaintive howl, like a small cat in great pain. Jenny's stomach twisted. She didn't think. She stumbled from the riverbank and followed a moonlit path through the unnaturally silent forest until it opened onto a glade, in the center of which was a stone circle. The smell of rot and decay surrounded her, but she pressed on, her nerves jangling. When she reached the stones, she found not a cat, but a tiny creature, wrapped in pale green-gray furs.

A baby, perhaps, but the child of what, she couldn't tell. Its tiny face was squashed and bat-like, the skin a deeper shade of gray-green than the fur. It shivered, its small lips pressed together so hard the lower one had turned white, and its dark blue eyes gazed up at her, ancient eyes in such a small face.

Then its somber expression crumpled and it wailed, a heartrending sound that evoked for Jenny every memory of being cold, alone, and afraid. Its open mouth displayed a row of tiny yellow teeth, sharp as pins, and a thick black tongue curled up behind them. It snarled at her, snapped at the air, vicious and terrified.

"Shh," Jenny whispered, steeling her nerve and leaning in closer. "Shh, it's okay. It's just me. I won't hurt you." The creature's eyes focused on her, and it stilled, its fierce little snarls turning to whimpers.

Before she could think better of it, Jenny scooped the baby into her arms, cradling it close. She had only held a cousin's baby before, but the little creature fit into her arms as if it had always belonged there. It turned its head toward her, the questing mouth open to receive milk she couldn't give it. A moment of panic seized her as it bared its teeth again. It was going to bite her, looking for blood like the Redcaps. But the little wet nose just nuzzled against her, and settled, comforted by her warmth.

Jenny shivered, holding it close and wondering what she was going to do now.

"Stop wandering off like that," Puck scolded as he stepped into the moonlight. Jenny jumped, her heart spasming. He glowered up at her. "Anything could happen to you and then what would I tell Jack? Where did you think you were going? What have you got there?"

So much for sneaking away in the night. Jenny turned to show him the baby, but on first sight of it, Puck's face paled.

"Put it back," he whispered. "Very carefully, put it back and move away."

"I'm not going to leave a baby—"

"It's not a baby. I mean, it is but it isn't— Trust me, Jenny. You have to put it back before the mother or the father finds us. Do you understand?"

The baby snuggled closer to her. Jenny smiled, smoothing down the silky hair. Her fingers brushed its leathery skin and the creature gave a tiny cooing noise. Ugly, yes, but a baby nonetheless.

"I'm not going to leave a baby alone out here at night," she repeated.

"It's not a human baby. It's a Leczi, and when its parents realize it's—" His feet tangled in the ferns and he went down, the air expelled from his lungs in a whoosh. He came back up, swearing loudly and his hands slick with blood, green blood. The conviction had gone from his voice when he spoke again. "I . . . I think I've just found its father."

Jenny approached the body warily. The Leczi had a thick mane of green-gray hair, the same shade as the fur covering the child. Now she realized that it wasn't a wrapping, but the child's own hair that covered it, long and silky. The adult Leczi's mouth was slack, open to reveal razor-sharp teeth, the same color as the child's but so much bigger. The fingers were tipped with long yellow claws. These were stained with more blood, a darker red than human, some old, but some fresh. Jenny could see raw, red, almost iridescent flesh trapped behind them. The Leczi had fought savagely, but it had still lost. Its stomach had been torn out. Claw marks gouged its skin.

Cradling the baby Leczi a little closer, Jenny let her eyes range over the broken remains. She'd never been close to a dead body before stepping into the woods. Now she'd seen two that had been all but torn to pieces. Her stomach coiled tight, her mouth filling with sweetness in a prelude to vomiting. She swallowed convulsively. She couldn't fall apart.

Upright, the creature would have been at least eight feet tall and terrifying, an ogre of legend, just as she had imagined a monster to be in her childhood. It smelled of corruption and decay, of rancid flesh, even though it could not have been dead for long. The baby gave off the same odor, she realized, just not so strongly.

"What could have done this?" she asked Puck.

To her horror, the hobgoblin was trembling. "I can think of one or two things, none of which we want to meet tonight. Jenny, we need to get out of here."

"Like the thing from the farmhouse? The one following us?"

But Puck looked away quickly. "Yes, possibly. Could be a Kobold. Or a troll. Maybe wood elves if they attacked in a swarm. And even a common ogre would have a pretty good chance at it too. None of which we would have a hope against. But there are other things. Much worse things . . ."

The baby stirred, opened its eyes, and then began to wail mournfully, the sound sharp and grating, tearing on the edge of their hearing to the very point of pain. Jenny hugged it closer, rocking it against her body as she shushed it.

The thought of the greenman chilled her, and despite Puck's attempt to deflect her question, she was sure it was still nearby—and not just since she had ventured out alone, she realized now. Ever since she arrived in this place, whenever the sun had set, when the darkness oozed up out of the shadows like oil, she could feel its eyes on her, feel it circling around her. It hadn't come so close by day. With Jack there, it would never dare to come so close, but at night, with Jack gone . . .

A chill etched its way down her back, little fingers of fear probing between her vertebrae. She could sense it.

Why had she ever thought she could brave this world alone at night?

But she had, she reminded herself. She had seen it, and faced it. She set her jaw a little more firmly.

"It's watching us now, isn't it?"

Puck tugged at her arm. "Leave the child and come back to the camp. It isn't safe here. *Whatever* killed the Leczi may come back at any moment. Please, Jenny. It's dangerous here."

"All right," she agreed, hiding her relief at the thought of their camp and safety. "We'll go back, but the baby comes too. I won't leave it here to die."

❧ ❧ ❧

They made their way slowly back along the path, Puck's eyes darting furtively from side to side. The baby slept now, curled like a kitten against Jenny's chest, its head on her shoulder, its breath coming in harsh little snorts. With tiny arms and legs bunched up against its torso, it held in its warmth. Jenny feared she'd disturb it with her own fears, so she hummed softly to it as they walked, and the creature slept on, snorting and snuffling into her shoulder. Puck glared at her whenever he dared tear his attention away from their surroundings.

"What's a Kobold?" she asked. She didn't know the word. Come to that, she didn't know what a Leczi was either, but something in the way Puck had said *Kobold* intrigued her.

Puck rolled his eyes to the branches and the stars above, growling under his breath.

"A spirit set to guard a house. First they were the dwellers in the trees, the living spirits of the forest. But their sacred trees were cut down and carved into figurines in such a way that the spirit was trapped inside. Then they were shut into boxes, locked away and brought indoors. Once there, they lived as slaves. Only if the box was opened by one other than their master could they escape, and if they did, they wreaked a terrible revenge." He leaned closer, enjoying this a little too much for her comfort. "They stole the children, spoiled the herds, blighted the crops, and set the house alight."

Jenny drew back from him, but he wasn't finished. He grabbed her wrist to pull her close.

"To protect their young, the masters created toys to teach the children never to go near a Kobold's prison—terrifying things. A box was simply but beautifully decorated in the manner of the shrine that trapped the spirit. The lid was held in check by a simple latch—unlike the wooden cage, which was sealed by magic. Ah, but if the child tripped that catch, just as if they opened the Kobold's box, something terrible leaped out, laughing like a maniac delighting in new freedom."

Disappointed, Jenny sighed. Was this Puck's idea of a joke? He did have that twisted sense of humor, after all. "A jack-in-the-box," she said. "I had one when I was little." They'd both had it, her and Tom, given to them by some great-aunt who should have known better. It had scared her half to death, which Tom had found hilarious, of course. Where was it now, she wondered. Lost and forgotten in the attic, gathering dust, probably. She couldn't remember when it had been put away, or lost. So many things blurred in her memory around the time Tom had vanished.

"A Kobold," Puck told her solemnly. "It's called a Kobold."

She shook her head. A jack-in-the-box. Another Jack. "Does everything come back to Jack?"

Puck grinned suddenly, the seriousness evaporating like morning mist. "Between mankind and the Realm, yes, of course."

⚜ ⚜ ⚜

Jack was back with the morning, just as Puck had promised. Jenny found him standing over her, his expression dark as a thunderous sky. For a moment she couldn't move. She stared up at him, suddenly afraid.

There was no shaking him, or Puck, she realized. No running away from them, no striking out on her own. But she couldn't let him lead her back home, or whatever else he had planned. She struggled to think of an alternative in that split second, faced with the anger blazing from his mismatched eyes. Nothing came. She stared up at him. Beside her, something warm and soft stirred, cooed, and then began to cry, a fierce snarling noise cut with knife-sharp wails. The baby! She sat up as quickly as she could, Jack forgotten, and gathered it against her.

But Jack was not so easily dismissed.

"Where did you get that?" he asked, his voice thin. She looked up. His jaw pulsed. His brows formed a grim line over tired eyes. He had not slept, then. Whether it was his duty as guardian, or hunting the creature in the forest to keep it away, he looked exhausted. In fact, she never saw him sleep. He didn't even doze when they rested. His eyes never left their surroundings, never ceased their patrol. And now he stared at the child in her arms.

"I found it last night," she replied, aware of the defensiveness in her voice. "Its father was dead."

"And where is the mother?" Jack turned away, moving with unsettling speed. She kept forgetting that whatever he was, he wasn't human. Now, with the dawn rising around them, his speed and strength seemed to grow by the moment. "Puck!"

But Puck was nowhere to be seen. Swearing, Jack searched the undergrowth around him, prodding all the likely looking hidey-holes. Puck was gone.

Lucky Puck, she thought.

When he turned back to her, his hands were clenched, his shoulders straight and hard, his chest rising and falling rapidly, and his face a blank, white mask. "Will you at least show me where you found it?" He bit out the request.

Jenny led the way, the baby cradled in her arms. She found herself drawn without conscious thought to stroke its face, to rock it against her as she walked. The baby snuggled, quiet now, lulled by movement. It had to be hungry, and yet, good little soul that it was, it never made a whimper. Jenny sang to it in undertones, gentle songs she remembered from her earliest childhood. When she looked at Jack, his expression mixed fascination and disgust. He flicked his dark hair from his eyes and turned away.

From the clearing ahead, they heard the sound of a woman weeping. Jenny stopped, hugging the child a little closer. Jack slid in front of her, drawing his wicked-looking knife.

The woman wore a simple white shift-like gown. She was sitting on the fallen tree trunk, her head and shoulders hunched over. She trembled as she wept, her sobs cutting through the still forest.

Jack came to a halt so quickly that Jenny nearly ran into him.

"Who is she?" she whispered.

He opened his mouth to say something when a dreadful cry split the silence. It sounded like metal tearing under pressure. Jenny's free hand went instinctively to her ear, to block the sound, but Jack seized her shoulders and pulled her into the undergrowth. The baby woke, its face reddening as it made ready to cry. Jenny hugged it close to her.

"Quiet!" Jack said. "Keep it quiet or we're dead."

Jenny pushed her little finger into the child's mouth, trying not to think of its teeth, and was rewarded by its frantic sucking. Hunger made it forget fear and it fell silent, but for the occasional grunt of frustration that no milk was forthcoming.

"This won't last long. It's too hungry. What was that awful noise?"

Wind rippled the leaves, set the forest around the clearing trembling and then, beyond the weeping woman, Jenny saw something alight on the ground as gracefully as a bird. For all that, the earth still shook beneath the weight of its enormous body.

"Elders defend us," Puck gasped. "It's a dragon." He wriggled from the bushes beside them, planting himself firmly at Jack's side. Questions of where he had been evaporated in the face of this mighty beast.

The creature was over twenty feet long, coil after coil of scaled body glinting red in the sunlight. Its great head moved from side to side as it tasted the air, a snake's tongue flickering between the massive teeth. Saliva dripped from its maw and it sucked in a breath. The roar bellowed through the clearing, rattling the forest.

"It's a dragon," said Jenny. "Jack, it's a real—"

"I know," he snapped. "Just stay down and be quiet. Maybe it won't scent us over the stench of Leczi."

"But that sound." She kept her voice low, no more than a breath. "Did it make that?"

"No. It was her. She called it."

On the far side of the clearing the fairy woman got to her feet, her pale face slick with her tears. There was no life in her eyes. Jenny knew that look far too well. Her mother wore the same expression. Her own mother could look right through Jenny, as if she weren't there some days. Perhaps she wasn't. Some days, anything could have happened and the only thing her mother would have welcomed was oblivion. Faced with that, the wretched boarding school had been a blessed relief. Faced with it now, seeing it in another . . .

"Jack, you have to stop her."

His glance, a mix of bemusement and disbelief, told her she was mad. "That's Titania's dragon, one of the most dangerous creatures in the Realm. If she wants to commit suicide, it's her affair."

"She's the baby's mother."

"Which means she's a Leczi," Puck interrupted. "And powerful in her own right. All the more reason to stay out of it, Jack."

Jenny turned on them both. "You can't! Look at her. And what will become of the baby? I know you'd both rather see it dead, but we aren't leaving it behind. So help her, or get ready for a life of Leczi nappies!"

"Jenny," Jack said in a calmer voice. "You don't understand. It isn't right for any one of us—"

"And what about the baby? Jack! You're a guardian. You have to. She wouldn't do this if she knew that the child was still . . . Oh God!" The decision was too terrible, but it blazed in her mind as if already made for her. "Oh God. I don't believe I'm doing this!" She surged to her feet, trying to shelter the baby, and ran into the clearing, straight at the dragon.

chapter ten

The dragon's roar shook the ground beneath her feet, almost sending Jenny to her knees. She scrambled forward, breathing hard. She was an idiot, that's what she was. The baby felt like a lead weight against her chest, dragging at her shoulders.

"Stop!" she screamed.

Claws scoured the earth to her left, and the Leczi's eyes flashed.

Then the mother saw the child.

Disbelief passed over her features, and then a light sprang into her eyes. She struggled toward Jenny, but the dragon brought one huge foot down between them and lashed its tail out, raking up the earth like a plow. Jenny threw herself back, but with her arms protecting the baby, she fell heavily, rocks digging into her shoulder. The dragon loomed over her, flashing red in the sunlight, each scale a shining jewel, and a wave of hot breath covered her, the smell of sulfur. She scrambled back, trying to retreat.

A figure leaped over her, waving a long tree branch. Jack yelled something incoherent, running right at the dragon with his makeshift spear as if his presence alone could drive it back. The beast exhaled with a shriek, and fire billowed toward this new threat. The branch burst into flames, but Jack held on, swinging it toward the dragon in an arc of light. The dragon shied to the left, exposing its flank, where a series of gashes glistened with crimson blood. Jenny thought of the dead Leczi, the blood and skin beneath its yellow nails.

"Jenny, get back!" he yelled. "To the forest!"

A line of flames burst toward him, incinerating the grass and turning the earth into a scorched scar. Jack dived to one side, rolled over the burning branch, and came up again, thrusting the end at the dragon's exposed belly. Jenny sucked in a breath, but the makeshift weapon only glanced off the glistening scales.

Squirming against Jenny's chest, the baby began to scream, its awful keening cry rising above even the roar of the dragon. Jenny struggled to her knees in time to see the Leczi running toward her, her face distorted with a vicious hunger. The baby screeched again and this time the mother joined in, their voices intertwining at the top of Jenny's hearing. Claws sprouted from the Leczi's hands as she bore down on Jenny.

Jack staggered back, still brandishing the flaming branch.

"Run, Jenny!" He drove forward again, aiming for the wounded side and the dragon lumbered away, on the retreat.

The Leczi shrieked and Jenny froze, staring at her, at the murderous claws and the teeth twisting her once beautiful face. But the creature wasn't looking at her. The piercing eyes were fixed on the baby alone.

"Wait," Jenny whispered. "Wait, please . . . just wait . . ."

She fumbled with the baby, cursing her own hands as she did so. The child cried out mournfully as Jenny lifted it out and offered it to its mother, holding it at arm's length.

The Leczi seemed to shrink down on itself, teeth and claws retracting. She edged forward, warily snapping her eyes up to Jenny, then back down to the baby. Jenny held firm, forcing herself to be calm and still so as not to frighten the mother.

In no more than a heartbeat, the Leczi snatched back the child, pulling it to her breast and crooning over it.

The roar of the dragon shook the world around them. Jack raced by Jenny and grabbed her shoulder, pulling her after him.

"I said run!"

Stumbling behind him, Jenny tried to catch both her breath and footing as they dodged into the trees. Jack pitched himself forward, rolling into the undergrowth and pulling her down behind him. She struggled through a tangle of limbs, fern, and bushes, and fell, finding herself face-to-face with him, their mouths a finger's length apart. His exhilarated grin faded, and his eyes widened, the pupils huge and dark. Her own face reflected there, mouth parted.

So much for her insistence that he never touch her again.

For a moment the insane thought that he would kiss her flickered across her mind. Jack stared. He swallowed hard, his Adam's apple bobbing in his throat. Her eyes followed its movement and then were drawn back to meet his gaze.

She'd been kissed before, once, by Peter Browning outside a school dance. It was rushed and disastrous, teeth clashing, wet. He'd tasted of beer and cigarettes and she'd frozen under the onslaught, then pulled away to find him laughing at her inexperience.

But this was different, wasn't it?

Jack leaned closer, his face strained, as if he weren't acting of his own free will. He reached out, his fingertips sliding into her hair, his palm cradling her cheek. Jenny's eyelids fluttered down and her breath hitched.

The dragon let out an earth-trembling bellow and the spell shattered as danger reasserted itself. Its wings battered the trees overhead and a shower of leaves and twigs rained down all over them. Jack snapped to a protective crouch, every muscle poised.

Free of his hands, Jenny's good sense slammed back into her head. The dragon whipped around in the air above the clearing, a new gash running down its side, a murderous gleam in its multifaceted eyes.

The Leczi still knelt in the clearing, cradling her baby, singing to it.

"Oh God, it's going to kill them!" Jenny started to get up, but Jack hauled her back down, pinning her there with his body.

"Don't move. Not if you want to live. Cover your ears."

She pushed at him ineffectively. "Get off me!"

He slapped his hands over the sides of her head, and she was surrounded by the scent of him—a combination of musk and forest leaves, of new growth and decay.

The dragon roared, then drew in a breath, the wind of its great wings sending a gale through the trees. Flames billowed from its mouth, boiling the air, making everything shimmer.

The Leczi lifted her head as if scenting the air. Her eyes were closed, and she smiled. She actually smiled. The flames enveloped her and she opened her mouth. Instead of a scream, she sang.

The fire transformed around her. It spread out like wings, billowing away in time with her song. The dragon recoiled, howling as it fell back, and the Leczi's note rose again, higher this time. Jenny's teeth ached with the sound. It pierced deep inside her brain. She winced. Jack's hands tightened around her ears, muffling her hearing from the full impact. Twisting her head, she caught just a glimpse of his grimace. He wasn't immune to the sound either, but he kept his hands where they were. His eyes showed discomfort, then outright pain until he squeezed them tightly shut.

The Leczi got to her feet, her child opening its mouth and singing in counterpoint now. She turned, her hair flowing out behind her in golden green strands, unaffected by the flames and the heat. They advanced slowly, the music of their magic tying the struggling dragon to the earth, preventing its escape. She wanted revenge for the death of her mate, for the risk to her child. She wanted . . .

"Blood," Jack whispered. The word ran from his body into Jenny's. She could feel it vibrate through her head. "I've given her blood. What more does she—"

The Leczi reached out her hand and pressed her fingers into the throat of the flailing dragon. She smiled her enigmatic smile and her song reached its highest pitch. The dragon convulsed, limbs, tail, and wings lashing out but failing to strike her.

Then it fell still and the world turned silent.

Breathing hard, Jack released Jenny and rolled off her. She gasped for breath, relieved to have him gone but cold now where the weight of his body had covered hers. She sat up, her heart frantic. Without the warm solidity of him, she felt oddly exposed.

Jack stared at her, as if struggling through the same tangle of feelings.

The sounds of the forest returned to her and Jenny looked up. The Leczi had turned back to face them. Even through the trees her eyes picked them out.

"Come forth," she said, and her voice seemed to ripple the air around them.

Jack got to his feet, wary as a cat. He spread his arms wide on either side, corralling Jenny amid the trees. He didn't look back.

"Stay behind me," he hissed. "And this time do as I say."

She didn't appreciate his tone, but she followed him, edging forward out of the trees.

The Leczi hummed to herself now, cradling her baby, rocking it back and forth. She swayed like a blade of grass, slender, elegant, nothing like a threat at all. Certainly not something that could destroy a fire-breathing dragon with just her voice.

"What's a—what's a Leczi, Jack?" Jenny whispered.

"Now you ask the right question," he replied. "Nature spirits, but powerful, especially when crossed. As you saw. If she speaks to you, if she opens her mouth, cover your ears and be careful. Be very careful, understand? *Try*."

Jenny couldn't help it—she almost smiled. Ducking out of the shelter of the trees, she followed him into the clearing and stopped next to him. When they were still, the

Leczi looked up. Her eyes were green, even more vibrant than Jack's green eye. They positively glowed.

The Leczi opened her mouth. Jack flinched, but Jenny didn't move. She knew Jack wanted her to run, or at least cover her ears, but when she looked into the Leczi's face, she couldn't. It would have been an insult.

Jack let out a long, low hiss, but Jenny ignored him. Let him scold her later. And he would. But she didn't care.

"You took my child." There was no doubt the Leczi was talking to her. Jenny couldn't look away. The music in the Leczi's voice compelled attention, as did her child's. Their magic, Jenny supposed. The same way the Leczi had repelled the flames, to defeat and kill the dragon.

"I couldn't leave it alone."

"*Him,*" said the Leczi's mother, lifting a hand to stroke her son's hair. "When I found his father, my mate, I thought—" She broke off and held the baby closer still, stroking the long silken fur. "My thanks."

"You're welcome."

The Leczi took a step toward her, her free arm outstretched. Jack stepped between them. Every muscle in his back and neck tensed, his hands stretched out on either side, fingers splayed. The Leczi tilted her head to one side, examining him.

"I have no quarrel with you, Jack o' the Forest. Nor with her. But I do have a question. Why would the queen send her dragon out where it could hear my call?"

Jack glanced at the Leczi, his eyes wary. "Why does she do anything?" he finally asked, raising one shoulder in a shrug. Jenny peered at him. If he hadn't known the dragon was nearby, it was clear he had at least suspected something. The exchange baffled her.

The Leczi looked past him now, straight at Jenny. Jack remained between them, looking from one to the other. "Step aside, Jack," the Leczi said.

Jack didn't move. Whatever the Leczi saw in his face seemed to amuse her. She smiled, but sorrow tinged the corners of her lips.

"You'll not hurt her," Jack said finally.

"No. Never for a moment. You have my word. It's just a gift, and a gift she deserves. Don't deny her that, Jack. Guardian or not, you cannot refuse to let her take my gift freely offered."

He breathed in, his shoulders contracting as he released the air in a long sigh. "Very well." He turned his back on the Leczi, glaring at Jenny as he faced her. "Come," he said, "take what's yours, Jenny Wren." He stalked behind her, but she had no doubt he was within reach.

Jenny took a step toward the Leczi, keeping her gaze lowered. When she glanced up, though, the Leczi's smile gave her nothing to fear. She took Jenny's hand and pulled her close. Warmth tingled in her palm and the Leczi leaned in to kiss her cheek.

"My gift is a spell that will work once only, little Wren. And it will choose the time. Kiss it, and bury it, and what you wish will be yours eventually."

She drew back and Jenny found a small, polished green stone in her hand. The color swirled across the surface, like the Leczi's eyes.

A stone. Jenny stared at it, then back at the Leczi. How was that a spell?

"Keep it safe," the Leczi warned. "Use it well. And keep it secret. Thus is my debt to you paid."

Jenny flushed, embarrassed by the gift, and her reaction to it. "I—I don't need—"

"A debt is a debt. It's our way, and always has been. Ask Jack. He knows all about debts. Especially debts of honor. Isn't that right?"

She cast an arch look at Jack, and when Jenny turned to look at him—still scowling, standing sullenly amid the trees like a lost boy—the Leczi laughed, her voice joining the breeze in the trees. And then she and her child were gone.

chapter eleven

Jenny was sure her legs were going to crumple beneath her. Blisters worried at her toes and heels. Each step burned. She didn't know where they were going. Maybe back to the Edge. Maybe just round and round in circles until he decided what to do with her. She didn't know what to say to Jack, wary of his answer. He pulled the cloak further around his body and stared off into the distance. Ever since Jenny had returned it to him, he'd had it wrapped around himself like a coat of armor.

"What's wrong?" Jenny asked, not looking at him. He'd been ignoring her, his mood darkening as the sun sank lower in the sky.

Jack just grunted.

Charming.

"I couldn't just leave the baby there to die, Jack."

"No, you had to blunder in without thinking instead. What were you doing out in the forest at night anyway? Why did you leave Puck?"

"You know why! I have to find my brother. And you and Puck aren't about to help."

Jack picked his way off the path and through the brush. Jenny fell in step beside him.

"You wander in the Realm at your own peril," he said, his eyes bright under the dark hair across his forehead. "That's why I'm here."

"Jack—"

"I have to leave soon."

Of course he did. Couldn't stick around and face an argument. "Why?"

"I can't stay with you at night," he told her, as if to do so would be somehow improper.

"Right. Of course, that explains everything. Where will you be?"

He hesitated, met her eyes for a second, and she sensed him biting back a short-tempered answer. "Elsewhere. Busy." He turned to Puck, who'd been watching them, his grin growing wider. "This is fine for the night. Go find her some food."

Puck didn't move, though. He plonked himself down at the edge of the tree, pretending not to watch them.

The little hollow, not far from the stream, was peaceful and off the beaten track. She sat in the long grass, watching him. Waiting.

"I have no choice," Jack said at last, stretching his arms

behind him, and then folding them behind his back. "It's a duty."

"What sort of duty?"

He looked at her, eyes metallic. "I don't pry into your thoughts, Jenny Wren. Why can't you leave me mine?"

"Because you never answer a question. You don't want me to go after Tom, so tell me why."

Jack sighed. But Jenny kept watching him. She ran her palms over the tips of the grass. Patience had always defeated her brother. Even when he had been in a bad mood, she always knew all she had to do was wait. Maybe it would work on Jack.

"Why are you doing this?" he asked at last. "It's dangerous, difficult. That's just ignoring the fact that you were probably lured over the Edge in the first place. Someone wanted to bring you here and they used your memories of Tom to do it. He's been gone for seven years, Jenny. That's a powerful long time, especially here."

"How do you know all that?" she asked quickly.

Jack tilted his head at her, raising his eyebrows. "It's common knowledge here. He's the piper. He belongs to the queen, body and soul. He won't go back. And you waited seven years. Why start this insane quest now?"

The question caught Jenny off guard. Her fingers tightened around a fistful of grass. "It's—it's the first chance I ever got. I looked everywhere. Tried everything. But it never worked, not until now." It wasn't quite true. She tried to hide the blush that heated her cheeks, but Jack didn't appear to notice. He made a dismissive noise deep in his throat.

"There are chances every day," he said, waving a hand in the air. "The portals are everywhere. I know. I have to keep people away from them all the time." He gave her a pointed look.

"You are so arrogant!" she burst out, ripping a fistful of grass from the ground and hurling it at him. It didn't have quite the desired impact. He looked at her, unfazed, and pulled a blade from where it dangled in front of his face. She grabbed another fistful, struggling to keep her voice even. "Maybe there are ways through on this side," she bit out, "but it's different where I come from." She pushed away the voice that told her she'd been too afraid to try, too terrified of forests and trees after what she had seen that night. She sat straighter, tightening her death-grip on the grass. "I owe it to Tom to try. I owe it to our family. You don't know what it was like, after he was gone. They think he's dead, but for so long, they thought—we all thought—" *The worst.* Oh God, the worst nightmares imagination and the media could conjure up. "But he isn't dead. And I'm *not* crazy. He's here."

Jack leaned against a tree and crossed his arms. "Perhaps. But maybe he should be dead. Maybe you should leave it like that for the sake of us all."

"Are you a monster? He's my brother! I love him!" she shouted. This time her fingers curled around a stone and she hurled it at him, her anger breaking her hold on reason. She didn't see Jack's arm move, but he snatched the rock from the air in front of his face.

Jenny recoiled as if she'd been struck herself.

"You loved him seven years ago," said Jack in a voice terrible in its calmness. "Now you love a ghost, a memory. You'll see. You don't even know your brother anymore. Seven years, Jenny, seven years in the court of the queen . . ." He tossed the stone aside.

"He's my brother, Jack. He was my best friend. We looked out for each other and I lost him. It was my fault. I went home and he didn't. And everything changed." Jenny struggled to keep her voice steady. "I want him back. I love my brother. Can't you understand that?"

Puck looked up from preening at his fur.

"Don't listen to him," he said with a laugh, clapping his hands together. "Jack can't tell you about love, fraternal or otherwise. He doesn't have a heart."

Jack pushed off from the tree he'd been leaning on. "Shut up, hobgoblin. You know nothing and understand less."

"What do you mean?" Jenny asked, ignoring Jack's darkening face. "Puck?"

"Just what I say," he chuckled. "Jack has no heart. Otherwise he couldn't perform his duty, do his job day after day, night after night. But he longs for a heart, don't you, lad? A heart of your own?"

"You're nothing but a miserable little—" Jack began, but Puck tutted him to silence.

"Of course I am. And you long for the heart you can never have. They won't let you have one."

"My heart is safe," Jack said, sliding down to sit at the base of the tree, like a puppet with cut strings. "There's nothing more to be said on that, Puck. As well you know."

Jenny watched him, his head bent, worrying a blade of grass in his fingers. She hesitated a moment, then got to her feet and approached.

The sun was low in the sky. The trees cast long shadows around him.

Jack suddenly surged to stand. He towered over her, a dark silhouette with burning eyes like gas flames. "I should go." His voice sounded odd. Something from her nightmares. Something momentarily forgotten and yet, because he was Jack, terribly familiar.

She took a step back, her foot pivoting in the dirt. When he didn't move, Jenny advanced on him quickly, before she could lose her nerve. Fingers fumbling, she managed to undo the clasp of her necklace. The little golden heart dangled between them. She stood before Jack and offered it to him. The setting sun made the gold gleam red, and she thought of the dragon's glittering scales.

"It isn't much," she whispered, "but . . . take it."

The marsh lights in Jack's eyes dimmed. His anger, his

darkness, seemed to die in him, like the calmness of the forest after a storm. He looked down at her, his eyes turning bright with confusion. "That's gold. It's a pure metal. I can't, Jenny."

Jenny frowned. "What's wrong with that?"

"Gold has a magic all its own." Puck laughed. "All things do. But gold is strongest of all. Noble, precious, magical gold. Even the earth itself can't corrode it."

Jack growled, baring his teeth at Puck, who grinned even more violently, as if that too was a taunt. For a moment she thought Jack would launch himself at the hobgoblin and stepped closer to part them.

Jenny swiftly took Jack's hand and pressed the necklace into his palm, closing his fingers over it. His skin was warm and smooth. She let go.

"If you help me find the one who gave it to me, it's the smallest payment."

"I asked no payment." Something flashed in Jack's face that Jenny couldn't identify. She looked at him, searching his eyes. "I have to go," he said again.

He stood there in the lengthening shadows, unmoving. Impossibly tall, unnaturally large. The light played tricks and gave the angles and planes of his face an appearance like polished wood. His right eye was greener than ever, a forest green of new leaves and fresh shoots. The blue of his left eye was the noon sky on a cloudless day.

"You will help me, won't you?" she asked. He uncurled his hand and stared at the heart. "You can't try to send me back again. Not after . . ."

Jack shuddered, the sense of menace leeching out of him, and looked at her once more. Changeable as the wind, her guardian. Like leaves in that wind, never resting. Jack nodded and fastened the chain around his neck. He tucked the locket carefully under his shirt.

"Very well, if that's your will. I'll take you to him, though I still think you won't care for what you discover. I'll make sure you get safely to the queen's palace and see your brother."

It rushed over her in a wave—relief, victory—but he looked so miserable she couldn't let the full extent of her elation show. She was sure he saw it anyway. "Thank you," Jenny whispered. It sounded like a prayer.

"I have to go."

"But . . ." She glanced back at the trees. Was it out there? Watching them? The thing in the forest. She sensed it, coming closer all the time. Following her. It seemed to remember her as clearly as she remembered it. "The creature . . ."

Jack followed her gaze, his eyes hard as precious stones. Then he turned away. "It won't bother you," he said. "I'll keep it away. I'll be back here when you awaken."

❧ ❧ ❧

The sun sank lower in the sky, only a slice of it visible above the tree line. Still Jack watched from the safety of the thickest foliage. Jenny sat, her hair twisted in a hasty knot, eating the last of the berries she had gathered. They stained her lips and her fingers. Every so often, she took out the stone the Leczi had given her, turning it over in her palm.

Her heart was too great for this place—he knew that now with certainty—and as such too open to being beguiled. The way she had rescued the Leczi child, and stood before the Leczi herself . . . The queen would grind her to dust. Oberon would use her no better.

She should go back to the Edge. But she wouldn't. He'd have to hand her over to one or the other.

And he'd promised to take her to Tom. To the palace. To the queen.

The thought was like swallowing iron.

Titania offered freedom if he obeyed her, if he handed Jenny over like a shiny bauble. He'd brought Titania lost things before . . . But that was because Oberon normally wanted nothing to do with the mortal world. This time it would be different.

Jack closed his hand over the gold pendant, felt it slide on the chain around his neck. Her heart, her mark on him in changeless gold. Had she bound him now as well? Or had he bound himself the moment he'd said *I'll keep a watch, I swear it.*

And bound himself further when he'd promised to take her to Tom.

He groaned, a deep creaking moan. Why had he said that? And she'd looked so happy. Like he'd just promised her the world instead of her doom.

The light had faded to almost nothing now. Still Jack lingered. Jenny settled down for the night, laughing at some of Puck's jests. The hobgoblin was positively courteous with her this evening, and Jack frowned.

Where had Puck gone when they'd faced the Leczi?

The weight of sunset pressed down on Jack, turning his rational thought sluggish and dull. Of a morning he would be able to figure it out, he was sure. But now . . . something else strained to get out with the growing dark. He struggled against it, trying to grasp the idea that was gathering momentum at the back of his mind. Puck had gone somewhere. Puck's attitude had changed. Why? Not because she'd saved the Leczi's child, surely. So where had Puck gone? And why?

The natural energies of the forest froze and contracted. Jack straightened, his bones aching as if the frost had gnawed on them. A wave of absolute cold burst through the trees, followed by the heat of a tropical night. He bent, his hands supporting himself on his knees, and tried to turn, but a force far stronger than him closed a mighty grip around him, holding him still.

"Well, what have we here?"

The voice resonated through his chest, as if it echoed off

stone in deep places. A figure stepped up to the edge of the tree line. Jack's body reacted in spite of itself, as it always did, as he was bound to do. He dropped to his knees and bowed his head.

"My lord." The words fell from his mouth, brought forth, whether Jack willed them or not.

Oberon towered over him, dark eyes glistening in his flawless face. Vines and fruit tangled in his black curls, and the antlers that formed his crown looked incongruous and yet as much a part of him as his strong arms or fleet legs. Some said he'd been a god once, in the mortal world, or as good as. Jack didn't know anything about that. All he knew, deep in the most sacred part of his soul, was that the king was to be obeyed. And even deeper, right down in the most secret place of all, a place he could never think of revealing, Jack hated him for it.

Oberon's full attention turned on Jenny, his eyes burning as he watched her lie down, watched her eyes close and her breath settle into the rhythm of sleep.

"Whatever have you found, Jack?" he asked, his voice rumbling like the earth itself.

"She's on a quest," Jack replied. "In search of her brother taken by the queen."

Oberon snorted at the mention of Titania. It was well known that they hated each other now. Arguments over servants, over boundaries, over anything at all . . . The queen was powerful, but she feared the king. And he in turn loathed her independence.

"But that's not all, I believe," the king replied. "Puck tells an interesting tale, you know? Of a great heart, of a battle with the Redcaps, of her rescue by a Kobold, no less, the rescue of a girl of pure spirit and heart. Of that same girl, risking her life for a fae child. The offspring of Leczi, who every other being here would have left to die. What do you make of that, Jack?"

The wintry cold inside Jack's chest spread into his limbs like frost across the forest floor. Puck had told. Puck had told everything. Worst of all, Jack wasn't even surprised. He'd been reckless. Now he bit down on his anger and tried to choose his words with care, though the compulsion to obey blurred his conscious mind.

"I'm charged with guarding the Edge, my lord, and with protecting those who quest in the Realm."

The trembling in his limbs warned him that the sun had almost set. His body ached, but Oberon's very presence held him as he was, on his knees. And would continue to do so until the king had extracted whatever he wanted. And then he would do whatever he willed. And not for the first time.

Elders preserve me, Jack thought, *this will hurt. He'll make sure of it.*

"Tell me, Jack," Oberon went on relentlessly. "Who do you serve?"

"You, my lord." *Best to get it over with quickly. Best to get it done.* "I serve only you."

Trailing brambles of agony began to stretch out through his limbs, tearing their way through the skin.

"Not . . . entirely true, that answer. Who else?"

"You, my lord. I serve only you." Panic touched him now, setting his blood rushing. Did Oberon know about Titania's offer? Did he know about the casket? He must, if he gave it to her. Or had she taken it? Could she do that? Jack hadn't told Puck any of it. What else had the king heard? What could he know?

Oberon chuckled and the pain sharpened still further, thorns puncturing him from the inside.

"Perhaps I misspoke myself," said the king. He reached down one huge hand to Jack's shoulder. It was the first actual physical contact, and it crushed him into the soil. "Who else *would* you serve?"

"My lord? I don't . . . I don't . . ." Jack clenched his teeth. He couldn't say it, not again. He'd made that mistake before and look where it had gotten him.

"Say it, Jack. I command it."

"The May Queen." He ground out the words. "When she comes. The . . . the Wren."

Oberon's smile broadened, triumphant. "She's beautiful this time. You choose so well, my Jack."

Jack drew back from him, fought not to cower, failed.

"But my lord, I didn't choose her. She isn't the May Queen. She's just a girl . . . just a lost girl."

"Then why are you bringing her to Titania?"

"I'm not!" He struggled again, his muscles straining, the thorns inside beginning to rip their way through even the king's constraints. It would be bad this time, the pain nothing to now. When the king allowed it, Jack knew his body would tear itself apart. But first he had to stop this, had to explain that Jenny wasn't a May Queen. She was just a girl. A stupid, thoughtless, stubborn, lost girl, with a heart too great for her own safety.

Liar, whispered the wind in the trees.

Liar, the shifting leaves replied.

"You don't understand, do you, Jack?" Oberon's voice ground him down once more. "Or you don't remember, perhaps. To say you choose them isn't strictly true. You just identify them. They are chosen by the Realm. Even in spite of yourself. Once upon a time, humans called it Hunting the Wren, when they sought her out and bound her, and carried her home. And if the spirits were willing she became the May Queen, the fairest of them all, so they brought her to the forest and gave her over. She came to us, to *me.* She must come willingly. That is the way of things, the oldest magic of all, the magic of earth and stone and blood. But the forest doesn't *choose.* It just *knows.* And so do you."

Jenny Wren. Elders help him, he'd called her Jenny Wren. And more than once. And Puck had heard him, and Puck had seen. And Puck had run off to their master with the news. The news of the coming of a Wren and a May Queen that Jack had found.

Puck had told him everything. And Jack had made sure he could, because he hadn't thought. He'd used words that had power without a care for the consequences.

"No, please," Jack groaned, and the pain burrowed through him, forcing him to yield through sheer force of determination, breaking him like roots breaking stones.

"So why bring her to Titania when you should bring her to me?"

He blurted out the answer. "That's where she wants to go."

"Is it?" The king laughed again. "Well then, by all means do it. Obey the May Queen . . ." He caught Jack's wide-eyed look of panic. "Oh yes, Jack, she is the May Queen. I tested her, had my lady's dragon kill the cursed Leczi father, and left the child to die. Who but the May Queen would hear its cry and respond? Who else would care so about a loathsome forest child like that? She is the May Queen. So let her face Titania. With all the queen's creatures spying and closing the net on the girl, it's only a matter of time anyway. The dragon was just the first. But just remember, my Jack in arms, in the end, willing or no, you'll bring her to me. You'll make her come willingly."

Jack's eyes ached. His neck strained. Everything in him wanted to refuse, but branch, root, and thorn wouldn't let him, all the magic woven around him over millennia wouldn't let him, all the magic that rose like sap inside him wouldn't let him. And if he couldn't say it, he couldn't do it. He'd have to obey.

What did she matter to him? She was just a girl. Just a stubborn, foolish girl. Great heart or not, she was nothing to him. Nothing but this pain. The king would have no reason to torture him if it weren't for Jenny.

No. That wasn't true either. The king would always find a reason to torture him. Because he was a Jack. And Oberon was the king.

"My lord," he whispered. "I'm yours. You know that."

"Of course I do, Jack." Oberon frowned at him as if he was a conundrum to be solved. "Whatever might have made you think otherwise? Go now, and remember, when the time comes: She is *mine,* guardian, not yours, or anyone else's. Not Titania's. Not Mab's. *My* May Queen. Allow nothing and no one to harm her, or I will watch your heartwood burn."

His heart? But . . .

If Oberon still had it— Was it all a trick, a lie, an empty promise? Jack had never seen inside the box. All he had was Titania's word. Which, he knew as well as anyone, was worth nothing.

He was a fool.

Oberon's voice grew gentle; he gazed down at Jack with a fascinated expression. "Does anyone want the old days back? The constant conflict, the endless cycle of violence and pain. No. That's past. A thousand years gone." His voice grew almost wistful. "No amount of wishing is going to bring it back."

He paused, a king indeed, staring down on a pitiful subject, a slave. His eyes narrowed to slits, endless darkness, cold as winter. "But just so as you remember, my Jack . . ."

Wind rushed through the trees, tearing through the leaves, beating against Jack's twisted form, and with it, like tiny white blossoms, came the shreds of cloth he'd tied to the tree. All his wishes. Torn away. They whirled around him and drifted into the distance, far out of his reach.

Jack's gaze followed them. All his wishes. Stolen and gone.

The magic released with a snap and the agony of night seized Jack. His muscles stiffened, ratcheting in a twist of anguish, ripping apart and re-forming anew. The scream that rent the air set the birds to flight, and he barely recognized the voice as his own. The thorns ripped through him, the pain of broken bough and torn meat.

In seconds he knew no more.

chapter twelve

An echoing shout jarred Jenny awake, like a night bird calling, a scream ragged with pain that faded even as she struggled to consciousness. She sat up, breathing hard, wondering in the silence if she had imagined it.

Puck was awake too, his eyes very wide in the dark, his fur bristling.

Something crashed through the forest to the left.

Jenny scrambled up. "What is it?" she whispered, but Puck put his fingers to his mouth and darted up onto his feet. He crept to the edge of the trees, where the forest crowded in on them.

"The wards have failed," Puck snapped, darting backward, trying to run and turn at the same time. "Something's gone wrong. Run, Jenny."

With a shriek like the splintering of ancient timber, a greenman burst from the trees, a piece of the forest given form, hurtling at them with the force of a hurricane. It lashed out at Puck and the trees echoed it, roaring with rage, twisting and writhing. Vines tangled around the hobgoblin's arms but he wriggled free, dancing from foot to foot across the clearing, deftly side-skipping the roots that burst from the ground to trip him. It was the nightmare of Jenny's last moments with Tom come alive again. She scrambled backward in terror, throwing herself out of the way. But Puck could move in ways Tom never could. Elusive, tricky, a creature of instinct, Puck leaped aside.

"Run, Jenny!" he yelled again. "What are you doing? Oberon's sent him after us and more could be on the way. Run!"

The ground bucked beneath him and he fell with a crash, the air knocked out of him, his eyes wide. Roots broke free of the earth, weaving around his legs, his waist. The greenman bore down on him, and Jenny froze, staring at it, at the winding vines tightening around Puck until he gasped, the shifting leaves, the harsh lines of bark and roots that covered its body.

It had taken Tom.

It had taken Tom, and now it had Puck.

Jenny's hands closed on a stone and she flung it at the creature's head, but her aim was off and it flew aside. Scrabbling around, she tried find something, anything else she could use as a weapon. She flung another stone as hard as she could and this time it bounced off the back of its head. She almost whooped with victory, but the creature didn't even flinch. It didn't even appear to notice. Her fingers closed around a branch, dead and abandoned on the edge of the forest.

The creature turned, Puck clutched in its arms. Its berry-bright gaze stole the breath from her lungs. And then she was running straight at it. Her voice broke as she yelled. She lashed out and the creature roared at her, the thorns in place of its teeth parting to reveal darkness. Jenny heaved the branch and struck, hitting the creature's raised arm with a terrible crack. It staggered back. She struck it again and again. Abruptly the greenman released Puck, dropping him like a pile of firewood. Jenny braced herself, the branch grasped tightly in her hand. And in that instant, everything slowed. She noticed her ragged fingernails digging into the bark, her knuckles bleeding and white with tension underneath. She felt the knotty heft of the branch in her hand. She saw the intricate web of twigs and branches that twined up from the beast's chest to its sinewy neck, where something, some bud or berry, glinted yellow. But instead of turning on her, the greenman retreated, backing away as quickly as it had appeared. Swallowed up by the forest.

Silence fell like snow, muffling the air, leaving Jenny facing the trees with her stick in hands, her breath coming hard and ragged.

Puck didn't move. He groaned when Jenny bent over him, muttered something and rolled onto his side with a whimper.

"Are you hurt?" Jenny whispered. "Puck."

"No, I'm . . . I'll be fine. Jenny . . . you—"

"I had to do it, Puck. I . . . Jack." Jenny straightened, adrenaline spiking through her. Jack was out there somewhere.

Puck sat up, a protest on his lips, but Jenny was already running.

The moon hung full and bright in the sky, framed by branches and leaves. Too full, too bright. A moon not for the real world.

Only this *was* real. All too real.

Everything lurched from side to side as she ran, the branch that had saved her at the ready, her heart thundering against the base of her throat.

An icy breeze blasted through the trees, cutting across the slick of sweat on her skin. She remembered the scream that had woken her. Had it been real? Had it been him? Was she already too late?

The moon seemed to have risen higher. It filled the sky over her, drenching the forest in silver. She slowed her pace, cautious now, trying to hear the crashing trail she'd expected from the fleeing creature. All was silent.

She'd chased it off.

The thought brought her up short. How on earth had she chased it off? Why had it run from her?

Reason told her to go back, to retrace her steps and

return to Puck. But she couldn't just leave Jack out there in the darkness. And which way was back anyway?

Jenny crept forward, pulling her hair into a messy knot as her eyes swept over the trees. Through the branches, little points of light flitted ahead of her like Christmas tree lights. She watched, almost enchanted by their dance as they darted in close and then fluttered away through the branches. Will-o'-the-wisps, like stars all around, so beautiful and delicate they reminded her instantly of the Foletti, and the prettiness died a little. If she followed any one of them she would leave the path.

Wander in the Realm at your own peril.

That was what Jack had said. She reached out despite herself to cup one of the lights, but it flew through her fingers. That moment, when he'd pulled her away from the dragon, when they'd hidden . . . He'd been about to kiss her. Hadn't he? She felt a burn in her face and looked around, as if the forest could read her thoughts. She pushed the memory down deep, locked it out of sight, raised her weapon again, and continued along the path.

"Where are you, Jack?" she whispered.

The forest shivered, leaves rustling in a world that was otherwise, in an instant, completely silent.

Jenny's heart lurched up inside her and she turned around, a full circle. No one appeared. The forest fell still, the will-o'-the-wisps gone.

They're only trees.

Jenny swallowed hard, her eyes squinting through the darkness. "I—I'm looking for Jack. Jack of the Forest—"

Laughter interrupted her, sweet gentle laughter, the kind she could trust . . .

But could she? Could she trust anything?

Jack's not here. Not anymore.

Jenny took a step back and a stick cracked beneath her heel, so loud she jumped.

"Where is he?"

The forest didn't reply, but the leaves of the tree before her shivered again. A silver birch, slender and elegant. She thought of the birch-boy. Was he here, or something like him? The Dames Vertes . . . Jack had called them gentle and kind. All she could see was a tree. But there was something watching her. There was something answering her.

She was talking to a tree. Just talking to a tree. Totally normal. People probably did it every day here. *They're only trees.* She fought an insane urge to laugh.

The undergrowth curled back, folding in on itself for her, revealing a narrow path. The leaves and stalks bent back out of her way and swayed, beckoning her inside. Well, at least the forest was answering back. That was good, wasn't it? Or maybe not. Maybe that was bad.

She turned around in a circle, and sighed. Might as well listen to the forest then.

Jenny crouched and headed down the path, aware that bushes and leaves were closing after her, sealing off her retreat. They brushed against her, a gentle touch, tickling but cautious. Another game, perhaps. They loved their games here. Jenny crept forward, slowing as she approached the silent heart of the forest.

And it was silent. Deep and endless, lit by the moon as it slid lower in the sky, filling the spaces overhead. Trees pressed closer, bushes and thorns crowding the edges of the path, like dark hands pushing her onward.

How long had she been walking? Time sometimes seemed to pass differently in the Realm. She couldn't tell if that was real or another of its illusions. It was dark underfoot and far too bright overhead. The world seemed upside down. But she pressed on. Time might be acting differently, but she wasn't. Stupidly, possibly, but not differently. She followed the path.

It opened out into another clearing.

And the greenman crouched in the center.

As she stepped out from the tree line, it looked up, its eyes burning behind the mess of leaves and briar of its face.

Run!

Tom's voice screamed at her down through the years. Puck's joined it until a cacophony of panic rang through her mind.

Run, Jenny, run!

But if she ran, it would chase her. And if she ran and it chased her—

It would run her down. It would catch her.

And then what?

Jenny paused just inside the tree line, holding her weapon before her. "Where's Jack?" It came out as no more than a whisper. She tried again. "What have you done with him?"

The thing crept forward, and she watched, fascinated, horrified. It was made of the forest, part of it. In a mostly human form, and not. It flowed and transformed as it moved—leaves, vines, briars, buds, bark, and moss. A thousand other things. The forest itself. Fluid, dangerous, alien . . . and yet not alien, not here in the forest where it lived.

Run, Jenny.

A small sound escaped her throat, her chest tightening so hard it hurt. The smell engulfed her, rich and moist, the scent of soil and mulch, of things springing to life out of things decaying and rotting away, back into the earth, returning anew with spring. She had smelled it before—the night it took Tom, in Branley Copse, in Sherwood Forest, in the night at the Woodsman's cottage. Tonight, when it had attacked Puck. She knew its scent.

"What do you want?" she asked.

It cocked its head to one side, a strange feline movement that made her start. And then it dashed away from her, leaves fluttering like rags behind it.

So fast, so fluid. It flew through the clearing and into the trees at the far side.

"Wait!" she yelled, and lurched after it, clumsy on mortal legs, her body not cooperating as she plunged along the path, into the shadows left long by the fading moonlight. What was she doing? What on earth was she doing? It didn't matter. She had to know. She had to know why it took Tom. And what it had done to Jack.

Red streaks rose in the sky. Dawn. The night was almost gone, but she couldn't lose it, not now. Reckless and wild with need, she rounded a curve in the path and there it was, just standing there, studying something in its gnarled hands. Head bent, shoulders hunched, it looked like little more than a mossy stump overgrown with ivy and mistletoe, speckled in the light of dawn through the trees. It turned, just as Jenny, unable to halt her headlong rush in the mud and leaves, skidded into it. She went down as if she had hit a boulder. Thorns snagged on her clothes and skin, tearing through as if they were barbed wire. A shot of pain went through her—or was it terror?—and she slammed into the ground.

"Jenny!" a voice like the cracking of branches in a high wind reached her ears.

Jack's voice, distorted with pain. Oh, thank God, he was alive. He was okay. But she wasn't. The image of the broken Woodsman flashed to her mind. She braced herself for that pain.

"Jenny." Jack's voice again. Jack, coming to rescue her from her own stupidity. Jack, who would be too late. Her stomach plunged and she tensed—

But nothing happened.

She forced her eyes to open.

The greenman was gone, as if it had never been. The next thing she knew, Jack gathered her in his arms. This time she didn't struggle.

"What happened? You're hurt. What are you doing out here?"

"I saw it." She gulped down air and tried to force the words out. "I saw the greenman."

He touched her scratched arms, the rip in her shirt, his fingers fumbling where he tried to be gentle. "Did it . . ." His voice caught. "Did it do this?" He was trembling, she realized, his eyes shining. Jack—grim and hard as stone— Jack was shaking all over.

"It was the thing that took Tom. It was— Jack? What's wrong?"

He pushed himself back from her, almost throwing himself away; all gentleness she'd thought she'd found in him a moment earlier gone.

"What were you doing out here?" His voice was a brittle crack. "Why can't you do what you're told?"

"I was looking for you!"

"You had no cause, no need."

"That thing attacked Puck. It came after us both. What was I meant to do?"

Blood drained from his strained face, leaving its stark contours prominent. "Puck? Is he hurt? Is he alive?"

"Yes. I stopped it and it took off. I went after it. We—Puck and I—we'd heard a scream. I thought it had—I thought you—"

"You should leave me be!" His voice broke against the trees and the birds took flight, crying out. He cradled his temples in his fingers, bent forward as if struggling for balance. "You are nothing to me but a weight around my neck."

She choked as he said the words and stared at him.

She was such a fool. Such an idiot. How could she have even dreamed that someone . . . some*thing* like Jack . . . How could she have allowed herself to feel anything at all?

No heart, Puck had said, and like a fool she had tried to give him one. Because she knew that feeling—like being broken inside—and she'd wanted to . . . to *fix* him, even if she couldn't fix herself. She'd wanted to feel something.

She got to her feet. Stumbled. Then let her legs take over and she ran, blindly, tearing her way through the trees without thought of where or why. She just ran. She had to put as much distance between them as she could. Time to think. Time and space and—

You are nothing to me but a weight around my neck.

chapter thirteen

Jenny ripped her way through the forest, using her arms to pull herself forward on trees and branches, her legs pounding on the narrow dirt path, while around her the light swelled and grew brighter, the sun rising on the Realm.

Her legs and lungs ached, and eventually she slowed, too exhausted to carry on. Jack had tried to trick her. He'd lied to her. He'd made promises, then rejected her. She owed him nothing.

Jenny stumbled as she broke through the trees and out onto a sloping riverbank. The river was much wider here, deeper too. The far side was blurred and indistinct. A waterfall plunged from the cliffs to her left, into a splash pool so dark at the center it looked bottomless. She slipped and fell to her knees, then crawled to the water's edge and scooped up the river water, splashing it onto her face, drinking it down.. It cooled her skin, her mouth, soothed her burning eyes. She lingered there, panting. For how long, she didn't know. The rushing of the waterfall filled her ears, its spray like a mist settling over her.

Then from somewhere far off she heard the music—gentle strains of an ancient melody Tom used to play. He had learned the tunes for her, when she couldn't manage them herself, and he'd played them, one after another, for her. Just for her. This version was sad, almost plaintive, like a voice calling her. It wasn't a flute, though. Not this time. Though for a moment she thought . . . like a memory . . .

Over the rush of the nearby waterfall, the sweet strains of music resolved themselves into the sound of a harp. Jenny sat up, wiping the water from her eyes. She had never heard a tune quite like it. After every second she thought she knew it came another where it was made anew. Old and fresh at the same time, beguiling. It stilled the trembling in her body, draining it out of her like the antidote to a poison. She got to her feet. Her mind drifted in a swirl of music. She knew the tune. Something struggled in the back of her thoughts—something she should know, something she should heed—but she couldn't really hear it . . .

Where the waterfall tumbled madly down the cliff, where the wide pool stretched out before her, impossibly deep and bright, she saw a young man perched on a boulder. He looked about eighteen, although she knew in this place that could mean he was anything from a day old to a thousand years. He had an odd flat red hat perched atop his head at a jaunty angle. Her first thought was that he didn't compare to Jack, but the idea slithered into the recesses of her mind before she could quite grasp it.

She stopped, hesitating, the music washing over her again. The boy before her was handsome. His golden hair hung around his ears in curls as full as wood shavings stripped with a plane. His eyes were closed, and his finely sculpted face lifted to the dawn. In one hand he cradled a golden harp, and the fingers of the other moved deftly over the flashing strings. A faint smile played on his lips, his own music enchanting him as it enchanted her.

Without thinking, she sank down to sit amid the reeds on the bank, listening to the melody. It evoked a dozen half-remembered dreams of pure joy. And though it was entirely new to her now, she felt she knew it, or that she had always known it, that it was part of her. Thoughts of anything or anybody else bled from her mind.

The final notes trailed away, leaving an emptiness she couldn't fill.

The young man opened his eyes, the color of cornflowers, so blue they seemed to glow from within, and he smiled a smile that made her smile back.

"That was . . ." She struggled for a word, but anything she said would demean it.

His glorious smile broadened. "It was," he agreed, and slid the harp into the safety of its leather case. "I didn't realize I had an audience. It's an old tune. They call it 'Hurry to the Marriage.'"

She knew it now. Though he played it as a tragic lament—not the jaunty, jumpy melody Tom had preferred—it still swept her along like the river itself. She knew it like she knew her own brother. Memory mixed with music; it sang to her of Tom and all she had lost.

The harpist must have taken her silence for ignorance, or dismay, and smiled. "Do you play? I could teach it to you."

She shook her head ruefully, remembering suddenly Mrs. Whitlow and the exasperated music teachers at St. Martha's. "I don't, I'm afraid. I've never been very musical." That had always been Tom's realm.

The young man climbed down lightly, and Jenny's eyes focused on him again. Only on him. He moved with the same grace as his music. Though water dripped from the hem of his loose white shirt, the rest of his clothes were dry. His feet were bare and she could make out a light webbing between his toes. The slight imperfection captivated her.

"I could teach you to play," the harpist said, slowing his approach. "I can teach anyone. It's my gift, and it's only right to share gifts with others." She smiled at that thought, tempted beyond words. Though she'd never admitted it, not even to herself, she'd always wished to be half as skilled as her brother. To have half his talent. To have people listen to her, to look at her with that kind of wonder. His gifts.

What would it be like to be able to do that . . . to make such music . . .

The harpist crossed the open space carefully, closer to the water than to the trees. One might say he crept toward her, but Jenny recognized it as the caution of any wild creature approaching something unknown. She swallowed hard. This close he was even more handsome. His skin caught the light and shimmered like mackerel scales. His eyes captured hers. "You're hurt," he whispered. "Let me help you."

Scratched and grazed as she was, she barely felt it anymore. Blood had hardened on the wounds, dirt smeared her skin and clothes. She couldn't think of what to say, so she just nodded.

She was meant to be doing something . . . looking for Tom? Yes. And someone was meant to be with her. Helping her. He'd promised when she'd given him . . . The musician knelt beside her, took out a white handkerchief—who used a handkerchief these days?—and dipped it in the river. Carefully, with the delicacy of a surgeon, he reached out.

Jack. Jack had been helping her. Hadn't he?

Then why did even just a thought of him sting?

The harpist touched her skin and it felt like the music returned, swirling around her, through her like water. Her heart was the rhythm that he needed, his music the melody her heart wanted to hear. For a moment, she wondered what his name was, wondered why she didn't ask, but it didn't do to question anyone too closely here. She felt the truth of this firmly, but couldn't quite say why. Besides, it was rude. If she started pestering him with questions now, he might take offense and leave. The last thing she wanted to do was lose sight of him. Everyone else she had met had been flawed, or plain, or simply ugly in comparison—except for Jack's eyes. The rogue thought sprang into her mind, but slid back down into its depths just as quickly. Jack's eyes weren't perfect. They didn't even match. Their brilliant green and blue drew her into his lies, deceived her. They weren't perfect and neither was he.

But this harpist was. She blushed, her cheeks fiercely hot.

Gently, he took her hands. Though cold, his touch sent shudders of warmth through her, an unexpected reaction that left her stunned. His gaze probed hers, pushing smoothly past her defenses, seeing all she had hidden away. He saw the turmoil and grief that had brought her here, saw her guilt and regret, and understood it.

"Let me help you, Jenny," he murmured. Slowly, carefully, he used the handkerchief to clean the cuts on her arms, to soothe her skin.

But once finished, the handkerchief laid aside, he didn't stop touching her. Fingertips traced chill lines from her temple to her jaw, marked the curve of her neck and paused at the hollow in the base of her throat.

She swallowed, found her mouth dry as sand and opened

it for more oxygen. Her tongue moistened her lips and his mirrored hers. He played with her hair and smiled. She couldn't see enough of his smile.

"Close your eyes," he whispered. "Beautiful maid, fear me not. I can make the pain leave. The pain in your body and the pain in your heart. I can take it away. Don't fear me."

She wanted to tell him that she wasn't afraid, even though her heart raced and he could surely feel the pulse leaping wildly where his fingers touched her neck. She felt her eyelids respond to his request and he pulled her toward him, even as she leaned in to his kiss.

The musician's lips were as gentle as ripples lapping against her skin. She sighed as he pulled her still closer. His hand cupped the back of her skull, his fingers burrowing into her hair, knotting its length in his fist. His other hand closed on her neck, the caress tightening.

"Jenny, no!" A voice rang out from the forest. "He's the queen's harpist. He's the Nix!"

Jack? She opened her eyes, tried to jerk back, but the harpist wouldn't release her. His hungry lips pressed to hers and his eyes, wide open, gazed on her, terrible in their greed. He held her against him, locked to him, body to body, mouth to mouth. Blue light blossomed deep inside his eyes, unnatural and horrifying. The sound of the waterfall thundered in Jenny's ears. She tried to scream, but her lungs could not draw the breath. Deep inside her something vital strained like taut tissue paper.

It held for a moment as she struggled to escape, her desperate eyes catching a glimpse of Jack sprinting toward her, his stone knife drawn, his face stretched tight in fury and fear.

It held for just an instant longer, one in which she realized that he would never reach her in time.

And then it tore.

As the river creature broke his kiss, some vital part of her was wrenched from her body into his. He flung what remained of her toward Jack. Her limp frame tumbled, unfeeling, into the long grass. It took a moment for her to realize she wasn't falling. She just wasn't there anymore. She was spinning in a void, lost and untouchable. Locked away, like a firefly in a jar. She was inside the harpist, trapped. He turned and dived into the water. She heard Jack scream her name, saw him gather her body in his arms, but she was far away now. Water roared around her. Water flooded her senses, drowned her, deafened her and blinded her. The harpist arced through the river like a pike, down to the darkest depths, where she knew no more.

chapter fourteen

Puck came running from the trees, but Jack didn't see or hear. He knelt over Jenny's body, calling her name and rocking her back and forth. Though she still breathed, her consciousness was not there anymore. Jack knew it. A hollow ache followed the certainty, a pain so deep it seemed to be gouged inside him. This was his fault.

Puck gave a cry. He came up short behind Jack.

They had both seen enchanted slumber before. There was rarely a cure. Cursing beneath his breath, Puck closed his hand on Jack's shoulder. He was trembling.

"What happened, boy?"

Jack opened his mouth and faltered. What could he say? He'd found her in the forest, hurt, bleeding, and he'd lost all control. The thought of her in danger, the thought of her hurt, of Puck hurt, of what the Kobold might have done . . .

Of Puck's betrayal of them both.

Jack rounded on Puck now. "You—*you* set the course for these events. You betrayed me. Her. You went to Oberon."

Puck shied back.

"You told the king." Jack's voice scraped along the sides of his tightening throat.

Puck paled, took another step back. "I had no choice, Jack. You know how it is. How *he* is. You could no more keep it from him than I could."

But Jack hadn't gone off in search of Oberon to greedily spill the tale of a May Queen in the forest. He'd been trapped. Forced to leave Jenny unprotected. Except for Puck, whom he had foolishly relied on.

And then the greenman, as Jenny called it, had run riot.

Jack squeezed his eyes shut. A sound escaped his throat. He opened his eyes to realize he was clutching Puck by the arm, his fingers tightening. The hobgoblin's eyes stared back at his, wide and shining, but he didn't make a sound.

Jack released him and looked away. At the waterfall, at the forest, at anything but Puck. He finally raised his eyes to the hobgoblin's, struggling to keep his gaze steady.

"It was the Nix," he said. "He lured her to the water's edge. I was too late." Answer given—not a full answer perhaps, but true enough for all its brevity. Jack shook Jenny again, searching her face for a response. It was empty.

Something in Jack's chest staggered as if struck from behind, an unfamiliar, unwanted sensation. The echo of a feeling that wasn't his anymore, no matter what he might dream. Dreams were just pieces of cloth tied to a tree and then scattered to the wind.

"He didn't take her body? Didn't drown her?" Puck asked quietly.

"No. I surprised him. But Puck . . ." Jack looked up at the hobgoblin, aware that his eyes pleaded like a child's. "Puck, he kissed her."

Puck groaned, burying his face in his hands. "Then she's lost."

"Just help me wake her up."

"You can't, lad. There's no waking her now. He didn't take her to be a servant in his halls. He did worse. He stole her soul. He's probably bound it in a golden cage deep beneath the water. She's gone, lad. As surely as if he had simply drowned her. Now the queen can collect her body whenever she will. And the Nix will hand over her soul for the reward. Her heart and soul together would keep her free of the queen. But this way—body and soul separated—Jenny is helpless."

"Titania . . ." The queen's name was fluid music and a bitter curse. "This was her plan all along. The Nix is her favorite, isn't he? Has she arranged all this, Puck?"

And why? Because she doubted him. And was she wrong to? How high a price would he be willing to pay for his heart? Perhaps Titania feared the price she asked was too high. Jack feared the same.

But Puck didn't answer. He touched Jack's shoulder.

"I'm sorry. It's my fault. I was to have watched her."

Of course it was his fault. If he hadn't told the king . . .
Anger like a lick of flame ignited again inside him, and he
glared at Puck.

"I'd give anything to take it back," Puck babbled. "I'd do
anything if I thought it would help!"

"How do I get her back?" Jack's voice cracked like ice on a
winter's night.

Puck stared at him in disbelief. "From the Nix? Jack, no
one so taken returns. Had he pulled her in bodily, to be a servant or a concubine, perhaps in seven or twenty-one years,
she'd come back, but he took her soul, boy. Look at her!"

Jack's gaze dropped back to her pale face, and grief
etched lines in his skin. He glanced at his friend to see it
reflected there. Puck felt some form of it himself, Jack realized, though he would never have dreamed it, not for a
mortal. Neither of them should feel anything like this.

It was as if she slept, but from this sleep there was no
awakening. Her lips were already turning blue. Her skin
looked like marble, traced with indigo veins.

"How do you kill a Nix?" Jack asked.

Puck sank to his knees at his side. "The river isn't your
place, Jack."

"Just tell me."

"You're an earth creature, a forest child, like me."

"If you won't tell me, someone will. Rusalka perhaps, or

Greenteeth. I'll find someone and pay the price. Even if I can't bring her back, the least I can do is kill him for her. I can let her soul go so the queen can't have her. Puck, I promised to protect her!" It was that more than anything. He'd promised and he'd failed to keep that promise. He'd failed Jenny. The thought left him shredded inside.

And yet it was still more than that.

What would Oberon do to him for his failure? What would Titania do? Any hope of his own freedom was gone, that was certain.

Those worries were pale ghosts compared to the one overwhelming truth.

He'd failed Jenny.

The hobgoblin said nothing. Enough that it was a promise. Enough that Jack had failed. Anything more would mean facing things that neither of them wanted to face, not now, not in anger.

"Steel," Puck muttered, as if even the word were a poison to him.

Jack looked up.

"You need steel for preference. Iron at a push. But a sword, not haggled for, given in fair exchange. And there's only one place to get it. Out there, along the Ridgeway between worlds, in the place of metal and fire from a hand that hates us and everything we are. The touch of impure metal is as foul to you as it is to me."

Jack swallowed down a breath and stepped over the Edge. The mortal world was wreathed in darkness, and a chill, constant drizzle misted the hilltop on which he found himself. He walked through a place called the Vale, crossing a road and climbing the steep incline, heading for an ancient pathway running through the sloping countryside. Beneath the mud, smears of pale chalk that formed the foundations of the land hereabouts were visible, like bare bones exposed. There was no sign of the folk anywhere. Neither mortal nor fae. But then, as Puck had warned him, the fae had no place here anymore. Not in the human world. Not in the places between.

"You'll have but one chance," Puck had said. "Oberon's protection is all that will keep you safe. And he didn't give it with good grace. He doesn't relish the thought of you stepping even a foot outside his power, no matter how much he wants the girl. He's turning your enchantment upside down for this one night so you can walk in her world." Jack had stared, unable to believe that. "Don't mistake me," Puck continued. "It's no favor. You owe him a great debt, Jack. He wants your word that you'll renounce what was yours, and your right to it, for once and for all."

Renounce what was his. Jack gazed down on the fields below, edged with hedgerows, a final line of wildness clinging to the edges of the mortal world, and the squat and flat-topped hillock where he had crossed through. There, Puck had said, a hero killed a dragon. Jack knew better. Dragons weren't killed so easily, certainly not by mortals. Not even by him. Another failure. More likely this hero was buried there.

Jack pulled the collar of his dappled green coat up around his neck against the rain. Beneath it, he wore a simple green shirt and loose britches. His boots were a sturdy leather fastened with synthetic laces. Puck's glamour was impressive. If he did encounter any mortals, they'd hardly give him a second glance.

Renounce what was his. The words rose again. It had been so long since he had even considered what was once his. And yet he never ceased to long for it. Titania's recent offer had made it more real by far. But he knew the truth. He was meant to protect the Realm. Yet he couldn't even protect Jenny. What was once his? That was a joke. Freedom? Knowing he could never take it back, or win it for himself, all this was a small thing to renounce.

No more dreams or hopes.

No more wishes.

His wishes had been torn from the tree. Puck had told Oberon everything and despite his regret, would probably do it again in an instant. The queen could come for Jenny at any second. With her soul in the hands of the Nix, there would be nothing she could do to withstand Titania. And

Mab. This one chance was all he had—and a slim one at that. He had failed in every way, in his servitude to the king, in his attempts to placate the queen, in his tattered friendship with Puck, his broken self-control, but most of all, he had failed in his primary duty—to protect those who wandered in the Realm. He had failed Jenny. He'd failed her from the moment he met her. His efforts to send her home had just served to entangle her in the Realm. To trap her there.

Better their paths had never crossed.

Resigning his claim to the last particle of his old self was a little thing in comparison to helping her now, a vain attempt to restore his honor perhaps, but the only thing he could do. And that meant approaching yet another king. A fallen one.

And then what? A voice whispered within him. *Win her back and hand her over? And to whom? There is no way to win this. Whatever you touch turns to ruin. That's your true curse.*

White Horse Hill lay dark beneath the clouded sky. And Titania's ward—the great White Horse itself—was blind without the moon. A small relief. Jack hurried past it as rain fell in gray waves, whipped up by gusts of wind that seemed to scratch at the sky. The clouds shifted then, and moonlight broke through. Almost at the summit of the hill, all Jack could do was stare. He lifted his face.

The moon hung high in the night's sky, cut by clouds, full and so very bright. He'd never seen it. Never thought to see it, not with these eyes. It was beautiful and vast, hovering so far above him.

The moonlight fell on him, and it fell on the horse. The White Horse. *Titania's ward.* He was a fool. So very much a fool. Jack cursed, pulled his hood up over his head, and hoped Titania wasn't watching. She'd no reason to notice him in this place, no reason to suspect that he was here or why. He prayed that the White Horse was not so mystical a thing after all, just a chalk outline carved into the living landscape. Someone had dug it out of the earth, clearing the grass to reveal the white chalk beneath, thousands of years ago. People, just people, he tried to tell himself. It looked like a sketch done by a child, and yet at the same time, profoundly powerful, as if a great hand had reached down from the sky—or up from the earth—to scour its mark into the land, long brush strokes that glowed with light when the moon spilled over it. He feared it. No simple thing of humankind. It was a ward. It kept things away. Things like him.

The moonlight called to him now. Almost as strongly as the trees. He'd never seen its light falling about him, never seen it silvering his hands. It made them like stone, strong and reliable. Hands that did their own work.

Jack thought of what Puck had promised on his behalf, and it made the pit of his stomach plummet. And yet, he would have done the same if he'd been the one to bring the news to their king, if he'd been the one to beg for help. That Puck had gone in his stead said much for their ruined friendship. Jack would never have asked it. He wasn't quite sure he should have allowed it. But Oberon now had his promise. It served them all.

Puck wasn't able to look him in the eye anymore, and some deep dark part of Jack was glad. That part of him took a malicious joy from the hobgoblin's shame. That part would be slow to forgive and quick to suspect. It always had been, and he should have known better and trusted it more.

Jack turned onto the Ridgeway now, the hilltop shielding him from the White Horse as he descended the other side of the summit, following the wide, ancient trail. Thick knots of trees and undergrowth pressed along the edges of this pale chalk path, lush and dark—rose, oak, holly, and hawthorn tangled together. The white mud was churned and rutted as if a great many people and chariots of enormous size had passed that way.

Nothing fae strayed along this road, not willingly. Not along the Ridgeway. There was no place for them here, and the place where it led . . . Well, the less anyone dallied there, the better. Humans too. Though the people of this place might think the Ridgeway was their oldest road, it was far older than mankind, older than anything. The path took him off the hill, into sheltered land where mankind farmed and tilled, where the Ridgeway met other, newer roads, but still carried on its own way, paying them no heed. At the cross-road, he tried to ignore modern man's way-markers, white ciphers on blackened wood. Each one was carved with an acorn, pure white like the chalk of the land, meticulously detailed. Even the things that showed him his path seemed to point at what a fool he was. Another of life's ironies? Or just fate's way of mocking him?

It was a place of magic, the Ridgeway, a place *between*. The only way to approach it was to step from the world of Faerie into the world of men, and from there into another world, one where both should fear to tread. This was the doorway to a place of another magic and other gods. This was Jack's destination.

The moon reappeared, just for a moment. The path ahead was overgrown, its center thick with grass. To the side of it, dense hedgerow surrounded a large field of swaying wheat. But then the hedgerow parted, broken by a gate, which revealed another, narrower path cutting its way through the crops. Beyond it was an unfarmed area, shaded by ancient beech trees. The dome of trees hid the interior from sight.

Only a gate stood in his way. Jack frowned at the chest-high barricade. That wouldn't stop him. It wouldn't stop anything. He climbed over it easily. Was it really meant to keep people from entering? Modern man should be more worried about what might get out.

Jack walked quickly up the narrow white path—chalk

again, smoother and less traveled, but not overgrown. He passed beneath the ring of trees and stopped, staring at the burial mound that now rose before him. It lay like a monster sleeping beneath a blanket of earth, fronted by its teeth of stone while its body sprawled back to the trees. The sign nearby named the place, giving facts, figures, and dates, and offered free entry for all. Humans had no idea of the true price demanded, but Jack did. No one had really entered this place in over a hundred years. They may have walked in the shadows of the standing stones, or made their way up onto the mound. They may have listened to descriptions of barrows and dates so long ago that they had no meaning anymore. But they would never be able to enter the smithy.

Jack felt the power of the place, the earth and fire energies seeping up through his legs even as the chill rain ran through his hair and down his face. He approached the mound, step by onerous step. All around him the beech trees swayed and whispered warnings that should have driven him back.

Every few feet, enormous rock slabs, standing upright like sentinels, guarded the narrow path cut into the mound. Once, it might have been a tunnel, but its roof had long ago been stripped off. A rock wedged across the opening before him gave the message loud and clear—stay away. Jack didn't listen, couldn't. He skirted up and over the cold, wet stone to the path inside and walked toward the black mouth at its far end, like a doorway, two upright stones and one on top, and beyond them darkness. Thick rocks on either side made walls that appeared to teeter on the edge of crushing anyone unwise enough to venture farther. But he couldn't stop now.

In the flat rock at the height of his eyes was a gap, barely discernable without fae sight. Jack reached for the pouch hanging at his belt, only to find it was now a portion of the britches themselves. Like in Jenny's clothes—*pockets,* she had called them. He smiled grimly, remembering her bemused expression in having to explain so simple a concept to him, the way the small line had creased between her eyebrows.

He tucked thoughts of her safely in the back of his mind and took out the first coin. It carried the image of a king on a horse. On the other side, the image had been worn clean away. Oberon had only given them grudgingly. He guarded such objects with a fierce possessiveness. The mortal metal sizzled against Jack's skin, but he could touch it, so heavy was the gold in it. The king had won it long ago, in a far-off land, in one of his many wagers. Oberon rarely lost.

Jack closed his eyes, murmuring his request, and set the ancient coin in the hollow, an offering to something far older than him. Then he leaned back against the nearest rock to wait, pulling his hood up over his head for shelter.

It didn't take long, but then, these things rarely did when you knew the way. He couldn't say exactly when it appeared, but between the blinking of his eyes to clear the rain, a ruddy glow appeared in the dry gloom of the barrow doorway. It stained the ancient stones, illuminating hidden runes around the entrance.

Jack read them each in turn. Old magic, as old as the stones themselves, foreign to him, but strangely familiar, as if he were finally seeing something he always should have known. Runes were not part of Faerie magic. But they were nonetheless powerful. They were the symbols of ancient things, things that Jack's absent heart would know intimately. Things stolen from him, perhaps, like his heart.

Is, it sounded like a voice, hissing in his ear, like water falling on a hot stone.

Rad, a distant shout, a violent urge, cut off too soon.

Ger, the growl of a cat, a murmur on the edge of sleep, a threat.

He might not understand their meaning, but that didn't really matter. It was magic, and the message was so very clear.

Know yourself, the runes seemed to warn him in the flickering glow, *before you enter here. Before you ask a boon you can never repay.* Kings were not patient. Not even the fallen kind.

The runes glowed a fiery red for a moment, the rain hissing as it came into contact with them and turned to steam in the frigid air. The shadows in the doorway to nowhere deepened, glowed red, and suddenly it didn't lead nowhere anymore. It led to a very definite place, the last place his instincts wanted him to go.

"Well," said a rough voice from inside. "You'd better come in if you're coming."

chapter fifteen

Something dark lurched between the stones and the fire, a huge figure, misshapen and hobbled. The rain worked its way under Jack's collar and ran icy fingers down his skin. He moved on reluctant limbs and stepped out of the rain, laying his wet cloak aside, shaking wet hair from his eyes. The center of the circular room was dominated by the forge, its fire bright and hot. The heat hissed life back into his skin. He hugged his arms around his chest and looked up into the black eyes of the enormous figure who stood on the far side of the forge, his features turned demonic by the glow.

He had gray hair, the color of smoke, but he didn't look old. At the same time, Jack knew, he was as ancient as the stones around them. This was no mere man. The relaxed stance did nothing to hide the strength in his hulking shoulders and arms. He wore a leather apron, and leather cuffs around his wrists. His thick beard was neatly trimmed, but the wildness in his dark eyes remained untamed. In one meaty grip he held a hammer. All around the edges of the room were workbenches, cluttered with objects in various stages of completion, each one so beautifully detailed that to look too long at them would draw tears from a stone.

"Cat got your tongue?" asked the smith.

Jack forced his voice out.

"Greetings and honor to you, Wayland. Peace be at our meeting."

"And at our parting." Wayland squinted at him. "I don't know you, yet there's something familiar to you. You have my name, lad. What's yours?"

"Jack." He found himself hesitant and then ashamed. He raised his chin defiantly. "Jack o' the Forest."

Wayland seemed more amused than surprised. "A Jack? *Is, Rad,* and *Ger* came for you, then? The first and last I understand then—a traveler from afar, a walker on the Ridgeway with the patience of stones, a creature of earth abroad on the way between worlds—but *Rad?* What has befallen a Jack that he needs to change so much? To call on such power, your need must be great indeed."

Jack's mind whirled as he struggled to keep up with Wayland's magic. This was another world, the magic of another kind than he knew. It wasn't like the way he heard the trees, the way the forest sang for him, the way the earth warmed beneath his touch. It was old and formal, a magic of iron and fire. A magic that threatened to burn him away if he leaned in too closely.

But he needed it.

"I need a sword. Puck said—"

Wayland surged to his feet, his features darkening still further. His eyes flamed red.

"What mischief is Loki making this time?"

Jack frowned at the unfamiliar name. "My Lord Wayland?"

The smith limped toward him, dragging his lamed legs one after the other.

"Or is it Alberich, whom your kind call Oberon?" He spat toward the fire and flames surged to a white heat. "Who sent you, Jack, and on what errand?"

"Puck—you call him Loki? He gave me the information on where to find you, and the means of crossing the Edge. But the errand is my own."

That seemed to give him pause, though Wayland still looked suspicious. The giant shuffled closer. "Since when has a Jack had his own business? You serve the king and queen of the elves, do you not?"

"I'm a border guard. I simply patrol the thresholds, the area around the Edge. A mortal in my protection was taken by the Nix and I need a sword—one of your swords—to rescue her."

A great rumble like the tremors of a volcano shook the forge as, to Jack's surprise, Wayland laughed.

"Ah yes, a girl. There's usually a girl somewhere along the

way. Come." He lurched away again and filled two goblets with ale from a skin on a nearby workbench. He handed one to Jack, who eyed it carefully. The cup, though gilded and studded with gemstones, was formed from a human skull. Wayland sat down, still laughing, and threw back his head to drain the liquid from its gruesome container. It flooded his broad mouth, glistening as it soaked his beard, turning the dark gray to black. His eyes met Jack's over the rim in challenge. Jack drank his ale more slowly, waiting to hear what Wayland would say next.

He lifted the skull-goblet toward Jack in a macabre salute. Rubies winked in the sockets. "They were the sons of my enemy, Nidung, the man who lamed me and trapped me on this waterlogged island. They came, like you, demanding mighty weapons to do great deeds and win fame. They were vain and arrogant." He refilled his cup and tossed the ale-skin to Jack. "Some may speak kindly enough of me, Jack, but they are few." He leaned forward, the fire demonizing his blunt features again. "There is a price for everything, from a sword to a human life, be they commoner, king, or queen. Or Jack. Are you prepared to pay that price?"

Jack drained the ale from his cup and refilled it. "I'll do what I must, Lord Wayland."

"Just Wayland, lad. I'm a craftsman, not a lord. And kingship?" He shrugged. "That is as it does. I learned my trade well and wanted nothing more than to live a simple life with my wife. So tell me about this girl you want to rescue. Is she beautiful?"

Jack closed his eyes, thinking of the faces he knew—the women of the Sidhe, Titania herself, the Dames Vertes and the River Maidens. They defined beauty and grace. And Jenny? How could a mortal compare?

"No. She . . . she's not like other women, the women of my Realm, I mean. She has hair the color of autumn leaves. She's gangly, like a newborn fawn, and awkward with it." A smile played on his lips. "She makes me laugh, usually without meaning to. Usually without realizing she's said or done something. She makes me want to be better, makes me think that maybe there's more to me than— She was lost and asked for help. I was duty-bound to give it, but the help I could offer wasn't what she wanted. We struck a bargain." He laughed bitterly at the thought and drank a little more, aware that Wayland's eyes never left him. The smith was studying him, examining him, intent on his every word. "I think she tricked me, but I'm not sure how. She gave me this." He fished out the necklace. The golden heart flickered as it turned, the light bouncing back into Wayland's face. It danced there, like a lure. "I promised to help her find her brother, stolen by the trees seven years ago. He's Queen Titania's thrall, her servant, but Jenny wouldn't listen to reason." He started to smile again, but his expression became a grimace as he felt his eyes burning. "But I can't.

I'm tied. Between the king and the queen . . . He gave me his protection to come here, to ask your help. He'd never done such a thing before. To get her back for him. I can't help but betray her. To one of them. I don't want to, but . . ." Screwing up his face, he turned away, tucking the necklace back into the safety of his shirt. "I don't think I can help it. It's part of what I am."

A huge hand took the goblet from him. To his surprise, Wayland squeezed his shoulder. Under the spell of the ale and the firelight, he hadn't heard the smith move.

"She sounds like my Alvit, my wife. Stubborn and impossible, not beautiful, but . . . compelling. And with that, more beautiful than any I had ever seen." He huffed and the fire blossomed again. "You might be as wise to let it go."

"I can't. Even if she's to be lost to one of them eventually, I can't. Not like this."

Wayland nodded slowly. "My ale has wondrous properties, they say. It never runs dry, always leaves you wanting more, and of course, makes you tell the truth, even if you don't know it yourself. Everything must be paid for, Jack. Mortals don't understand that, but we do, you and I, all our kind. I fear the price asked of you will be too high. If she's in search of her brother, aren't you just a means to an end?"

And what was she to him? A way to gain his freedom? Maybe once. Not anymore. That option was gone. Titania lied, and Oberon had made him promise to give up everything for this chance to save her. Freedom was a dream now lost. And if he could still reach for it . . . if the option was still open to him, he'd still turn away. For Jenny. The realization tasted of ashes and regret.

Was that all he was? A means to an end?

For so many people throughout the Realm, yes. Jenny was the least of it. Just the latest and most gentle noose around his neck.

"Probably," he admitted. "But now she lies in an enchanted sleep, watched over by the forest folk, and her soul is caged in the Nix's hall, his plaything and trinket. Just waiting for the queen, helpless. She'd hate anyone to think of her as helpless."

He fished out the remaining two coins, older by far than the first. Pure gold, they didn't sting him, but they were unnaturally heavy. Each had a hole in the center and the gold bore a red hue, as if bloodstained at their minting. Both surfaces were worn clear, but at the sight of them Wayland froze.

"Where did you get them?" The words came out in a desperate rush. A fierce hunger filled his blazing eyes. The forge became incandescent, illuminating the barrow as if it were full daylight.

"From my Lord Oberon."

"Alberich's rings," the smith breathed, and stretched out a trembling hand. He stopped, a low hiss coming from between his teeth. "*My* gold. The gold he stole from me. And what price did your king demand? He would never relinquish them lightly. What other bargains have you sworn?"

Jack closed his fingers over the rings. "She's the May Queen. What choice do I have?"

"You're a fool," said Wayland at last. "And a traitor to boot. A self-confessed traitor to yourself, and the folk, and, aye, to her as well. Like as not she'll curse you before she takes her leave of you, or let you rot in your own coffin. Help her, obey him, accept what's offered . . . You can't keep all these vows."

Jack remained silent. Wayland heaved in a sigh, his chest like bellows. Then he seized a huge sword from the wall where it was mounted. Runes glistened like water along its length. The counterweight was shaped like a flame.

"This is Mimung, once called Hrunting, the Jester's sword, the Blade of the Fool. That alone makes it suited to you. With it you may slay any foe, and save your May Queen. It was mine once, then I lost all use for it. I'll give it to you for the rings, but I fear it will bring you no joy."

Jack stared at the smith, surprised to find the deal was done. Wayland cradled the red-gold ring-coins in his hand, turning them over and over, marveling at them in the firelight, while Jack took the Jester's sword. It was fantastically light to hold, perfectly balanced. Radiance rippled in the steel, making the endless folding that had created it appear like the age rings of a tree. As it sliced through the air, he heard the steel sing, and it brought a grim smile to his face. He'd never held such a weapon before.

"What do the runes say?" he asked.

"Know yourself," said Wayland, his gaze fixed on Jack's rapt expression. "Advice to live by."

Jack couldn't take his eyes off it. It was what he'd felt at the doorway, the same feeling, the same warning. Flint and bronze were one thing, but this . . . Its music sang to him of mighty deeds, of heroes and valor, of Jacks who had transcended what they were, what they were made to be, to become instead legends. It sang old stories and lost stories, and things that never were. Couldn't be. Dreams, some might call them. Lies with a kinder name.

"'Ware its song," Wayland's voice warned. "Mimung, like your elf king and his queen, or indeed like the Nix, has the power to beguile. It is a tool, Jack. You must wield it, not the other way around."

The words were like a punch to the stomach. The vision shattered, cracking like ice in a thaw, leaving him open-mouthed and breathless. The sword murmured on, but its effect lessened now. Jack bowed his head, his face warming with embarrassment, and he nodded, sheathing the sword. It was a dangerous thing, as Puck had warned, dangerous to all of the folk, but perhaps to a Jack most of all. Jacks could dream. It was part of their tragedy.

He strapped it across his back and thanked the smith somberly as he made to go. Wayland, still entranced by the gold rings, gave no answer. Perhaps, Jack thought, he should heed his own advice. Jack slung his long-dry coat on, covering the sword. It wasn't until he made for the door that the smith straightened up.

"Wait. The runes *Is, Rad,* and *Ger* greeted you. You heard them, didn't you? At the door? Man of earth come to the crossing, to the places between, with a need to change . . . to change everything he is. And it can be done. But only at a great cost. *Is,*" he said with the same sibilant whisper Jack had heard outside. "The ice before spring, the bridge between worlds—this is where you came from. Winter has its mark on you, Jack, and will cling to you. *Rad,* the change, the quest, the need to act—this is where you are now, and the need will drive you. And finally *Ger,* the earth, the harvest, the final reckoning, when all things are tallied and winter starts to reclaim its own, the grave—that's where you're headed. From earth you came and to the earth will you return. You have no place in the water. If you go in after her, you won't come out again. Not as you were."

Jack frowned. "Is that a prophecy?"

"Yes. And it cannot be turned aside, unless you turn aside. Your bargains and your honor, however, will not allow that, and something more. Something that, being what you are, you cannot understand yet." Wayland sighed, shook his head. "I was a king once. Do you know what that means?" Jack didn't answer, his voice lodged in his throat. The world around them—this world, Wayland's world of rune magic and fire and iron—shivered as the old king spoke, and Jack could only listen, though all his instincts told him to flee. "Don't even recall that much of the stories, eh? I was a god and a king, and I lost it all. Through a trick. The kind of trick Alberich, whom you call Oberon, plays so well. The kind he used on you. I know what you are, Jack. Better than you do."

Fires flared around him, melting the ice inside him, freeing Jack's voice at last. "And what am I?"

"Now? You're a Jack. You are a guardian, bound by duty and obedience. He'll want his price too, as I wanted mine. You aren't like your Jenny. When she finds out what you are, and what you've promised to secure the sword—"

"I know. Puck has already warned me half a hundred times."

"Pah," Wayland spat into the fire, which sizzled and spat back. "You place too much trust in that trickster. At least you'll betray with the best intentions. He'll do it just for the fun."

Jack, who had known Puck all his life, withdrew. "He's my friend." Perhaps not entirely true, especially in light of recent events, but what did that matter now? He might doubt Puck himself, but that didn't mean he would listen to someone else say it. "My thanks, Lord Wayland, and all honor to you, but I must go."

Wayland narrowed his eyes as Jack turned once more to leave.

"Wait!" His voice held a plaintive undercurrent, yet was still commanding.

Impatience gnawed at Jack's guts, but Wayland was holding something out to him. He hesitated, feeling the chill that emanated from the small, spiked object in the smith's hand. Jack's skin recoiled from it.

"What is it?"

"Your payment exceeded the price. Give it to your Jenny. It'll make her smile, I promise you." He produced a piece of soft leather and wrapped it around the dreadful thing. Jack's revulsion subsided. He took it hesitantly, half expecting the sensation to return when he held it, but there was nothing. The leather protected him from it. He slipped it carefully into his pocket. "Don't touch it yourself, Jack. Nor allow any of the folk to touch it. Just give it to her. She'll understand. It may even be of use to her."

"Why?"

"It will offer her a protection you cannot. It's made of iron." Jack winced, thinking of the thing now as a poison vial at his side. "If she really is the May Queen, they'll all want her—the queen, the fae, your lord and master most of all. If you love her . . . You *do* love her, don't you, boy?

I can see that much on your face. Are you prepared to do that, though she be the Wren? You are more than a slave, you know. Or you were once, weren't you? Before he captured you. Before he created you anew and made you simply one of many. Practiced and practiced until he had it perfect and then turned his arts on you. But now the holly wears the crown. And the May Queen comes. Will you abide her thorns to hear her voice?"

Jack had no answers to give. Every sentence presented another riddle, and yet everything Wayland said was true. He drank the ale as well. They were things to puzzle out perhaps, when he sat in the full sun of the Realm and could turn his face to its touch. When he wasn't lost in this gray world anymore. Jack pulled the green coat around himself, noticing for the first time that it was patterned chiefly of oak leaves. If Jenny was the May Queen, that marked her as a child of the hawthorn, the May Tree. The two would never mix, or so the forest lore went.

Oak and thorn. Mortal and fae. And the king and queen. Everything stood between them. Everything.

chapter sixteen

In the watery depths, Jenny regained some sense of consciousness, but a consciousness like nothing she had ever known. She was cold, cold to her core, and deep water surrounded her—water and weeds. She tried to turn, but found her body unresponsive. It was like one of those dreams, the kind where she ran from something monstrous only to find that she couldn't move, that her own body was betraying her. Something from the forest, part of the forest, with burning eyes and leaves, moss and vine. In such dreams, she felt she had lost all power, all control. Like now. Just like now.

Something glinted in front of her. As her vision adjusted, she could make out bars, golden bars, no thicker than a wire, woven close together in a glimmering net. They twisted around her, enclosing her completely. High overhead she could see light moving on the surface, a shifting, chaotic pattern that she longed to escape toward. To fall upward, to float to freedom. But the golden bars held her fast and her world was upside down. She was trapped, what there still was of her. Her body, whatever insubstantial form she held now, was not her body. That lay somewhere on the shore, abandoned, shaken off like old skin. Or worse, drowned in the river.

A figure surged out of the darkness beneath her. Her abductor was even more impossibly beautiful in the water that was his home. His hair flowed around his face, framing it like a halo, and his body was lithe, graceful as a golden eel. He loomed over her, impossibly large, and then he smiled, baring small fishlike teeth, inserting a finger into her cage to prod at her, as one might to encourage movement in a reluctant pet. She shied back from his chill touch. It seared her skin, like bleach in a cut. But she didn't have skin, not anymore. The pain felt vivid, even though she knew she had no substance down here. Her disembodied spirit still tried to cry out in pain and fear at the touch of this fae thing. No sound came out. The Nix smiled as if he knew anyway.

He was joined by two others, women so beautiful Jenny wondered if she was looking at the source of all those legends about the mermaids' beauty. Golden hair undulated around the cage as they leaned close, their long fingertips rippling the water to agitate her. Their smiles lit up their faces, glittering like the lure on a fishing hook.

The Nix took out his harp, strumming his fingers across the strings. Music swelled beneath the water, the vibrations stirring up more ripples, which lashed against her flimsy form. Each touch shivered through her, burning, both plea-sure and pain. She wanted to weep, but there was no weeping in this watery grave. She darted around, desperate to find some escape. But there was nothing, no way out.

The Nix's sisters interlinked their hands and swam around her cage. Their voices rose in song, buffeting her and cajoling her frantic senses, lulling her until she felt her lim-ited strength draining away. In the final moments before she slept she was reminded of another story of mermaids—that of the sirens who lured men to their death with the beauty of their voices.

⚘ ⚘ ⚘

Led by Puck, the forest folk had raised a bier for her, layer upon layer of sticks and stones, topped with soft moss, herbs, and grasses. They had decked it with every flower imaginable and Jenny lay upon it, her hands lightly folded on her stomach, her face turned up to the trees overhead, her eyes closed, her skin pale as the cherry blossoms scat-tered around her face.

They'd laid her out for burial. The significance of that didn't escape Jack. But it had been done with respect. And that was a comfort, however small. They stood at the end of the trees now, tall and small, beautiful and ugly, all the fae folk. And in front of them, Puck sat with his back to Jack, his shoulders hunched and eyes downcast, while the others watched avidly, some in view, some out of sight amid the trees.

Jack dropped to his knees beside the bier, staring at Jenny's unmoving face. He could feel the fae watching him, the warmth of their gaze, their closeness and affinity. And not just him. They watched her too. It was a kind of love. She'd saved one of their own, shown true kindness. Now they offered her respect, and honor.

The girl lay amid flowers and fragrant herbs, her chest moving only shallowly now, her skin so pale that the freckles stood out like stars in the night's sky. So pretty. He had never managed to tell her how pretty they were. Perhaps he never would. On a glance anyone would think she was dead, but not the forest fae. They knew all about appearances and just how deceptive they could be. Puck had called them and they had come. For Jenny. And for that Jack was grateful.

"I'll find you," he said to her now. He didn't know if she could hear him or not, but he wanted to believe she could.

You have no place in the water. If you go in after her, you won't come out again.

The chill that had dogged him since he sat before the blast of Wayland's furnace and heard those words returned again. He wasn't coming back from the water. He was a thing of earth. He knew that. It was ingrained in the most basic part of his being.

The Nix was too powerful. He knew that as well. And the water would only aid its own creatures and hinder Jack.

But he'd failed Jenny too many times. If he could get her out at least, give her the opportunity to continue her quest, then maybe his part in this wouldn't have been in vain.

Jack sat back on his heels and took Wayland's gift from his belt pouch. Then he leaned forward and tucked the leather-wrapped iron into her hand, closing her fingers gently around it. He noticed for the first time that her nails were ragged, the earth of the Realm blackening underneath the tips. Her hands were covered in small, partially healed cuts that stood out against the pale skin and freckles. They were strong hands. They'd endured so much already. The gold heart necklace suddenly felt very heavy around his neck. It seemed to strain toward her. He winced.

"What is it?" Puck asked. Jack hadn't noticed him move from where he'd sat with his back turned. He'd thought Puck would ignore him altogether.

"It's for her alone, Puck," he warned. "A gift from Wayland and it's made of iron. Keep your light fingers under control. That goes for the others too." He glanced toward the line of trees. "It could kill any of the folk, even the strongest."

Puck shied back as if burned. "What were you thinking, bringing something like that through?"

Jack ignored the outburst. "It's hers. Wayland wanted her to have it and it might be . . . I don't know. He said it would make her smile." He so wanted to see her smile again, and frown too. If she threw a handful of grass in his face again, he'd welcome it. Puck didn't look convinced, but Jack didn't particularly care. "I should go." He pushed the cloak from his shoulders and draped it over her. The sword was unnaturally heavy across his back. It dragged at him. Steel was almost as dangerous as iron to any from the Realm, and this sword called to be used. It murmured a song of war right on the edge of his hearing. "Keep a watch over her for me, Puck . . . This time—"

Puck bowed solemnly, a courtly bow. It was easy to forget how high he stood in Oberon's court. The stunted little hobgoblin had the grace of an elf when he put his mind to it. As if he noticed Jack's observation, Puck tried to smile reassuringly.

"I won't let you down again, Jack. I'll watch her from morn 'til night. I'll keep her safe."

Jack looked at him. Puck had told Oberon everything. There was no doubt he would do it again if the situation demanded it. But the forest fae were here, at least, and—

"Just hide her, and keep her safe until I . . ."

The words choked in his throat. *Get back?* He was leaving earth and sunlight behind, the source of any strength he had in him. He was going into another element, one that didn't love him.

Puck nodded and pulled the leaf cloak up to cover Jenny's face. With a wave of his hand, he muttered a few words and the cloak shimmered until the bier appeared to be no more than a small raised area of fallen leaves and flowers, a mound of earth that blended flawlessly with the forest. Jack frowned again. It looked like a well-tended grave.

"I'm sorry, Jack." The hobgoblin's subdued voice snapped him back and Jack turned. He watched Puck's bowed head, waiting for more. "I had to tell him."

Jack held himself perfectly still as a fury like an inferno surged through him once more, threatening to incinerate the logic he had carefully built up. He could not lose control. He didn't have time for it now.

Slowly, every movement measured and careful, he closed his eyes, breathed deeply, and opened them to find Puck gazing up at him like a kicked dog.

"And what will Oberon do to her, Puck?" His voice was quiet.

Puck winced, pursing his mouth. "She has to go to him willingly. Why would she do that? He can't touch her otherwise. I thought . . . I hoped . . ."

No hopes. No dreams. He had bargained them away. They were fools. And Puck hadn't answered him either. But it didn't really matter. "You were wrong."

"We were both wrong," Puck said miserably. "And neither of us can stand against the king now."

Jack grimaced and turned to look out at the river. What could he say to Puck? He was right. None of them could possibly resist their duty to Oberon. Not without suffering a dreadful retribution. Part of Jack wanted to wring the life out of the hobgoblin for telling, but another part of him understood profoundly why Puck had done it. And that hurt more than anything.

He'd thought they were friends. Even though he knew better. He didn't have any friends. Not really. But he'd thought, of all the friends he didn't have, Puck came the closest to transcending that barrier.

He took a deep breath. It didn't matter now, though the thought made him acutely aware of the gaping hole the lack of that particular loss left. Puck had failed him, just as he had failed Jenny. Puck was trying to apologize, to make amends. Much as Jack himself was.

So what else was there to say?

"Help her," he whispered to Puck. "Find her brother and get them out of the Realm safely." If it sounded like a command, so be it. They both knew it was a plea.

Puck's pained expression collapsed still further. He bowed again. "I will. On my life, Jack."

On his life. Even Puck couldn't break that vow. And so simple a promise couldn't be twisted into something else. He had to believe Puck in this.

Jack hesitated for another moment trying to think of something more to say, and then, finding nothing, he turned away. Stripping off his boots and adjusting the sword for ease of movement, he prepared himself. He knelt to the earth and pressed both hands and his lips to it. The warmth was fleeting. He looked up to the sun and then slipped into the water's chill embrace.

If you go in after her, you won't come out again.

His skin contracted around his bones. It was colder than he had imagined it could be, forcing his breath from his body in a single gasp of shock. Used to the summer sun and the woodland's gentle breezes as Jack was, the cold teeth of the river gnawed at him. The waterfall thundered in his bones, threatening, taunting. Weeds tugged at his legs, the mud sucking at his feet, claiming him. He stood on the edge of a drop. Another step would take him into deep water. The Nix's world.

He looked back over his shoulder at dry land. The forest folk, Puck foremost amongst them, had gathered at the tree line. Great and small they stood there, watching him. Elegant Dames Vertes in gowns the same colors as the leaves of their trees, the brightly hued sparks of flighty Foletti, the gnomes, birch-boys, and the leaf-clad pixies . . . The light of their ancient lives burned brighter than he had ever seen it. They stood still for him, bearing witness.

Jack drew the Jester's sword from its sheath—the Blade of the Fool, Wayland had called it—and the blade rang out in challenge, a pure note that echoed around him. He could sense the hunger in it, could feel the enchantments woven into it as if they were now a part of him. They promised glory and fame. Things he neither wanted nor needed. But its song was as charming as that of the Nix. Powerful too. Lifting a sword changes a man, or so the old saying went. And it was truer in the Realm than anywhere else, as most stories and sayings were.

The sword's energies touched him and he knew it had faced the Nix before, or something of his ilk. It was ready. Jack swallowed hard as the sword drained away his doubts and fear. Better to die nobly than to eke out a pathetic existence as a slave, the sword sang. Better to save Jenny, even if it cost him everything, than to continue on knowing how badly he'd failed. He had to try. A grim smile spread over Jack's face. He looked into the troubled faces of the folk, one after the other, and wondered if he was seeing them for the last time.

"Wait for me here," he said, then turned, and with the great sword held above his head, he plunged into the depths.

chapter seventeen

Beneath the waterfall, the Nix stirred and Jenny came to herself again, woken by his movement. One of his sisters knelt before him. Jenny watched her, feeling the water's ripples differently now. Somehow she could read it as they did, could feel an invasion in their world. The Nixie spread her arms wide, her finger undulating with the current. Her hair billowed around her head, moved by the same disturbance. Her eyes were wide and she searched the water overhead relentlessly.

"What is it?" the Nix asked, his voice drifting through the water like whale song, an eerie, beautiful sound that rocked through Jenny's consciousness, leaving behind the impression of the words and the sorrow of a thousand years.

"He's coming."

Was it Jack? It had to be Jack. Jenny's spirit soared at the thought, and the next words dashed her down again.

"Then he's yours. Yours and our sister's. Do what you will."

The Nix turned back to Jenny, thrusting his hand into the cage, toying with her, running his fingers through her warm and radiant light. It would destroy her in the end, drain all the energy she held. She knew it instinctively, as surely as she knew herself. Each time it was worse. Eventually, she would just melt away. Not released, not set free, just gone.

"You stir the sentimental side of my nature," the Nix said, his voice winding through the water. "You're a tragedy, a tiny, glittering tragedy, locked away in my gold cage."

Jenny struggled, trying to avoid him.

"You're stronger and more brilliant than any I've snatched away for centuries," he continued, his voice lulling her like his music. "Mortals don't stray to my riverbank anymore. So pretty a thing. So delicate. So amusing."

His sister was watching them, gray eyes ravenous. Jenny knew that look. Cats wore it as they stalked their prey. She only wanted to feed.

"Have you sent word to the queen?" she asked.

The Nix scowled at the interruption. "I have. She knows where the body lies, but this fancy is mine until she pays my price. And she would want to hurry. She can't have both without the promised gold." Still his sister didn't move. He narrowed his eyes. "What else?"

"The queen isn't here to protect us. He's coming for her." She nodded toward Jenny's cage. "He's coming to kill us. You know what he is, what he can do."

The Nix narrowed his blue gaze to icy shards.

"In the water? I think not. Take your sister with you and sing to him. Drag him into your embrace and then he is yours. Now leave me."

☙ ☙ ☙

Jack was almost at the waterfall itself when he first heard it. It was a whispering in the water . . . a noise like a dream in audible form. And then a voice rose in a half-remembered song, and though he could not make out words, he felt compelled to listen. After a second, it faded. He turned in a circle, treading water, and then in another, until the spray of the falls once more rained onto his face.

To his left, a second voice took up the refrain, the tone trailing to laughter as he splashed around in search of the source. Behind him, he heard the first voice begin again, and his body relaxed in the water, the song soothing him, the river cradling him.

Both voices joined together in harmony, the sound of all his desires, from the simplest to the most complex. The song worked on his body, on the taut muscles and lines of tension. These were creatures who understood what he was, for they were the same. He had no need to fear them, or hide from them. Magic knows magic, his mind murmured, lulled by their music. It sang of freedom, of dreams, of never struggling again.

A hand ran up the column of his leg. Another encircled his shoulders. Golden hair spread out in the water like the fronds of some exotic plant. Chill fingers played with the tender skin over his Adam's apple, while another hand ran down the length of his arm. The hairs on his skin shivered.

The song was everywhere, in his ears, in his mind, in the water that played against his body. A woman surfaced before him, her heart-shaped face pale as porcelain, shimmering with a touch of silver like scales on a minnow. Blue eyes gazed at him, liquid with desire and need, her pupils wide. Her mouth parted, revealing a flash of white teeth, and her song grew louder. Under the water, another circled him, her hands unfastening the baldric, uncurling his fingers where he held the sword. Their song was wound about with secrets and enchantments. Even knowing that, Jack wilted beneath the onslaught, his body betraying him. A traitor to the last. As the first laid her frozen lips on his, their grip on him tightened to silver bands, drawing him under the surface of the river. Wayland's great sword slipped from his loosened fingers.

The cold shock of the water drove breath from him and brought a frightening moment of clarity. The Blade of the Fool . . . He knew it now, as the water closed over him and the river sisters drew him down. *He* was the fool. Wayland had called him as much, had given him the Jester's sword as if to prove it. It glinted several feet below him, sticking out of the black, consuming mud. Mud that would suck a man down and trap him forever.

The second sister pushed herself between him and the first, her kisses even more savage. His breath felt caught, stolen. His energy drained and diminished. Her hands traced lines across his bare skin. She pulled at his leaf shirt to get beneath it, murmuring a song of sweet seduction, saw the bright glint of gold around his neck and her eyes widened. A new fascination entered them. She smiled, her full lips parting to reveal small, sharp white teeth, and her grip closed on the chain, ready to rip it from his throat.

Jack's hand came up, forcing its way through the water, closing on her wrist and wrenching her away. Her shock fragmented the spell. He flipped over, diving straight for the sword before their song could engulf him again.

The play of seduction dissolved with his escape. He was their prey, in their element, and he had gold. They circled him like predatory eels, their long bodies brushing against him, trying to disorient him and knock him away from the weapon.

His fingers closed on the sword hilt, closed into a fist, and he pulled.

Mimung stuck fast, lodged in the clinging mud. He heard laughter and the Nixies stopped their circling. They hung before him, beautiful and terrible, waiting for him to move. He would need air. The moment he broke for the surface, they would be on him. He could see the intention in their flawless faces. He tugged at the sword, but it stayed where it was, wedged in the riverbed. Panic rose in his throat like bile.

Please. You have to come out.

His lungs ached, his eyes burned as he glanced for the surface. He needed air. He didn't belong down here. His muscles strained, tearing, the water leeching his strength from him. Closing his eyes, he placed both hands on the sword hilt again.

By oak and holly, he prayed, *by ash and thorn, you're earth, no matter how the water holds you down. Help me.*

The sword jerked free. The Nixies gave twin cries of rage and flung themselves at him, but the blade was still moving. His muscles strained to control it, fighting the water even as he fought its creatures. The Nixies rushed toward him, teeth and claws bared. Mimung, who had fought and destroyed water spirits many times before, arched toward them. The impact shuddered up his arm. The blade swept through them, leaving a long line of blood in the depths, billowing out and dispersing like ink. The Nixies shrieked, the steel destroying them. Dragging the sword back against his body, Jack pushed skyward with all his strength, forcing himself toward light and air.

He broke the surface, his mouth distended, the sword still gripped in his hand. Blood burst around him, a huge bubble that polluted the clear water, churned up by the crashing waterfall. Jack heaved another breath and held the sword close, treading water desperately as he fought to keep from vomiting. When he could bring himself to dive again, the Nix's sisters were gone.

He surfaced and breathed. Breath was all he could cling to. His breath . . . and the sword. The waterfall thundered down, agitating the water around him. The Nix was down there somewhere. Had to be. He was down there. And so was Jenny.

Jack took a series of rapid breaths, filling his lungs nearly to the point of bursting, and dived under the waterfall, letting the force of its descent drive him down to the lair of the Nix. Amid tangled weeds and misshapen stones, he felt his way, the sword icy cold in his hand. Through the gloom he saw a flash of light, golden, as bright as newly restored hope. He caught it for only a moment before his lungs betrayed him and he was forced back to the surface for air. Treading water, breathing calmly, he tried to fix the light's location in his mind. Then he dived back into the depths.

The light was gone, but he pushed himself toward its last location. The unfamiliar weight in his hand dragged him down, but at the same time the necklace tugged him forward, as if Jenny's golden heart guided him to her. He allowed it to lead him, following the pull until he saw the riverbed. A line of jagged rocks ran across the base of the waterfall, and overhead, the surface boiled.

His strength was failing. Out of the sun, away from the earth, out of his element, he couldn't keep going. But he had to.

He wasn't sure what he had expected. Though the tales of the Nix had spoken of a stately hall and cages of gold, Jack had thought it a fancy. But under the water, his eyes adjusted. He felt the subtle shift of a magical charge and before him, the riverbed fell away, dropping down to reveal polished marble, columns and terraces. A palace spread out before him, shimmering in the water like mother-of-pearl. There were no roofs, no need for them here under the water, and mosaic floors and decorated walls spread out like intricate ruins that had never decayed. He dived deeper, passing beneath row after row of ornate arches, past faded frescos and into the largest chamber of all. Gold and precious stones decorated the walls and floor, each one glinting in the shifting light from high overhead. He glanced up. It was so very far to daylight, to air, to safety.

Standing on a plinth that had once been a jagged rock but had been polished by water and smoothed by magic-wielding hands, stood a small and intricately crafted cage made of gold. It was the type of thing in which a queen might keep a songbird, but inside it he saw something like a will-o'-the-wisp, a single point of flickering light. It was the only light down here that wasn't reflected from above.

Jenny.

He grabbed the cage, tearing the door open. The light shied back from him, colliding with the far side of the cage, desperate to avoid his touch. He drew back, willing her with his eyes alone to understand him, to seize her freedom. She darted clear of the cage, circling him like a frenzied firefly. She was lost, bewildered and terrified.

Did she even know or recognize him? Could she in that state? She was so small, so fragile. She'd be furious to be seen as such, he knew that. She'd stick out her chin, ball up her fists, and raise herself straighter. Then do everything in her power to prove him wrong. The thought of it almost made him smile. He wanted to reach out, to gather her to him, but she was light, dancing through his fingertips.

A roar shook the pool, the concussion throwing him back. The water twisted in a maelstrom and her soul-light was torn aside. A wave of hatred tossed Jack back toward the surface and he managed one brief, desperate lungful of air before the Nix closed hands around his throat and dragged him back under again.

Had he been on land, Jack would have had no fear of this creature. He was a guardian, a warrior by nature, created to fight. But this was not his element. He needed earth and air. More than that, he needed sunlight, and beneath the surface of the river the sun diffused to a pale and distant glow. The Nix moved sleekly through the water, formed from it, a part of it, while he, ungainly and flailing, was forced to fight it as a second enemy.

Jack's back slammed against the side of a boulder. The remaining air exploded from his lungs in a chaos of bubbles. Black spots danced before his eyes. He saw the Nix snarl, revealing a row of savage teeth, and close in for the kill.

Golden radiance exploded before his face—Jenny's will-o'-the-wisp. She darted toward the Nix and he lunged for her, his prey forgotten for his prize. His grasping hands were claws around her, but at the last minute, she darted between his fingers, distracting him and leading him away. Jack broke for the surface and sweet air filled his lungs.

But precious little light.

He emerged in a cave behind the waterfall. The sound was deafening. The air hung with moisture. There was barely enough light to see at all as he hauled himself onto a wet ledge, gasping for air. It felt like someone was levering his ribs apart with each breath.

The sword clattered from his hand, and even as he clawed after it, he didn't have the strength to lift it anymore. Desolation drained his hope away. Moisture plastered his hair in strands over his face.

Wayland had been right. Water would be his death.

Light swelled in the river behind the falls. He gazed at it, a fire rising from the depths, like the sun he so desperately needed to feel on his face once more. Lying on his back, he saw Jenny's light break the surface of the water. It darted toward him and then to the sword. He tried to sit up. He could barely breathe. It was like he was still there, at the bottom of the vast river with the full weight of water pressing down on his chest.

"I can't, Jenny Wren," he told her, his body failing him. Failing her. She buzzed around his face angrily, a little glowing wasp of rage. It was Jenny all right. No doubt about that. He tried to shift his weight, to get leverage from his arms. Useless. He closed his eyes. Felt a coldness spread through him. Too late. The water had stolen whatever life was left in him. He was fading. Without the sun, without the earth, he was nothing.

He opened his mouth to tell her that his strength was gone, then opened his eyes to see her flying straight at him. Before he knew what was happening, she shot into his mouth and his body swallowed reflexively.

Her voice exploded into his conscious mind.

"Get up! He's coming to kill you!"

The Nix erupted from the water, his mouth distended in a roar. Inside Jack's head, Jenny screamed garbled instructions as the water demon bore down on them. Like a wave, the Nix seemed to hang there, just for a second, before crashing down against the rocks.

"Move!" Jenny yelled, and Jack could do nothing but obey her.

He rolled over the icy stone. The Nix's claws slashed toward him. Jenny's light flared in his chest, warm and brilliant as a star, right beneath the point where her locket rested against his chest. She was like the sun, the thing he needed, like the earth beneath his feet. She was breath and strength, everything.

She was his May Queen.

Jack came to his feet, snatching up the Jester's sword as he did so. It filled his grasp, its song flowing through him, loud and new, and Jenny gave a shout of joy. His stance slid, the ground treacherous with water beneath him. But earth surrounded him, earth and rock and mineral. He felt the steel blade hum with expectation and tightened his grip. He was a creature of the earth. The sword was a thing born in fire. Water was the enemy of both.

He had to trust the sword. To know it and let it be what it was.

The Nix faltered for a moment and a slow smile spread over Jack's face.

"*Jack?*" Jenny whispered nervously when he didn't move. "*What are you—*"

The Nix lunged forward, intent only on carrying Jack back into the water, where he would be strong and the guardian would drown. Jack twisted before his assault and brought Wayland's sword up to greet him.

Like earth, like rock and steel, unmoving, rooted deep.

Jack reached for both earth and sword and linked the two with his body. Earth and weapon, and the warrior between.

The Nix tried to stop his rush forward, his eyes flaring at the sight of the blade. But nothing could stop the oncoming flood, nor move the earth itself. The Nix crashed onto the Jester's sword, its full length passing through him.

The creature shuddered, his blue eyes wide and liquid. He slid up the blade, toward Jack, reaching out with lethally sharp talons where his fingernails had been. Then his form lost cohesion. Jack watched the blood melt away into the river, and like his sisters, the Nix was gone.

The spell of strength snapped.

He sank to his knees, cradling the sword. Every part of him was wrung out, broken. He needed to sleep, for just a while. He laid his head down. The world went black behind his closed lids, then crimson. His eyes snapped open.

Gold-red light warmed his face. Sunset filtering through the curtain of water. Something stirred deep inside him, something ancient, scrabbling to get out.

Oh Elders. He had to get her back to her own body—*now*.

"Jack? Can you still hear me?"

Sunset . . . And then night . . . Greedy fingers of exhaustion worked their way through him, as insidious as the icy water and the cold of the stone burrowing in from outside. Jenny was with him, her presence a bright spark in his mind.

But if he didn't move now, if he gave in to the great silence, she'd know him for what he truly was.

And then?

Puck was right. Wayland too. Even now, she'd never understand.

He forced himself up, heard her sigh of relief. She thought the Realm a place of monsters. And he could hardly blame her for that. Sometimes he believed the same himself.

"We haven't much time," he wheezed, praying that she couldn't see his thoughts.

"But he's dead, isn't he?" Fear sharpened her voice to a point.

Her innocence glowed within him, cleansing him by virtue simply of touching him. For the first time, he could understand why those with souls were so highly prized by all of Faerie. Why she fascinated him, why Titania feared her, why Oberon wanted her . . . The knowledge chilled him. He didn't want to understand how Oberon thought.

It was her heart that did it, that made them all notice her, that made her stand out like the only still thing in a world of movement. Her heart, the very fact that she cared at all after everything she had been through, that beauty of spirit, the heart of a May Queen. No wonder Titania wanted it so badly.

"The sun's setting," he said. "That's all I meant." He

closed his eyes. Opened them. Struggled against his own exhaustion. "It isn't safe."

"*I know,*" she replied and he heard the fear in her voice. Not fear of the Nix now. Just . . . fear. "*I . . . I'm losing myself.*"

She could feel it too, he realized. The silence, the endless dark. She wasn't losing herself, not really. *He* was losing *himself.* To the evening shadows. To the night.

Jenny shrank back somewhere in the center of his chest. It was just as well that her fear kept her from examining her surroundings. Jack wasn't sure if he would be able to maintain his control long enough as it was, let alone if she fought him. He lowered himself back into the river, flinching in expectation of another attack. But it was calm now. Except for the churning of the waterfall, nothing moved. The cold helped. So did being in another element. It distanced him from the earth, helped him to hang on a little longer. But even that wouldn't last. He swam as quickly as he could for the shore.

Strength was fading fast. It wasn't far, but that didn't matter if he couldn't make it. The water might stop him changing but not for long, not forever. And in the meantime it might just kill him instead.

"*Jack? What's happening? Jack?*"

Kill them both.

Spots of light danced before his eyes. The world around him blurred and twisted. He was almost there, but the river was pulling him down, cold fingers as strong and insidious as those of the Nixies. He wasn't going to make it. Water filled his mouth and nose, choking him, sucking him under. The light was going, his vision dimming, flooding with water thick with weeds, darkening. Water closed over his head. Sound and light faded away, leaving only darkness.

Strong hands closed on his, a grip like a tree root, impossibly strong, dragging him to shore. He took a deep breath, choking and coughing up water, then blinked as his sight returned and saw the nut-brown face and copper eyes, as familiar to him as anyone's, but full of fear. Puck, soaking wet, dragging him through the mud.

"You're all right, lad. You're here. You're safe."

Jack coughed up more muddy river water, choked, and pushed himself up on his aching arms. Puck? Puck had saved them? No time to riddle it out, but the relief on the hobgoblin's face spoke more than could ever be voiced between them. Back on dry land, Jack hung on his hands and knees, breathing hard as the pull of earth and forest returned, slamming into him with renewed force. Puck tugged at his arm, trying to get him to stand. The sun was a blood-red orb hanging over the trees. Jack's body creaked as he hauled himself upright. The change was sweeping through him now.

"That's it, lad," said Puck. "All will be well now. Take it slowly." But Jack pulled away from him. He staggered for the trees, aware that stiffness was coiling beneath his skin.

"Jack?" Jenny felt his panic. He couldn't disguise it from her now. She wasn't a fool. She could feel it as clearly as he could. And it terrified her as it terrified him. *"Jack? What's wrong? What's happening?"*

In the midst of the glade, the forest folk saw his frantic approach and scattered. They could sense it too. He fell to his knees before her body, jerked back the cloak so he could see her pale face and those wondrously human freckles.

"Go," he gasped.

"I—I don't know how."

"Jenny, now! Go!"

"But I—" She fluttered within him, a firefly in a jar.

"Old ways," said Puck, laying a small, gnarled hand on Jack's bent shoulder. He spoke softly, in calm and measured tones that Jack found too disturbing for words and far too great a comfort to say. "Old ways. Though they are never without danger."

Jack stared at Jenny's still face. He knew of what Puck spoke. It was never without danger, just as the hobgoblin said, but he couldn't think of anything else that might work. He took in Jenny's features with his eyes one last time, then seized her shoulders, pulling her limp body up, and kissed her.

It was hardly romantic. He could sense Jenny's outrage at such a savage touch, her shock, and then . . . Nothing.

She was gone, no longer inside him. But her body remained

still and unmoving. Panic raked through him, even with the encroaching dark, even with the threat of what was to come. It hadn't worked. Jenny was gone.

With a gasp, she convulsed against him, her eyes opening, her mouth stretched, hiccoughing for air. He dropped her back down and saw her outrage turn to shock, to horror.

It's time, his mind screamed. *It's time. She'll know.*

She scrambled back from him, and with a snarl of despair, Jack threw himself heedlessly toward the trees and their dark, welcome embrace.

chapter eighteen

Shivering, Jenny huddled against the flowery bier—it might have been her grave if it hadn't been for Jack. She wrapped his leaf cloak tightly around herself, twisting her fingers through the material. The moon had risen and the trees whispered on and on and on. There was no sign of Jack. No sign of anything moving in there. No monsters in the darkness. But she couldn't be sure . . .

The forest seemed exceptionally dark tonight, or was it that she just couldn't see its beauty anymore? The Nix had left her afraid. Again, afraid. Of the shadows, of the water, of the distant sound of the waterfall. Afraid of—of everything. Always afraid! She was sick of it.

And Jack had come. He had come and gone . . . and left her with a—with a monster in his place.

She was confused, that was all, her mind addled from everything that had happened. Waking up, she'd seen her nightmare made real and screamed. Puck had eventually calmed her down, but by then it was too late.

It was gone. And so was Jack.

She was an idiot, so afraid of the greenman, so angry with Jack, so thoughtless. She'd kissed the Nix—not willingly perhaps, but she'd done it, all the same—fallen under his spell without a moment's resistance. So upset, so angry, so stupid and blind. But like the Goodwife and her husband, she'd slipped into a fairy trap, and almost lost everything.

She was no better than them, it seemed. The thought made her shiver more than the cold.

And then Jack was gone. And in his place, the monstrous forest spirit that haunted her, hunted her. But she knew Jack had saved her. That she had somehow been inside him. That he had kissed her. And changed. She lifted shaking fingers to her mouth, as if his kiss still lingered there.

What had happened? What on earth had happened?

But of course, deep down, she knew. She just didn't want to.

"What ails you, lass?" asked Puck, gently enough.

Jenny looked up as his gnarled little hand brushed her cheek and came away damp. Tears streamed from her eyes. Strange, she thought. Up to that moment she hadn't realized they were there.

"Will he ever forgive me, Puck?"

"Forgive you what?"

"The . . . the Nix . . ." she began uncertainly, unable to voice another reason. "Will Jack . . . will Jack come back?"

He had to. Moments flickered like lights through her mind. The exhilaration of their escape, rushing back from the river, Jack's hard kiss, opening her eyes to find . . . not Jack, but the greenman standing over her. She hadn't been able to help herself.

He'd lied to her all along. He wasn't protecting her from the monster at all.

Puck nestled himself beside her, his warm earthy scent a comfort; even that reminded her of Jack. No matter that his kiss had been brief and desperate, hurried. No matter. Its effect was the same. It wasn't shy or uncertain. It wasn't seductive. It had only served a purpose. And yet . . . it was like nothing she'd ever experienced.

She smoothed her fingers over Puck's wiry fur and he rested his head against her shoulder, warm as a sleeping cat. Who would ever have thought a hobgoblin could be such a comfort? Only to someone like her, she thought with a grim smile.

"Jack would never hold another's enchantment against you," said Puck. "He knows that within the Realm, one's actions are not always—"

"When I woke up, when he had to kiss me like that . . ."

"Shh . . ." Puck pulled his head away, his eyes bright with grief. "He'll come back. Jack must patrol at night. That's in his nature. Surely you've realized that by now, lass."

A childish need rose inside her, a need to hide from everything, to make the world normal again, to pretend at least that none of this was real. It was what people had tried to tell her for the last seven years, wasn't it? That she'd been hallucinating, dreaming, that somehow losing Tom was all her fault and if she just told them the truth—their truth—it would magically make everything better.

She could try one last time, to pretend everything was normal, couldn't she? To pretend this wasn't happening and make it go away. "And the—the creature?"

"What *creature?*" A hint of impatience entered Puck's voice with the word.

She bit her lip and pressed on. "The beast he's hunting, or that's hunting us. The thing that killed the Woodsman, the"—she had to whisper the word—"the *greenman*. Is he—is Jack holding it back from us?"

There was a long pause as Puck scanned the trees with catlike contemplation. Was that disappointment in his face? Whatever it was, he decided to veil the truth, if not lie outright. He sighed. "You could say that, lass."

Jenny paused. "What is it? I saw it before, when Tom was taken. A monster."

"Aye." He smiled as if he were talking to a child, or an idiot. Perhaps that was what he thought of her. And perhaps she was. She wanted to think that. To hide for just a little longer, to be normal, to be sane, not someone who was falling for a— Puck's voice trembled just a little with regret. "A fairy-tale monster. Nothing more."

Jenny sagged forward, her chin against her chest. She was an idiot indeed if she chose to believe that.

She drew in a deep breath. Puck would lie to her, for her, but she couldn't lie to herself. No matter how badly she might want to.

"But it isn't. Not really." She closed her eyes and let her head tilt back against the bier. Jutting from among the neatly piled layers of sticks and stones a stray twig poked into the back of her neck, snagging her hair. She pulled it free, twisting it in her hands. She couldn't hide any longer. She couldn't be a child in this world, or it would swallow her whole. Hers was not the truth of psychiatrists and drugs, of her parents and their world. Their truth— human truth—had never been enough. Her truth was Jack's truth and everything that couldn't be real. "Jack is . . . it's him, isn't it? Somehow? The greenman. He turns into it at night."

Puck didn't stir. She could sense him watching her. "That . . . that is perceptive, Jenny Wren," he said at last.

She sighed, the sound wrung out of her body. Puck would lie to her as long as he felt it comforted her. "Not really. I should have realized. That's what you meant, isn't it? When you told me about the jack-in-the-box. A Kobold."

"Yes. That's the truth of it. A curse, or something as near as like it. They were tree spirits once. Wild creatures, reveling in that wildness in the moonlight, but hidden in their trees by day. Jack was the strongest of them. Their leader. Their king. Oberon took them prisoner one by one, and broke them, carving the wood of them into the semblance of men. He breathed new life into them and they are his servants, his knights, some might say"—his voice grew strained—"his slaves. The last one, the strongest of them all, the Oak King was Oberon's eternal enemy. But even he fell, at the last, alone, the wild king of the wild places." Puck breathed deep. "Oberon didn't just subjugate him. First Oberon destroyed all his people, and then took him as well. He carved his wood into the same figure as all the rest, made our Jack one of so many slaves, took away all that made him different. His spirit, his fire, his heart. Oberon took them all. Oberon made Jacks of them all. His slaves. All the fearless trees."

Jack's tree flashed through Jenny's mind—the May Tree, Puck had called it—tied all over with fluttering white. "You said he wished for freedom," she breathed. "Not just freedom for him. For all of them." She turned to look at Puck, a hope rising behind her eyes. "Then he . . . he wasn't there that night, when Tom was taken? It was one of the others."

"No."

That single word crushed her.

Puck looked at her sadly, intently. "It was Jack," he said. "He guards the Edge. The others guard other edges. But the forest is still his. Even when he isn't Jack, when he's in his natural state, the trees are his, Jenny. And they took your brother. Jack . . . Jack found him a home here rather than leave him lost."

Tears needled her eyes but she pushed them back. "I don't believe you."

He shook his head slowly, so sadly. "Then you must ask him."

"But he's helping me."

Puck didn't answer at first. When he shifted his eyes to look at her, she caught the flash of guilt across his face. "He *wants* to help you, lass."

Puck pulled away from her then, getting to his hoofed feet and stretching like a cat waking from sleep.

Jenny's heart stuttered. "Jack is bound by vows. To *him*. To *her*. To do what, Puck? And why? Why would he make such vows?"

"You must ask him that, Jenny Wren."

Lines wrinkled Puck's face and suddenly he looked old, as old as the stones on the riverbank. Sorrow lined his features and changed him from a mischievous sprite to something ancient and unfathomable.

"Only he can give you an answer to that. I'll tell you this, though: I've never known Jack—I've never known *any* of the Jacks—to do for another as much as he has done for you. Though I was the one who begged our master's protection, he crossed to your world, walked the Ridgeway between, and risked himself before our master's enemy to get that sword. I imagine it burns against his back every second he wears it. Even setting foot in your world could have killed him, for without the protection of Lord Oberon, it is fatal to us. And Oberon exacted a price from him too. A terrible price for a forest king. His freedom, any chance of winning it for himself, and his kingship too. But he gave all that. For you."

Dawn crept through the trees and fell, dappled, on her face. Jenny woke and there he was. Jack. Sitting across from her, watching her, his gaze troubled. She tried to smile at him, tried to give him the thing he needed most—proof of her trust.

But her smile wavered. She felt it, right before she saw the effect on his face.

And in that instant she knew the damage was done.

"You came after me," she said. Her eyes stung. There was a tingling across the bridge of her nose, tightening her skin and closing her throat.

I will not cry, she told herself.

"I'm bound to protect you," Jack said. *Nothing more.* The words were unspoken but hung between them. She was nothing but a weight around his neck. He'd told her as much already.

She tried to think of something to say but Jack beat her to it.

"We wouldn't have got out if it hadn't been for you. You thought quickly, and you were strong." He hesitated, staring down at her, his features emotionless. "You did well."

Jenny swallowed. His gruff praise should have made her proud, but instead she felt wretched. All she could think of was the expression on his face a moment earlier, and the stiffness there now.

Silence dragged out between them, the long, agonizing death of Jack's trust. She had to say something. Anything.

"Where did you get the sword?"

Jack flinched at the mention, glancing behind himself at the weapon still strapped across his back. It looked old, even by the standards of the Realm. Saxon, perhaps. She'd seen them in the British Museum on various school visits, studied them in history class, and they had fascinated her. This one was different, more ornate, special somehow. She'd seen what it could do.

Well, not seen, exactly. But she knew; she had watched it all unfold before her, through his eyes.

"Wayland," he grunted, looking away from her.

"Wayland's a legend." Her laugh made its escape and he glared at her. But the sound made that expression melt to a smile.

Such a wonderful smile. It sparked in his eyes, crinkled the skin around them, and made him handsome.

"Yes. He is. And more."

She shook her head, still smiling. Well, why not? Why not any number of old gods and forgotten stories? She looked at him again. "Can I see it? The sword?"

His face fell again into that stone-cold seriousness, and her heart fell with it. He pulled the sword out of the scabbard. Though he held it out to her hilt-first, she hesitated to take it. Light glinted off its edge, razor sharp. Most of the weapons she had ever seen—apart from being safely locked behind glass—were blunted and marked, nicks taken out of the edges, the metal tarnished and dull. This sword didn't just gleam, it dazzled.

"Is it magic?"

"It's one of Wayland's, so . . ." He shrugged, and came closer, hunkering down beside her, back to the bier. They sat there, side by side, studying the weapon. "I suppose it is," he said finally.

"And this?" Jenny uncurled her fingers to reveal the tiny star of iron he had given her. She lifted it in her palm and, seeing it again, felt a smile overtake her face. It was the smile she should have given Jack in the first place. She raised her eyes and offered it to him now.

But he was staring at the thing in her hand, eyeing it as if it might jump from her palm and bite him. "I'm not sure what that is. But Wayland said it would make you smile."

It did. Or rather he did. "It's a jack," she said. "That's probably what he meant. You play a game with them. Throw them on the ground, bounce a ball and see how many you can pick up before the ball stops bouncing. But you need more than one."

Jack dipped his head, dark hair hiding his eyes a moment. Then he turned to face her. "Puck told you what I am. There are always more than one of me." One green eye, one blue. Both searched her face now. "Jacks . . . Jacks are endless, identical. Someone's creations."

Oberon's. He couldn't say the name.

Jenny looked at him steadily. "What is a Kobold, Jack?"

He drew in a breath and his eyes grew distant, as if focusing on something far away. "I'm a . . . a servant. What he made me to be. A slave."

"A slave?" she asked.

His eyebrows drew in, the skin between them knotting. "I don't know what else to call it. He made me. I live on his whim, act according to his will. I'm bound to obey him. He has power over whether I guard the Edge or toil beneath the earth, or if I'm simply locked away for the rest of my days. What else would you call me?"

Jack looked up at her and Jenny's heart twisted. She reached out, her fingertips touching his cheek. His skin was warm, smooth over the cheekbone, speckled with a faint roughness across his jaw. He shuddered and turned toward her again. His mouth was inches from hers, her fingers millimeters from his lips. So very warm. His skin moved, tightening beneath her touch, and he stared at her, eyes blazing, blue and green rings encircling his pupils, huge and black. Her face was reflected there.

Jenny leaned forward, pressed her lips to his. A startled breath warmed her skin, but he didn't pull away. The sword fell between them, forgotten now.

"Jack," she whispered, and he kissed her, making her head swim, making her want to press closer. No, not want. *Need.* She leaned in against him and his hand closed on her shoulder, his thumb brushing the skin at the collar of her shirt.

Deep in his throat Jack gave a muffled groan, something between submission and resignation, and he gathered her into his arms, deepening his kiss, while his hands moved to her hair, her shoulders, the curve of her side. She could smell him—forest and sunlight—taste him—salt and sap. Her body melted against him, something unknown awakening within her. It unfurled at the base of her stomach, spreading through her body like electricity until her fingers tingled against his skin.

"Jenny . . ." His lips fumbled against hers. "We can't . . . We shouldn't . . ."

No. Something in her rebelled. Something she didn't want to control. And for that one moment she would have done anything. A blinding disappointment crashed over her, and the longing in her sharpened to a point of pain.

He was right, or at least determined enough. And it almost broke her heart.

"You came for me," she said, though her voice wavered, betraying her. She tried to smile. "Don't I even get to reward you with a kiss?"

Jack withdrew a few inches, his manner at once chivalrous and profoundly cold. The fire inside her dimmed. She stared at him. He couldn't be doing this to her. Not now.

"Beware a kiss," he told her. "Kisses are powerful things. You expose part of your soul. Have you learned nothing?"

Of course she had. She'd kissed the Nix.

A weight around my neck.

His words were meant to hurt her, to drive her back. She knew that. Her fingers still lingered on his face and as she pressed them a little closer, he shuddered, his eyelids half closing until his will reasserted itself and he opened them. She looked into those fascinating eyes, steady, asking him to believe her. "I know what you are, Jack. I'm not afraid of you."

The frown came back, with eyebrows raised. Such a strange combination of an expression—infuriated and confused—and the same feelings flooded her in a second. Was he going to deny it, then? Was he going to deny what he was feeling too? Because he had to be feeling it. He couldn't kiss her like that and not—

"You may not be afraid now, Jenny Wren. But you will

be. I saw your face. I saw what you felt in those moments, before . . . before I lost all knowledge of myself. Because that's what happens. I'm not *me* anymore. Or rather I am . . . the real me. I'm not this. Not a sentient, feeling creature but a—a wild *thing*."

Jenny wrapped both hands around his and found them trembling. "I've been in your mind, Jack. I don't believe that."

"But you must. For your own safety. I hurt you already. I attacked Puck." He swallowed hard as he said the words. "I could have killed him. Or you. And you came after me, and anything could have happened. I could have hurt you— worse, I could have *killed you,* Jenny. Don't you understand? I didn't want to, I didn't even know it, but . . ."

He brushed his fingers over the cuts and grazes on her arms and hands, and her skin shivered. She'd almost forgotten they were there. She'd almost forgotten the encounter with the greenman that had sent her running to the river.

She narrowed her eyes, as if focusing more sharply on him would help her understand. When she lifted his hand to her mouth, he didn't resist, but he shut his eyes, as if he couldn't look. Jenny kissed his fingers while still holding them. His grip tightened, almost to the point of pain, but not quite.

"But you didn't. You'd never hurt me, Jack. I know that."

"*I* don't know that. How could you?"

She pressed his hand to her cheek and he relaxed. "I just know. It wasn't you, that night at the Edge. Puck was lying."

He gave a growl of frustration, even as he put his hand over hers. "It was me, Jenny. That night. It must have been. Because when I came back to myself the next morning, there was Tom. His music had woken the forest and it took him. He was too dangerous to leave walking around, so I took him to the queen. And that's where he's been ever since."

Jenny flinched, pulling her hand away. "Puck told me—" she whispered, her voice failing her.

"He told you the truth." Jack let his arm fall to his side, but kept his eyes fixed on her, like shining knots of polished wood. He stared at her, watching her reaction. "It was my duty. And Oberon had no use for him. He isn't—he isn't kind to those he has no use for, you see?"

"But he— I saw it happen. I saw you. You! Jack, it—it destroyed my life. It shattered my family. It—" She drew back. Then reached for him again. It couldn't be real, but what else made sense? Only he patrolled the Edge, that's what Puck said, its guardian, its Jack. She wanted it to be a lie, or a mistake. But no. It had been him.

It had been him.

Oh God, it had been him.

Jenny scrambled to her feet. She wanted to hit something, wanted to scream, wanted to—

"It was for the best," he said, bowing his head, unable to look at her.

She turned, her shoulders sagging. With an effort, she straightened. "Then keep your promise. Take me to him and help me get him back."

chapter nineteen

They stepped out from among the trees, and the forest fell away. The sky stretched everywhere, so brightly blue, and meadows dotted with wildflowers unfurled before them. The long grasses swayed and butterflies danced at their tips. In the distance, where the river ran down to a lake like a pool of molten silver in the sunlight, the glittering towers of a palace rose.

It was so beautiful, she should have gasped, but Jenny couldn't. After a day of walking through dark tree cover and brambles and briar, under a leaden silence that not even Puck dared disturb, she could only stare at the fairy-tale structure before her, squinting in the bright sunlight. So impossibly graceful, it hardly looked real; rather, it appeared to have been spun from dew drops and gossamer. Ash trees lined the path leading toward it, slender and pale as beautiful maidens bending as if to tend it. Jenny and Jack walked between them, like vagabonds coming to the feast.

It hadn't taken long to get here, and in truth, she wasn't

ready for it now that she'd arrived. Her stomach twisted with dread, and Jack wasn't helping. He kept his gaze straight ahead, or looked past her, never meeting her eyes. Not that she helped either. She didn't know what to say, or how to feel, or how she'd explain it if she did.

It didn't matter. She would get Tom and get home. That was it. That was everything. That was all that mattered now.

The gates to the palace stood open, and Jack hurried her inside, nodding at the guards as he did so. He seemed to dart from place to place, moving almost too fast for the eye. Puck clung to the shadows, trailing behind them. Perhaps he blamed himself for telling her. Jenny didn't care. She didn't care about anything now but Tom.

"Bringing up the rear," Puck grunted as they passed through a courtyard.

"Ready to be first out the gate as soon as there's trouble," Jack replied without humor.

Not "*if* there's trouble," Jenny noticed. But she let it pass. *It was for the best,* he'd said. *The best for whom?*

Not the best for her. Not the best for her parents. He couldn't possibly mean it was best for Tom.

Jenny closed her eyes a moment. It was exhausting, this pinwheel of doubts. She turned her thoughts away from Jack and traced her hand along the nearest wall, smooth and iridescent as mother-of-pearl. The castle bustled quietly with the life of an early morning. She could smell bread baking, and all around them, strangely silent servants, dressed in the muted gray of a dove, moved from place to place, carrying trays, pitchers, and whatever else the queen and her court wanted.

They passed the stables where the long-legged white horses they had seen out hunting snorted and stamped. Jack skirted around the far side of the next courtyard. Close behind him, Jenny heard dogs snapping and snarling, and turned to stare at a group of stone buildings.

"Kennels," Jack told her without looking around.

A series of dull-faced men carried buckets of raw meat inside and a shudder ran through her, remembering the hunt, the hounds, and the tracker they'd killed, remembering her confusion over Jack, her anger. She smiled, though it was bitter, and followed along in silence. Behind her, Puck spat on the ground and muttered charms for luck.

It suddenly occurred to her that, for all the activity, the place was deadly silent. "No one is saying a thing," she whispered as they passed more servants.

"They have no will," Jack said. "They're caught in the dreams she weaves, happy to serve her."

"Are they fae?" she wondered, a sadness coming over her at the thought of them mindlessly toiling away day after day. She frowned, not having meant to speak aloud. But this time Jack didn't answer.

"Hardly," said Puck. "They're human. Some of them have been here for thousands of years, some only just arrived. And they're all hers."

"Human?" Could that be true? But then, all those stories of men, women, and children stolen by the fairies, in every culture, every age—from changelings to abductions . . . "You mean . . . all of them?"

Puck shrugged. "She wouldn't have the same hold over one of us. But over your kind . . . well . . . She's awfully good at that. She can stop them aging if she wants, hold them in her web, keep them for as long as they amuse her or are of use to her. She doesn't need guards to stay them. They wouldn't dream of leaving. They don't even know they're here. In their minds they're the hero of their own fairy tale—killing giants, fêted as warriors, marrying the handsome prince, dancing at the ball. You see?"

Jenny's stomach sickened. Every story, all those tales she loved as a child, all her escapes . . . were they all twisted and changed to something dreadful here? And yet, wasn't that where they came from, all the oldest tales, from blood and pain and misery? She pulled her hand back from another pearlescent wall.

"Is everything a lie?" she asked quietly.

To her surprise, Jack's hand folded around hers, squeezing softly. He pulled her into him, held her there a moment, a small and unexpected comfort. More surprising was that she let him. She didn't mean to, but even if she hated what he'd done, could she ever bring herself to truly hate him? It would be so much easier that way . . .

Then she heard it. Music drifted on the air. A light and airy reel that trilled like a blackbird's song. She pulled away, looked around, her heart beating fast.

"That's him," she said. "That's Tom."

Jack exchanged a glance with Puck. "Are you sure?"

"I'd know his playing anywhere. Where's it coming from?"

Jack lifted his head as if smelling the air. "The rose garden, I think. Stay close, and . . . please, just remember, Jenny . . . he's been here seven years. He's changed, just as you have. And probably not for the better. Few do in the queen's embrace."

Jenny shook her head, impatient. "But he tried to run away," she said.

"Maybe." Jack didn't look convinced. "Or maybe . . ." A shuffle of emotions slid over his face. He opened his mouth and paused, his gaze flicking warily over her expression as if to gauge her reaction, as if praying for something other than what he expected. "Maybe he ran for the Edge knowing he couldn't cross. Maybe he was looking for someone to take his place." He let a long, low breath out and studied her for another moment. She kept her face still.

How could he say something like that? Jack didn't understand this, any of it. He wasn't human, didn't have brothers or sisters, couldn't possibly fathom all he'd put her through for the last seven years. She needed to find Tom, to take him home, to make amends—for her family, for her brother, for herself.

A new emotion—disappointment?—dragged Jack's gaze toward the ground. "Just stay wary, Jenny. And please . . . please just know, I'm sorry."

Jack bent his head toward her and with a stray thought, she wondered if he would kiss her again, not sure what to do if he tried. She didn't want him to. Still, her mouth parted, her breath catching in her throat. Jack stopped, just looking at her like he was trying to imprint her on his memory.

"Let's go," he said, and turned sharply away.

Baffled, Jenny fell in step behind him. She cast a glance behind her at Puck and raised her eyebrows. The hobgoblin just shrugged. Great. Really helpful. Such a comfort. Her chest tightened, shortening her breath, but she kept her face smooth.

I will not cry, she told her body as it threatened to betray her.

They followed the music through a gate wound about with roses. The thorns gleamed and the petals' luster was red as blood. As Jenny and Jack passed through, the gate swung closed. Jenny glanced back. Puck was gone.

"He never stays where there's danger," Jack muttered,

without bothering to look around. "I'd say we're lucky he came this far."

Jenny barely heard him. The music of the flute grew louder. If Tom had been good before, he was a master now. It was like birdsong in the morning, like soft rain after a drought, like the sound of dreams made real.

But then again, she thought, he should have improved after seven years. He'd be twenty-one now, a man and not a boy. Would he even recognize her? The Woodsman and his wife had seen a resemblance, or so they said . . . if anything they said could be trusted. Would she still be able to see her brother in this person, this piper? No one seemed to hold him in very high regard. He served the queen, and no one seemed to care for her at all. From their brief encounter, Jenny could understand why. She was more an addiction than an object of affection.

Leaving the courtyards behind them, they passed by immaculately manicured lawns edged with sparkling granite curbs.

They followed the path through an arched gateway into a walled garden crammed full of rosebushes, where blossoms of every color tumbled over each other, fighting for the sun. The path wound like a snake through the sea of bright, heavy blossoms, and the music drew them on. Gravel crunched beneath their feet and that was the only other sound. That and the music.

There, on a low stone bench in the center of the garden, sat Tom, dressed in the splendid jewel-colored clothes of the royal court, his hair still light but darker than it had been, curling against his neck, and his eyes closed, the better to concentrate on his music. The breeze lifted her hair, played on her skin. The petals of the roses seemed to whisper to each other. The flute was silver, and not just in color, Jenny thought. His fingers danced over the instrument and the silvered sound rose like a spell.

A spell she promptly broke.

"Tom?"

His music faltered, ending on a bum note. He swore with a violence that was shocking after the sublime music, and turned around, quick as a wasp, to face her.

For a moment there was nothing, and then his eyes widened, his pupils dilating and shrinking in an instant. "Jenny?"

Relief swept her forward. Jenny tore past Jack and flung her arms around her brother. "Tom! I heard you in the forest. I came to get you—to take you home. I've—"

He was stiff in her arms, awkward and unresponsive. He heaved in a breath and she pulled back, lifting her face to see him. His eyes burned, and when he spoke, his voice was appalled.

"What are you doing here?"

Jenny's arms slipped to her sides. She stepped back. "I . . . I came to take you home, to—"

"This is my home." He frowned, his mouth a tight line. Then he swallowed hard and shook his head, studying her.

"What are you talking about? Our home. To our family. How could— Have you forgotten?"

"Jenny . . ." Tom shook his head, and his eyes slid away from her face. When he looked back, his features were filled with confusion. "You have no place here."

"I came for you, Tom. To take you home."

Tom stared at her, his mouth parting, his eyes dazed. He looked like a child in that moment, like the boy she had known and remembered, the boy in all those photos at home. But he had never looked so confused, or so scared. He had always been the fearless one, never afraid of anything. Except for the night he was taken, except for that one night, when the trees had wrapped him in branches and roots and vines and dragged him away from her.

Looking at her now, he seemed as terrified as he had then.

Jenny reached out her hand to—what? Touch him, comfort him, to assure him that this time everything was going to be all right? She wasn't totally sure she believed it herself anymore.

His mouth twisted abruptly and a hardness filled his gaze, as if a different person had slipped beneath his skin. He jerked back from her, folding his hands around his flute. "Jennifer, I live in a palace. My lover is the queen. Not just any queen, the Queen of the Realm. Why would I want to go back?"

She stepped away from him, her heart beating so hard she couldn't be hearing him right. "What? Tom, I—"

He pushed himself to his feet, towering over her, a man, not a boy. Jenny took another step back as he filled the space before her.

"Why would I want a life striving to create music in a world that doesn't value it? Play in some second-rate orchestra? Do a turn in the Christmas show in the village hall? Get married to some second violinist and squeeze out a few kids we can't afford to keep on a musician's pay? Why? *Why?* When here"—he swept his arm in a circle, taking in the garden, the palace before them, the woods beyond— "I'm a prince."

Jenny stared at him, this stranger. She realized her hands were up near her shoulders, as if to ward him off. She made them fall to her sides. She wouldn't be bullied, not by Tom of all people. But before she could gather together a reply, another voice answered.

"Here, you're a fool," said Jack. "You know what happens to mortals who belong to her. You aren't a drone. You couldn't create music for her if you were trapped in one of her dreams. But you aren't exactly free either, are you, piper?"

Tom stiffened his shoulders like a dog about to fight. "That's none of your business, *Jack.*" He said the name like a slur. "I wouldn't have thought you capable of doing Titania's will so well, yet here you are. And with the promised pay-

ment in tow. Did her bed, her threats, or her empty promises tempt you more?"

Jack stepped forward, his shoulder sliding in front of Jenny. She stared at her brother. What was Tom implying? Tempt Jack to what? Panic filled her mouth with a metallic tang.

"Where were you trying to run to the other day?" Jack asked. "Why were you at the Edge?"

These were Jenny's questions to ask, but the words wouldn't come. She'd dreamed about Tom for so long, remembering only the good, and now he was nothing like her memories of him. She stood there, her body betraying her just like everything and everyone else. She had to get control. She imagined two strong hands pressing down on her shoulders, stilling them, and took a deep breath.

Tom shoved the flute into a loop at his belt. It dangled there, gleaming against the embroidered blue velvet. "That's none of your business."

"But it's mine," said Jenny, stepping around Jack. He jerked after her, trying to stop her. "You're my brother, Tom." She frowned. "I love you. What's happened?"

"You have no idea what you're doing here, Jenny," he snarled, the expression so foreign on his face. "She's bored with me, and seven years are up. I'm going to be tithed to hell, handed over as part of the pact. The Realm must be protected, and this is the only way. Blood must be paid,

the debt, the tithe. And now, it's me. So"—he shrugged—"I had to find someone else, someone to take my place. And who better than you?" He looked at her, eyes wide, challenging. "The forest wanted you to begin with. *He's* the one who turned it on me instead." Tom pointed at Jack, his finger shaking wildly. "It's his fault I'm here. And now he's brought you instead, as he should have years ago. It should have been you." Tom shook his head, glancing at her with raised eyebrows as if to see what she'd do next.

Guilt fell over her, his malice almost sweeping her feet out from under her. She staggered back, her eyes burning. She'd thought it so many times over the years, wished it even as she blamed herself, but to hear him say it—

"No," she said. He was lying, he didn't know what he was saying. She shook off her uncertainty and started forward again. Jack's hand brushed her shoulder, but he didn't stop her. Jack, at least, understood this.

Tom smiled, a gleeful, vindictive expression that made him look like one of them, like one of the Sidhe. Jenny's feet slowed to a faltering stop. Disdain blossomed in his face like an infection, his mouth turning down to mock her. Tom was gone. Only the piper remained. The realization shivered through her. In this man who had been the boy she'd searched for, Jenny saw at best blank disregard; at worst, contempt.

There was no sign of her brother at all.

Tom dodged toward her, as if to attack, but he didn't. She flinched and he laughed into her face.

Behind her, Jack's sword hissed as he drew it.

Tom went very still, just for a second, and his face transformed, a nasty sort of triumph flickering over his features. Then he moved in a blur worthy of one of the fae. He lifted not a weapon, but his flute, pressed it to his mouth, and sounded three sharp notes that shot through Jenny like blades.

There was a muffled grunt behind her. She turned to see Jack pinioned against the garden wall, his feet kicking in the dirt. Cords of roses entwined his limbs and torso, squeezing, snaking around his face to gag him. When he struggled, thorns tore into his cheeks, his hands. The stems turned slick with blood. It slid down the length of his sword to drip into the soil below his thrashing feet. Jack's mismatched eyes stared at Tom, wide with surprise and sharp with rage.

chapter twenty

Jenny ran toward Jack, but a tendril lashed out, a barbed whip, striking her face and drawing a line of blood. Jack bellowed, straining against his bonds. They tightened still further. Strands of ivy slithered across his skin to bind him more securely. They wound around his throat and squeezed. Crushed beneath them, his skin torn by the thorns, he was forced to fall still, gasping for breath.

"Jacks shouldn't stray here," said Jenny's brother, or what little remained of him. "They aren't at all welcome. Though I'm glad you brought my replacement." He had lowered the flute. It was back on his belt, seemingly innocuous.

Jenny whirled on her brother. "Stop it," she hissed. "Let him go."

"Or what?" asked Tom. "He's just a Jack, Jenny. It's not like he's of any value. There are hundreds, even thousands, in Oberon's service. He isn't human, if that's what you think—" He broke off suddenly. "Oh," he said, giving her a pitying look. "You thought he was? Best not to get too attached, Jenny. He isn't good for much more than firewood. A puppet with invisible strings, made only to obey Oberon. But, interestingly . . ." Here the piper cast his eyes over Jack. "Interestingly, not this time. This time he obeyed my queen, Titania." His gaze slid back to Jenny. "He brought you here just as she asked."

Jenny narrowed her eyes at him. He was lying, clearly. She studied his pale, sculpted features, the courtly clothes and the silken curls of his hair. His face was soulless. This wasn't her Tom, her brother, her friend. This was one of Titania's thralls, a shadow that happened to resemble the boy she had known.

"Let him go," she repeated, her decision made. She lifted her chin. Imperious, she thought vaguely. He might respond to that. How did a queen command a servant? Only she wasn't a queen. Just a little sister. "Let him go, and I'll do whatever you want."

His eyes came alight with a hunger that chilled her.

"Without a fight?"

"Yes." She glanced back at Jack and saw the panic in his face. Whether caused by his predicament or her words, she couldn't tell, but it didn't matter. Something in her heart gave a little twist of pain. "All right. Yes. I'll do what you say. Just let him go."

Tom lifted the pipe again and blew three shrill notes. The ivy and roses snapped back and Jack dropped onto his feet, off balance, and fell. He landed on his hands and knees, wheezing and coughing. He pulled the sword into his hand.

"Don't," he managed, shaking the dark hair from his eyes. "Please, Jenny Wren. Don't trust him."

"Like she trusted you, Kobold?" Tom asked. "At least I'm honest about what I want her for, Jack o' the Forest. At least I want her for myself."

"I thought so," Jack wheezed. "That's why you ran from the queen—not to escape, but to draw another in. To bring someone over the Edge." Jack struggled to pull himself up, dropped his sword, but finally stood, his eyes hard.

To Jenny's surprise, Tom's face crumpled. "It wasn't like that," he protested. "It wasn't meant to be *her!*" His voice shook and he tightened his fists until his knuckles turned white. It lasted only a moment. When he looked at her again, his expression was cool once more. "But since it is—"

"He wants you to take his place, Jenny," Jack said. "To be a sacrifice in his stead."

Tom's voice was hard again, unrelenting. "And he wants to hand you over to the queen, little sister. You're the price for his freedom. Is that any different?"

Jenny stood between them. The piper on her left. Jack on her right. She looked from one to the other, feeling suddenly trapped. The distance between her and them appeared to lengthen. Jenny was alone. Then in an instant reality came hurtling back at her with the force of a collision.

She'd seen a chink in Tom's armor, just for a second. Even if she couldn't trust him, she couldn't ignore that. And Jack . . . What was she supposed to think? She wasn't sure she could trust him either. But her treacherous heart felt differently. And now this, an impossible choice. Jenny tried to pull herself straight, shoulders back, chin up. But she didn't even fool herself. Yes, she'd spent the last seven years pretending to be strong, pretending it all slid off her like soap in water. But here she was, *feeling* far too much. Tom was still her brother. If anything happened to him—if anything happened to either of them—

But . . .

An idea was tugging at her mind, struggling to break the surface.

She grabbed at it, caught it, held it, turned it over in her mind so she could see all its facets.

Decided.

"It's going to be okay, Jack."

Distantly, she heard her own voice say the words. She saw herself move, taking the sword from his hands and sliding it back into the sheath. Safe. Out of the way. He didn't protest or fight her. He did nothing but frown, confused, afraid. She hadn't seen him afraid before.

"No, it won't," he told her in a whisper. "I can't let you be damned for me. He's right. I'm not worth it, Jenny Wren."

She smiled and shook her head. If Tom was safe, and the

queen had Jenny in his place, then Jack was free too. She saw it so clearly now. How had she not seen it before? She just had to get them both out of here.

The piper seized her arm and pulled her roughly to his side. He was stronger than she would have imagined, certainly stronger than she remembered, but that was so long ago now.

"Of course he isn't worth it. He's one of Oberon's creatures, made of lost dreams and savagery. Didn't he tell you?" The piper started to laugh. "Oh, you fool, Jenny."

"Don't listen to him," Jack said. "You have a heart like no other. You are strong. Stronger than you know."

Jenny let their words wash over her, even as Tom shook her, his glare malevolent. "Don't you see, you stupid, weak-witted girl?" She refused to meet his eyes. "That's why his king wants you for his new queen. It's the only reason Jack o' the Forest helped you in the first place. But then . . . *my* queen wants you too. Jack was always going to sell you out to one or the other, little sister, don't you see?" Jenny struggled to keep her emotions under control. "And you, you fell for his charm. But he's nothing. Nothing but old wood and rotting leaves wrapped up in lies and curses. You thought he was like you and me."

Jenny struggled free and swung around, her fist striking the piper hard across his perfect face. His head snapped back and blood spurted from his nose.

"I'm nothing like you, Tom," she spat. "And neither is he. And aren't we blessed for that?"

Then he hit her. The blow to her own face was three times as hard. Light exploded before her eyes and she dropped to the ground, blind with shock and pain. Her mouth filled with blood as she gasped for air. Tom stood over her, waiting. Her brother. Her own brother. The flute dangled from his belt and she grabbed at it, intent on taking the wretched thing and using it to beat him. Tom's fist descended again. But it was knocked off course as Jack sprang at him and they went down in a tangle of hatred.

Jack pinned Tom to the ground, trying to grip his arms, but Tom kicked out, catching Jack with a glancing blow. They rolled, tumbling across the gravel path in a scrambling of stones. Tom's fist struck Jack's face, snapping his head back, but Jack grabbed his arm again, slamming it down onto the ground, holding him there with his knee. His knife seemed to leap to his hand. Jenny screamed and ran at him as he brought it up to Tom's neck.

"Stop this at once!" The queen's voice rang out across the grounds. She stood in the gateway to the garden, her companions behind her. Jenny's eyes latched on to Jack. He still had his knife pressed to Tom's throat but he seemed to freeze, hand trembling. Tendons stood out in his arms and neck. Panic entered his eyes as he stared past Jenny at the queen, somehow trapped by her glare.

Titania's slender figure approached with the grace of a bird. Wherever her feet fell, flowers opened to greet her passage. In her wake they withered and died. Jenny's eyes took her in with unexpected yearning, but Titania swept by her without a glance. The queen touched Jack's shoulder and he cringed away, his chest hitching as he fought for breath. She gave only a flick of her hand, but he was flung back to sprawl on the grass, the knife still clutched in his hand.

"I thought we had an agreement, Jack," Titania said, loosening her riding gloves one finger at a time. "That didn't include destroying what is mine already."

"I never agreed," he gasped, forcing out each word. His eyes sought Jenny, wild and pleading. "I swear, I never agreed."

"Jack," Titania purred, holding out her hand to him like a gracious monarch. "Be reasonable." Jack's muscles tightened, twisting to agony.

The words wrenched their way out of his tortured body. "I never agreed. No matter what you offer, I will never agree."

The queen's eyes widened, liquid with surprise and . . . Jenny stared, but the emotion that had flickered over the queen's features was too brief to capture. Her face had already hardened like the surface of a mirror, smooth and perfect, impenetrable.

"I see. Well, if that's the case, begone, forest thing. You have no place here. Return to your master and tell him of your failure. Take your punishment. And tell him not to meddle in my affairs again."

Flowers burst from the earth and roots shot out like a thousand serpents. If the roses had been powerful, these were a hundred times so. They moved like sentient creatures, with no music to cajole them. They tangled around Jack, snaring him in seconds, twisting around his body to bind his knife in his hand and with the Jester's sword still sheathed uselessly at his back. Where Jenny had put it. The ground began to part, churning and heaving as though it struggled to breathe, and Jenny realized with sudden horror what was happening.

"Let him go!" she screamed, and tried to grab his free hand. Her locket glistened around his neck, the gold her last guide. She ripped at the stalks and stems, pulled them back from his face, but there were too many, they were too quick, too strong. The queen's magic was far too powerful. The earth of her garden parted and closed, sucking Jack under like quicksand.

"Jenny." He spat dirt from his mouth and trapped her gaze with his eyes. "Jenny Wren, listen to me. Don't believe what they tell you. Don't even believe your own eyes. Trust your heart. Please, Jenny. I'm . . . I'm sorry I lied—I didn't tell you everything I should have, but trust me now. *Trust your h—*" The earth consumed him, dirt falling into his mouth, his eyes, grass closing over his face, the ground sucking his fingers out of sight, and Jenny was left kneeling on the ground, her hands clutching at spring flowers and nettles.

In the silence that followed, she heard the Sidhe murmuring among themselves, the birds in the trees, the insects, and the distant sound of the forest folk. A keening lament echoed over the walls, and above it all, one cry rang out, so close to her ears it hurt. It wasn't until she snapped her teeth together that she realized the sound had come from her. Jack was gone.

From the royal court, there came no sound at all, not a movement, not a breath. They watched her tears fall to the ground. It wasn't until Tom reached out and touched her shoulder that she became aware of how many flawless faces gazed at her.

Jenny dragged her arms over her eyes, scrubbing the tears away with her hands. "What have you done?"

But he didn't answer. He was looking at her like a cat trying to fathom how to get food. Her brother, her betrayer. She shook him off.

Titania's voice was sweetly precise. "I did what you asked," said the queen, as if it were the most obvious thing in the world and the girl kneeling before her a simpleton. "I let him go."

chapter twenty-one

On her knees in the dirt before Titania, Jenny dragged her shirt sleeve across her bloodied face and struggled to quell the tears stinging her eyes. She wouldn't cry, not here, not in front of them. She wouldn't give Titania the satisfaction.

Neither would she stay on her knees.

A leaden resolve fell over her. Jack was gone. Swallowed up as his precious forest had swallowed Tom seven years before. The bitter irony wasn't lost on Jenny, but it did her no good.

Was he dead? No, he couldn't be. He was part of the forest. He was . . . He was Jack. He'd saved her from the dragon, rescued her from the Nix, had tried to protect her even from himself. Jenny took a deep breath. It rattled through her. If Jack was dead, if Jack was gone—

Please, no.

For all his tortured loyalties, his ties of duty and honor pulling him in every direction, he had proved himself more trustworthy than anyone she had met in the Realm.

You are strong. Stronger than you know.

Jenny rose. Standing there in jeans and a shirt that had seen too many days of scrambling through forest, that had been washed in river water and dried in the sun, she felt like something half wild, especially under the eyes of the flawless Sidhe court.

"We were just about to go on our morning hunt," said Titania. "And look what we already caught. The so-called May Queen, here and waiting for us."

"Jack and I meant you no harm," Jenny said, aware that her voice trembled, and furious with herself for showing weakness.

Titania laughed. "What sort of a fool do you take me for?"

"I only came for my brother."

Tom blanched as Titania turned her viper's gaze on him. "I'd forgotten that," she said in tones that said nothing was ever forgotten. "She's your sister, Tom. How sweet. You called and she came to find you." She laughed again, a bright and merry sound, but no one joined in. "And do you find him unchanged, May Queen?"

"No," Jenny said coolly. "I find him very much changed. And my name is Jenny. I want none of your ridiculous games."

"*Games?*" The amusement was gone. The queen bared her teeth and stalked toward Jenny. "You have not seen *games* yet, girl. Look at yourself. Is this how you appear before a queen?"

Jenny couldn't help it. She glanced down at her clothes, and her skin pricked with shame. Tangled hair, ragged clothes, dirty face, earth blackening her fingernails. She could imagine if she turned up at home or school looking like this. But this was worse. She stood before a queen.

Swallowing hard, she opened her mouth to apologize and then caught herself. What for? How was any of this her fault? And why should she care what Titania thought of her? She hadn't cared about those who didn't believe her, who wanted to put her on meds, or who constantly told her she had imagined everything. She had taught herself—*forced* herself—not to care. She struggled past the queen's enchantment and lifted her eyes to meet Titania's.

"I want to take Tom and go home. You can have your fantasy kingdom and everything that goes with it." And more, so much more, she wanted this to be over.

"Really?" The single word scraped the air.

"She doesn't ask much, my queen," Tom interrupted, his voice plaintive and weak. "Just to go. Just for the two of us to go."

"*You* aren't going anywhere. You have an appointment in two days' time, *tithe*. You should never have run from me. I might have kept you forever, the way you make music, the way your music makes magic. But I can't stand betrayal. Such treachery. You brought *her* here."

"Let her go, Majesty," he continued, actually wringing his hands. "I didn't mean to. Not her. Please. I swear, I'll go willingly, give myself up for you, to protect you. I'll be the tithe. Wipe her memories and let her go."

Jenny stared at him. What was this change? Minutes ago he'd wanted to send her as sacrifice in his place.

"For me? Really?" Titania simpered, but her sugar-sweet voice devolved into cruelty. "Or to protect *her*?" She laughed. "Someone get the piper something to drink. He forgets himself. Or rather, he remembers."

Two men—tall and willowy Sidhe lords—grabbed Tom by either arm and pulled him away, laughing at his protests and easily overpowering his struggles.

That left Jenny alone with the queen and her court, and her heart sank. In spite of all he had said and done, the changes wrought on him by his time here, Tom was her brother. Something in their food and drink changed him, made him . . . made him more like them. And when it wore off, for a moment he was Tom again.

Jack had told her not to take their food or wine. That was why, she realized. It changed you forever. Made you their slave. She thought of the servants in the palace, lost in their dreams, mindless drudges, doing the will of the Sidhe for eternity. He hadn't lied about that, then. He hadn't actually lied about much at all. She just wished that he'd told her everything.

Jenny closed her eyes and forced Jack from her mind. Her mouth dried as she brought her eyes back to Titania's face.

The queen studied her for a moment and then made a subtle pass of her hand in front of Jenny's face. When she looked down again, she wore the same dove-gray clothes of the servants. A fitted bodice, high neck, and long sleeves, all edged with buttons covered in the same fabric. The full skirt was heavy and awkward. Around her waist was a pristine white apron with deep pockets. She could still feel her own clothes beneath. Another illusion.

Titania's eyes glittered like shards of glass, hard and devoid of feeling. Her beauty was unreal, harsh in its perfection. Jenny remembered the glimpse of the dark thing lurking inside her, the thing she'd seen in the forest when she first laid eyes on her. Mab. It was Mab. The evil inside Titania. Beyond the cool beauty. Now she circled Jenny, examining her work, her every glance critical.

"There," she said at last. "I thought you could be improved. What do you think of her now, Thomas?"

He stepped back through the attendant Sidhe and Jenny saw at once that whatever they had given him, he was the heartless piper once more.

"You'll make her a skivvy?" asked Tom.

"I can't think of a better occupation for a would-be queen. She needs to learn her place."

Jenny stiffened but remained silent. What good would it do to argue now? She couldn't outrun them all. *But later . . .*

"I know what you're thinking, little Wren," the queen mocked. She snapped her fingers and someone passed her a bottle. The glass was a brilliant green, and little dints of light glittered on the surface. Its round bottom caught the sun, but from there it tapered up to a long neck, closed with a stopper made of silver, shaped like a rose.

"Lethe water," said the queen. "Although I doubt you, in your modern age, know what that is. We make it ourselves with honey and valerian and . . . oh, a thousand special things. It has no effect on the folk of Faerie, although it tastes like nectar, but on humans . . . well . . . You'll see."

Jenny clamped her lips together and shook her head. Whatever that stuff was, there was no way she was drinking it. She'd seen what it had done to Tom.

"Stubborn, obstinate child," the queen growled, and nodded to two more of her courtiers. They seized Jenny's arms, forcing her to her knees so Titania towered over her. One of them pinched her arm hard and she cried out in spite of herself.

That was all it took. Titania thrust the mouth of the bottle between Jenny's lips and upended it. A stream of sweet, cloying liquid filled her mouth, choking her as she coughed, spluttered, and tried to pull away. Someone held her head and they forced her to drink it, draining the whole bottle until she fell, coughing and gasping for air.

The Sidhe pulled Jenny back to her feet and she hung limply between her captors. Titania pressed her hands on either side of Jenny's head. The last thing she saw was the queen's victorious smile.

It was like falling into dark water, like being dragged down by the Nix all over again. The soft fragrance of night closed over her, a cushion of down, a cocoon. Music surged around her, beguiling. As Jenny opened her eyes, she found the world had transformed.

Laughter pealed around a great stone hall. On a family holiday, long ago, she had visited Mont Saint Michel and stood in the banqueting hall, a vaulted room with glass windows looking out over the treacherous sands, twin fireplaces her whole family could stand in. Tom had been a pain that day, bored with the whole thing and out of sorts, but Jenny had fallen in love with the romance of the place. It had been hers alone, the palace she dreamed of where she was a princess and nothing could harm her or any of her family. She had hopped from slab to slab across the floor, pretending she was dancing, until her mother had made her stop, telling her to consider what people would think.

Now the hall inside her dreams was filled with a fairy

ball. Fires blazed in the fireplaces, candles burned in the chandeliers. It was dark outside, not the dark of night. No moon or stars were visible. The windows showed nothing. They might have been made of stone themselves. Laughter and the sounds of amused conversation entwined with the music, swirling up to the ceiling so far above her. The stone slabs covering the floor seemed to move, even as she looked at them, twisting in the unnatural way things did in dreams.

This wasn't real. She knew it couldn't be. This palace was not Titania's palace. This was cold stone, not polished marble. This was a world away from the queen's shining palace. Yet it had its own beauty.

Strong arms caught her shoulders, twirling her around. The gray servants' gown had vanished, and something spun of diaphanous silk took its place, a confection of lace and captured light. A snow-white dress swirled about her legs, the bodice clinging to her torso, lifting up her breasts like an offering to the man dancing with her.

His hair was the color of coal dust and his eyes so dark as to appear endless black. On his head he wore a golden crown, styled like antlers, leaves, and berries. A king, then. Her king. A face from her dreams, sending a shudder of recognition through her, a face she'd known all her life, and yet never known at all. He smiled, a seductive, indulgent expression. His eyes captured hers and she stumbled under the impact of his gaze, falling into his embrace. That look promised so much, things she didn't dare to want yet, things for which her traitor body yearned. He caught her, turning her so that her clumsiness became part of their dance, transforming her into a being of grace in spite of herself.

His long fingers caressed her bare shoulders or entwined with hers, and her heart beat faster. With him pressed so close, the heat from his body swept over her, the elegant washed silk gown felt like nothing more than a veil, and a flimsy one at that. She could have been naked before him. A smile curled the corners of his mouth, as if he could read her very thoughts.

"Gwynhyfer," he murmured. His voice rumbled deep inside his chest and her heart beat in response, a bird trapped in a cage, a wren. The single word echoed on and on, twisting and resolving as she listened to her name. *Gwynhyfer* . . . *Guinevere* . . . *Jennifer* . . .

Entangling his hand in her hair, he pulled her close, kissing her deeply. He tasted warm and earthy, of forests and undergrowth, but unlike Jack, beneath that initial touch, he was cold, icy cold. The cold of deep beneath the ground, of places that had never seen the sun. It was the cold of winter, clawing deep inside her. There was magic, but not the magic of Jack's kiss.

Beware a kiss, Jack had told her. *Kisses are powerful things.*

You expose part of your soul. Have you learned nothing?

She tore herself free with a gasp. The memory of his voice was so clear he could have been standing at her side, whispering in her ear. Her smiling partner didn't seem fazed by the abrupt movement. He took her hand and led her forward, twirling her on the end of his arm. He made her dance now, though she wanted to escape, moving her around him, dancing with her despite her resistance. And how could she resist him? He overwhelmed her with just his presence.

"Stop," she whispered breathlessly, her head spinning, her stomach sickening. It still churned from the Lethe water having been forced down her throat, and she couldn't think straight. She needed him to stop, all of them to stop, just for a minute, to leave her alone and let her be. "Please, stop."

But no one was listening to her. The crowd parted to watch them pass, some laughing good-naturedly, some applauding. Through all the unreal masks and smiling faces she couldn't spot a single one she recognized, a single soul she could trust to help her. She didn't know any of them, but every eye was upon her. Studying her, waiting for her to falter and fail so they could laugh. How they loved to laugh.

The throne was fashioned from the gnarled trunk of a hawthorn tree, the branches twisted to form the arms and the ornate crest on the top. The roots plunged through the stony floor beneath it, and white blossoms hung in heavy clumps from the branches. There was no sunlight here. Nor moonlight either. Only the dark and the flame. So how could the tree still be alive?

Her dance partner spun her around one last time, the glossy surface of his green cloak catching the light. It looked like leaves, like holly leaves, rich and dark, glistening. Jenny felt herself falling into the living throne as he released her. She landed, the gown billowing out around her, and the music fell silent at last.

His figure loomed over her, a silhouette with small horns or antler points poking through the curls, and eyes bright with unspoken threat. He gave her that dangerous smile again and lifted a coronet of tiny white flowers. He cradled it in his long fingers, bruising the flowers a little until a heady scent rose from them.

Jenny shrank back against the wood, but it was useless. There was no way out. If only Jack were here. He'd help her. Jack would draw his great sword, shout a battle cry, and fight their way out. She closed her eyes, wishing he were there, knowing he was gone. He'd betrayed her, hadn't he? Brought her here. And she'd lost him. She had seen the earth swallow him whole. He was gone.

She was alone. If she was to escape, she'd have to do it herself. But the throne drained away all her will.

Don't listen to that, a voice in the back of her mind whispered. *You are strong. Stronger than you know.*

She'd rescued the Leczi, stopped the dragon, helped Jack escape the Nix, she'd fought and struggled and done her best to find her brother. It couldn't end like this.

Tears wet her cheeks and she heard the onlookers give a collective susurration of appreciation. She looked up as her dance partner placed a crown of flowers on her head. The thorns scraped her scalp, tearing her skin.

"Greetings to you, May Queen." His deep voice rumbled again and the crowd echoed him. With a curious tilt of his head, he reached out to touch a tear on her cheek. Then he smiled again. "Perfect," he told her. "Just perfect. I was certain you would be."

"I—I'm not the May Queen," she stammered.

"Oh, but you are, pretty one. The guardian named you so. And besides, the throne of thorns accepts you. Look."

The throne trembled beneath her and then shoots erupted from it, bright green, growing as she watched. The roots swelled, cracking through the stone floor. She twisted, looking for a gap to flee through, but the hawthorn throne embraced her, growing around her, trapping her in a cage, in a human shape made of twigs and branches.

"There's a mistake!" she cried. "I'm not a queen."

The king—for she couldn't doubt that's who he was, Oberon at large in her nightmare—laughed and stepped aside. A defeated figure knelt at the front of the throng of dancers, his head bowed, his pose immobile. A cloak of leaves covered his back too, but these were dying, turning to autumn colors even as she watched. All around him, even as the other beings of her dream continued their celebrations, the guardian remained locked in his abeyance.

"Tell her." The king's command boomed through the room. No one could fail to obey him. No one. Not even—

"Comes the Wren," said this broken knight. "Comes the May Queen. Comes the spring."

Only one person had given her a pet name in years. Jack had called her Jenny Wren.

Comes the Wren.

Jenny's tears flooded her eyes, and with each one she shed, the hawthorn tree grew, its thick limbs wrapping around her. She threw back her head and screamed. There was but a single intelligible word in the sound, the name of the boy clad in leaves and bearing a Saxon-like sword strapped across his back. His cloak of dying oak leaves spilled across the floor and the guardian, her guardian, raised his mismatched eyes to look on her. There was nothing in his face, no love, no affection, not even anger or annoyance or pained disappointment.

Jenny Wren.

She had trusted him. She had let him lead her through

the Realm. She had let him make of her whatever the Realm demanded.

"Jack!" she screamed, struggling against the tree even though she knew there was no escape, not since he had put her there. Her certainty wavered, unsteady as the twisting ground beneath her. Jack had betrayed her after all. Puck had been right and so had Tom.

"*There now,*" came a voice, slightly rattled but trying to hide it. "*She's deep inside now. Just another drone. Someone take her to the kitchen and put her to work.*"

The queen's voice, echoed through the hall, or maybe it was through Jenny's head. No one else reacted to her, or the words she said.

"*Majesty, please . . .*" Tom spoke now, his voice smoother than Jenny ever remembered, almost seductive when he tried to get his way with Titania. "*She's a danger to you. Send her away. It's safer that way. Get rid of her.*"

Laughter echoed around the hall, bouncing off the ceiling, but the dancers carried on as if it were just another part of the music. The dark figure of the king watched her, and Jack still knelt on the ground like nothing more than a lump of wood.

"Jack!" she called. "Jack, please."

Somewhere, she knew, she was being led away, though Tom still argued.

"*She's the May Queen. We all heard it. And Oberon will know*" *as well, since the Jack was with her. Majesty, please, just send her away or send her home. Let her go."*

"You don't understand, Tom. If she's the May Queen, then I need her. As much as Oberon does. Perhaps more. She came here willingly, so here she stays. Don't try my patience, piper, or it will go the worse for you."

"And how can it go worse?" he snarled, but Titania didn't reply. Their voices faded away and the world of the ball reasserted itself around her, swirling skirts, spiraling music, laughter and voices raised in delight.

Then she noticed it. Starting with her hands, her fingernails. They grew as she watched, oval and perfect as pearls. Her fingers too—they lengthened, changing to more elegant versions of her younger hands, a woman's hands, pampered by creams and oils. The cuts and scratches healed themselves and vanished.

"What . . . what's happening?" she whispered. Her body itched all over, as if her skin were shifting over the surface, and she thought of the Redcaps from long ago . . .

"You're becoming what you were born to be," said Oberon. He clicked his fingers in a single sharp gesture, and a mirror was brought forth. Old and marked, black flecks marring the surface, and yet she could see herself as clear as day. "It's part of the magic, you see? The transformation. You're the Wren now, but soon . . . soon you'll be the queen."

Jenny leaned forward, her eyes widening as she saw her

face transform, re-form. Her skin grew paler, freckles fading, and her cheekbones lifted higher, sharpening. Her
face took on an alien cast, her eyes elongating even as she
looked, and her hair staining with gold until . . . until . . .

"No," Jenny whispered. And she heard Titania's voice.

No, she realized with dawning horror. Not Titania's. It
was older than that, more powerful, more dangerous. This was
the reason the queen wanted to keep her. It wasn't Titania's
voice at all.

It was Mab's.

Jenny closed her hand on the arm of the throne, digging
those sharp nails into the wood, and the wood fought back.
A thorn dug into her skin, hard and unyielding, a sharp pain,
deeper and harder than anything else. It dug into her palm
and with a burst of light, she was herself again.

Barely. Her stomach twisted and she tried to rise. The
dancers protested, but she tore the hawthorn away from
her, breaking free of the throne. The king snarled, but he
didn't move to intercept her. Blood dripped from her palm,
where a black thorn still jutted from her skin.

Jack looked up as she approached him, his eyes begging
forgiveness, emptying with heartbreak as she came closer.
Lost. What had he promised as his price to save her from
the Nix? This? Had he renounced her for Oberon? Wouldn't
he even fight for her?

Jack opened his mouth to speak, but only dirt fell out.

He extended a hand, a shaking hand. His limbs creaked and she watched in horror as his skin hardened, transforming to moss-covered bark. He lifted his other hand to the glinting touch of gold around his neck, closing wooden fingers over the heart she had given him. Sap leaked from the corners of his eyes.

Stronger than you know.

He tried to smile. Like he knew she'd understand somehow. Like he'd do anything for her if only he could. Like he trusted her with all his heart. She reached for him, to help him, to save him, to tell him—

The pain in her hand sharpened, changing from a thorn to a spike, something cold like ice. The fairy-tale world in which she was lost shifted and then melted away, like rain on a windshield.

She pulled her hand out of the pocket of the apron. The iron jack dug into the torn flesh of her palm.

Jack . . .

Delicate hands caught her shoulders, shaking her awake. Not Jack. Jack's grip was firm and strong. Jack had never been so rough with her. Besides, Jack was lost.

And then in her dream—was it only a dream? He had turned her over to the king. He'd just knelt there, looking at her, holding the golden heart like it was the most precious thing in the world as he turned to—

It was just a dream. But visions had a way of making

themselves come true, didn't they? She gasped out a sigh, broken by a sob and her eyes snapped open. Pain stabbed at her head, the pain of a migraine, and deep into her hand with the iron of the jack. Someone dropped her, releasing her so abruptly that she fell to the ground. She landed face-down on cold, hard stone.

"Snap out of it," a distant voice said. "You have to get out of here."

chapter twenty-two

Jenny blinked around and saw what must be the palace kitchens. The place reeked of stale grease and rotting food. She was on her knees, a scouring brush in hand. Large slabs of stone spread out like a chessboard before her, and in the cracks between, foaming soap lifted out scraps and crumbs. She looked up to the enormous range dominating the wall before her, the tiny barred window high overhead, the grime smearing the walls. Finally her eyes found her brother's face.

"Snap out of it," Tom said again, shaking her. "You have to get out of here."

"No. I came . . ." Her throat was too dry and her voice grated. She tried again. "I came to get you."

"You're a fool. No one leaves the service of the queen. No one would want to." But he no longer looked convinced. How long had it been? There was no light here, so she didn't know if it was morning or night. But her hands were raw from scrubbing the filthy floor. Except where her palm bled.

She tore a strip off the apron and wrapped it tightly around the wound.

Can you get tetanus in fairyland? she wondered idly. *Or something worse?*

"It wasn't meant to be you," he blurted out. Jenny looked up at him sharply. His eyes glistened like broken glass. "I thought . . . I thought I'd find someone to take my place. But I never meant for it to be you."

And that was supposed to make it better? She paused for only a moment. "Well, it was. And I came."

"Why?"

"For you. To come home. Come home, Tom. Please."

"Home?" He faltered, his eyes flickering away from hers. The Lethe water must be wearing off, Jenny realized. Otherwise, why was he even here? Please, she prayed, please, let me get through to him. But he shook his head. "This is my home."

"This is an illusion."

He laughed and Jenny realized what she must sound like, kneeling in a filthy hearth in a kitchen with no escape. If this was an illusion designed to snare her, the queen had a lot to learn. Somehow, she doubted that. No, the ball had been an illusion. The awful embrace of the throne, the king's touch, and Jack . . . All illusions.

But it didn't matter now what they said, or what she feared. Her heart knew the truth. Jack hadn't betrayed her, not willingly, not in truth. Jack—or the memory of him—had given her the strength to break free, Jack and the little iron jack, which he had given her despite its danger to him. Tears stung her eyes. She was so tired of this. She forced them back, focusing instead on Tom, on the reason she was here.

He blinked and for a moment she saw her brother in his eyes. "I can get you out of here, Jenny, out of the Realm, or at least as far as the Edge. You have to leave, though. It isn't safe for you." Wasn't that what Jack had said all along? *Go home, Jenny. Leave. It isn't safe.*

"Jenny?"

Tom's voice was different now, familiar, and at last she saw Tom, her Tom. Relief surged through her and brought a smile to her face, quickly replaced by a determined frown.

"I'm not going without you. What else can she do to me now?"

Tom sighed, suddenly exasperated, and began to pace. "You're a threat. If you continue to be a threat, she'll kill you, drink your blood, eat your heart, and then she'll . . . and then she'll become you. She's done it before. Countless times. With each May Queen she conquers. And she is not known for her patience."

Eat my heart? "But . . ." She remembered the queen's stare, her strength and beauty. Nothing could harm such a woman. Nothing was a threat, especially not Jenny. "Why would she?"

Tom stopped and pulled her to her feet.

"You're the May Queen. Your vision proved it. The forest found you, the king chose you, and the May Tree Throne accepted you, as your Jack must have known they would."

"My vision?" She stared at him in amazement. "How . . . how do you know what I—"

Guilt reddened his face and he turned away. "Everyone saw, Jenny. It's part of the magic. She peered into your mind and projected it as an—an entertainment for the court. She wasn't expecting what she saw, though, and she's *displeased*." The coldness with which he said the last word made Jenny's chest contract. "You're the May Queen, little sister. Her rightful heir. One chosen by the land, by the Realm itself, found by the forest. And it'll mean your death. When she's ready, she'll take your body, but you . . . you'll be gone. Only the king himself can stop her. So far, he's remained aloof. But from what you showed her, that's all about to change. He knows, if Jack knew, for he's bound to have told his king. And Oberon will come for you."

Exhaustion swept through Jenny like a sudden sickness, and she swayed on her feet. Tom turned just in time to reach a hand out to her. "I don't understand," she whispered. "I saw myself changing, becoming . . . her. Becoming— What is the May Queen?"

Tom looked at her, his eyes serious.

Jenny became scared. "Tom, what is the May Queen?"

He dropped his hands to his sides. "Titania's—Mab's rival, one of the few creatures who can withstand her. Everything is tied to nature. The old is continually replaced by the new. Mab is a very old queen, Jenny, though she changes her name, alters her appearance at whim. She has ruled for a very long time. But it begins and ends with the May Queen."

"I don't want to be the May Queen!"

"You don't have a choice." Tom's face crumpled at the words, and Jenny found herself suddenly wanting to comfort *him*. "Titania was a May Queen once"—he took a calming breath—"a May Queen who won. A thousand years ago or more, she stepped from our world into this one of dreams and shadows, and she too defeated Queen Mab. She ate the old queen's heart, as had been Mab's way."

Jenny's stomach twisted in disgust. "Why?"

Tom shrugged, again composed. "A tradition, perhaps, a victory rite. They were different times, violent and dangerous with old and bloody magics. Or maybe it was a trick. I don't know. But like a snake coiled beneath a stone all winter, Mab came back, even stronger." Tom's eyes were distant now. "And Titania wasn't the victor anymore. They were one and the same. There were many others, whose names we haven't heard, names no one has heard since the day they came—they weren't so lucky. They lost and were consumed, defeated."

"Titania and Mab—they aren't the same person?"

His eyes snapped back to her. "They are now. The May Queen is like a mold into which the power is poured. And with power comes new life, fresh power. They haven't seen such power as they see in you in a thousand years, Jenny. The forest didn't come alive for me. It came for you. She can't let you go. And Oberon won't let her keep you here."

"Then we ask him for help." Even as she said it, she knew it was ridiculous. How could she hope to outwit even one of them, let alone both?

"Oberon?" Tom sighed, and his eyes hardened the way Dad's did when he had to explain something he thought she was deliberately failing to grasp. "There was a time when there were two kings and they fought for the May Queen. Until Oberon. He started the imbalance when he defeated the trees and trapped his rival king rather than kill him. He does not allow freedom. That's why Titania fled from him in the first place. And now he wants you in her place. He sees you as a queen he can control."

"I won't be controlled by anyone." Anger flared in her voice and Tom looked back at her, a curious expression on his face.

"You sound like Mother," he murmured. Then he shook his head and the moment was gone. "He'll find a way to control you. They always do. Mab's approach is simpler. Kill you. Use you. Become you. Or, failing that, have you become her."

She swallowed hard and took his hand again. His skin was too warm, covered in a light sheen of sweat, as if he had been sitting in the noon sun for too long.

But it *was* Tom . . .

"Come with me."

He shook his head. "I belong here now."

"If you could only see . . . Mother and Dad . . . If you could have seen what they went through when you disappeared— the endless searches, the pleas on TV, the newspaper report- ers everywhere, the Internet—" She studied his face, trying to see something more of the boy she had known again— the warmth and gentleness that had allowed him to create such beautiful music, so beautiful that it touched the souls of all who heard it. The music that was the very reason he had been taken.

"Mother and Dad." He laughed bitterly. "You don't remember what it was like, Jenny. Mother and Dad and their child prodigy. All I heard was how talented I was, how that would open so many doors. But they weren't the doors I wanted to open. You were the only one who didn't care if I could play or not, or who took pleasure in the music just for the sake of it, the way I used to."

A smile formed on her lips. "I don't have a musical bone in my body, Tom."

"Yes you do. You may not be a musician, but you loved music. It's inside you. You loved . . . you still love so much."

"I loved you. I still do. You're my brother."

It was a plain and simple answer, the honest answer, but he clearly wasn't expecting it. The moment dragged on too long. Tom backed away from her, freeing his skillful hands.

"You wouldn't claim me so easily if you knew what she—" He stopped at the door, lost in the shadows again. "I'll take you as far as the Edge, Jenny. That's all I can do. I can't leave her, and you can't remain here. They need me. She needs me. She might not have gone about it the right way, but that doesn't change things. If they don't tithe—"

"What? What happens if they don't send some innocent person to die?"

He drew in a breath, as if she'd uttered some terrible blasphemy. *"Innocent . . ."* he scoffed, but the word was tainted with regret. "No. It's not like that." His voice shook, suddenly childish. "It's a sacrifice to save them all, not just the Sidhe. To keep the whole Realm safe."

Jenny shook her head. "Why can't she do it herself? Come back with me, Tom," she tried, a last desperate effort. "She's going to kill you, no matter what. If not now, then in another seven years. You aren't one of her people, and she tires of new things in the blink of an eye." Jenny's voice was rising. "You're old to her now! She's just using you." She took a step toward him, but stopped when he shied back as if afraid.

"Meet me at midnight, when they're all feasting. I'll be in the rose garden."

Her brother stepped outside and slammed the door behind him. The sound was final, but Jenny couldn't stop now. She threw herself against the wood. "Please, Tom. Listen to me! Come home. You're a grown man, not a child. They can't make you do anything you don't want to. Tom! Please. It's a lie. Everything about this place is a lie!"

But the only sound that came back was his retreating footsteps. The cut in her palm made her whole arm ache now, and a deep weariness went alongside it. The jack dragged at the pocket of her ruined apron, pulling at her until she sank to the ground.

She breathed. Jack had been right. If only she could tell him that. If only she could see him once more.

But if she was going to get herself and Tom out of the Realm, that wasn't going to happen. Perhaps that was what Jack had been trying to tell her.

chapter twenty-three

Jenny waited, clutching the iron jack, until she heard the footsteps coming toward the kitchen. She didn't have much time. And if they guessed even for a moment that she was no longer in their thrall . . .

She scrambled up from where she sat with her back against the kitchen door, took three breaths, and forced herself to be calm. She had to make sure she played the part to perfection.

Somewhere far off, a clock chimed midnight.

Three other servants opened the door, different ages, a man and two women. They smiled at her and set to work carrying out trays of food Jenny could not remember having been there before, and she smiled back, the same beatific expression that spoke of nothing but bliss, and headed for the door with a similar tray in her hand. She moved as if she were a puppet, mimicking them exactly. And smiling.

Smiling, smiling, smiling, until her face ached.

Still holding her tray, she drifted down the halls as if her only thought was to carry it to her masters and mistresses. The palace was a maze. She passed room after room, some filled with revelers, some empty and eerily silent. Turning corners and following the hallways, she found her way to the ground floor of the palace, to the outer wall, and finally to a way out. Awkwardly opening the heavy doors, the tray still balanced in one hand, she stepped into the night.

Cool air washed over her. The midnight chimes fell silent, the last one echoing after her as she tried to find her way to the rose garden.

She had almost given up hope when she heard the flute. The tune began slowly, an invitation, and sped up, elaborating on its main theme until she knew it, better than she knew her own heartbeat. "Haste to the Wedding," Tom's favorite, the same song that had brought her—and him, she realized now—to the Realm in the first place.

The silvered notes rang out clear and bright. They carried over the evening air and she followed them, determined this time to make him listen, to make him come with her across the Edge. The tune guided her back to the rose garden, and she couldn't help but pick up her pace. She ran through the courtyards and cloister-like paths, slowing to a sleepwalk when she encountered someone, her blissful smile pasted onto her face, her tray her excuse.

When she stepped into the rose-scented air of the

garden, she was almost convinced she had gotten away with it. Almost.

Titania's presence sent her heart into the pit of her stomach like a lead weight. Ducking down at the last moment, she crouched out of sight behind one of the flowerbeds, waiting.

"You seem tired," Titania was saying. "I brought you a drink to help you sleep."

"You're too kind to me," Tom replied dreamily, and Jenny's heart sank still lower. He was back in the queen's power, lost to her. "I should practice, though. I want my music to be perfect for you."

A smile ghosted across Titania's face. The moonlight made her even paler, an angelic being in the darkened garden. "Your music is always perfect, Tom. You never fail me there."

"Then where do I fail you? Help me serve you better, my queen."

"It isn't a punishment to be the tithe, Tom. Some consider it the highest honor. You will preserve all of the Realm by your sacrifice. Hell . . . Hell is not as people imagine it."

Tom frowned, and Jenny saw something else in his eyes. Doubt. Only for a moment, but there.

"But hell is torment, my queen," he murmured as calmly as before. "Hell is being without you."

Titania sighed. "I would that I could keep you, Thomas.

Even at your most obstinate and headstrong, you are unique . . ."

She leaned in to kiss him, a gracious lover, a queen among queens, and Tom returned her kiss with unexpected passion. Jenny remembered the kiss she had shared with Jack, though, and could see that both of them were lying. Too many things were between them, too many resentments. Even in their intimacy, they lied.

Titania pulled back first, and smoothed her hand through Tom's hair, curling it around her long, elegant fingers. "Drink down the water, my sweet Tom, sleep and dream of me. Dream of wanting nothing but to serve the good of the Sidhe. And die well on the morrow. Like the prince you are."

Tom nodded, drugged and enchanted, helpless before her. What was Jenny going to do with him now? What was he going to do with her? He lifted the glass to his lips as Titania left him there.

But he didn't drink.

Sitting still, waiting to see if she returned, he didn't tip the glass up, but held it there at his lips. Only when she was gone did he pour the glistening liquid onto the ground behind him.

"Tom?" Jenny whispered, rising cautiously.

"Jenny? You're here. Are you okay?"

"I'm fine. Are . . . are you . . . ?"

He sighed, and she saw his age in his face. More than his

own age, the weight of the years he had spent here. "I'm more myself than I have been in seven years. I don't know how you did it."

She smiled and held out the iron jack for him to see.

"Iron? You brought iron in here?" The shock on his face made him look young again, the brother she remembered. Then he laughed. "God, Jenny, only you would have the gall. If she'd found it . . ."

"Can we go now?"

He nodded and lowered his eyes. "About what I said, I'm—I'm sorry, Jenny. I didn't— I wouldn't—" He stared at the ground and rubbed a hand over his face.

Jenny walked over and put her arms around him. She felt her brother's arms tighten around her in a bear hug. But Tom's voice was solemn.

"It took the look on your face to make me see what Titania has made of me. I—I can make music to wring out a soul, but I can't feel it myself. I'm a—a waste . . . I'm sorry, Jenny. If I have to die tomorrow, so be it, but I'll get you out of here."

She pulled away and turned to look beyond the garden walls. "No," she murmured. "We're getting out together."

Jack would know the way, would help them. Jack—

Jack in this very garden, Jack swallowed up, Jack in her dream trying to speak, but only dirt falling from his lips. The lips she had kissed. Jack, holding a golden heart.

"Jenny?" Tom asked.

Cold slicked through her veins. "I have to find Jack."

"The Jack o' the Forest?" Confusion filled his face. "He's gone, Jenny. Back to the earth, back to Oberon."

"But I can get him. I'll get him back."

"Jenny." Tom's voice soothed her, cajoled. "Jenny, he's gone. And we have to go now, no matter what. She's going to realize you're missing. You're too valuable to her for her not to check on you."

He was right. God, he was right. Jack would tell her to go. All he had wanted was for her to leave the Realm, to be safe. And yet he had helped. Despite his duties and the temptations laid before him. He'd risked everything for her. And he'd lost. He'd lost everything.

But if she didn't flee with Tom now, she would never have another chance to free her brother. Come the morning, the queen would kill him.

Jack or Tom. That was what it came down to. Jack or Tom.

All the choices she might have had were gone, like water held in cupped hands.

"Come on, then," she said. Jenny took her brother's hand and they hurried out of the rose garden, through the moonlit meadows, and onward toward the waiting forest.

⚘ ⚘ ⚘

The call of the hounds cut the night and Tom tensed, his head lifting like a stag sensing the approach of the hunt.

"They're coming," he said. Dawn stained the eastern sky and filtered through the forest, giving them much-needed light at last. But with it . . . with it came their enemies.

"We'll have to run for it," Jenny said.

"No, we should hide. Maybe if we . . ."

Jenny broke into a sprint ahead of him. She heard him curse and pick up his speed to match hers.

"They're tracking us!"

Let them, she wanted to say. *Just run.* But she didn't have the breath to spare. She tore through the narrow forest path, brambles and twigs catching her skirt, pulling at her bodice. The dress was awkward and constricting. She wished it would transform back into her jeans and shirt. Branches tangled in her hair, and something sent her crashing to her knees in the dirt. Tom picked up her, hefting her onto her feet again with barely a pause.

"Hounds and horses. She's coming and she's angry. Can't you feel it?"

The wind rushed through the trees around them and the hounds howled as they caught the scent.

"Run," she told him. "Faster!"

"Jenny . . ." Tom's voice faltered and broke on her name. "Jenny, you go. If she has me, maybe—"

"No!"

"No," said a new voice, a gloriously familiar voice. Jenny turned, her heart almost bursting within her, to see Puck standing there in the forest path. "No, she won't be content with you now, piper. Not with the new May Queen here. She wants your sister. You're little more than an inconvenience now. The sooner she's rid of you, the better. She wants Jenny. And we can't allow that."

Jenny dropped to her knees, scooping Puck into her arms like a child. He gave a cry and stiffened, shocked at her behavior, but she didn't care. Not anymore. She held him, tears welling in her eyes and her chest tightening.

Puck patted her back, laughing at her exuberance. "It's all right, lass. We'll get you and your brother to safety now. All will be well."

"Where's Jack?"

He pulled back from her, his face full of confusion and grief. His brown eyes flicked up to Tom. "Why didn't you tell her?"

"I tried. I swear, I tried, Robin, but she—my sister is stubborn."

Puck sighed. "Come, the forest will hide you and I'll show you the way home."

"But Jack . . ." she tried again.

Puck held up a hand to silence her. "To the deep forest now. And be quiet. There are things in here that would not welcome you, not even if I vouch for you."

"Some would say *especially* not if you vouch for us," Tom muttered, but he followed them nonetheless.

~ ~ ~

Folletti and sprites clung to the trees as they passed. Jenny watched them cautiously, aware of other eyes following them, unseen, some benign and some hostile. Not to her, she realized, but to Tom. The piper. They knew him too well to trust any apparent change in his nature.

It sent a chill through her. What had he done under the power of the queen to make them hate him so? And just what did they expect of her? Because clearly the forest fae were looking for something.

Other creatures flitted around her, their voices rising in song as she passed through the trees. Slender girls in white and pale green shifts drifted through the forest, smiling at her and bowing their heads. Little gnarled figures like living mushrooms crawled from the ground to watch her go by.

The sound of the hunt fell away as they passed deeper and deeper through the trees. The path was easier now, as if it opened up to admit them, to let them through. The forest had done it before, Jenny realized, remembering the night the trees had unfolded, ushering her toward the greenman, toward Jack. And maybe even before that as well. The forest had known, even if she hadn't. She glanced back to find a tangle of briars and undergrowth in their wake. The forest had closed around them, sealing off any possibility of pursuit, or escape.

"Puck," Jenny murmured, keeping her voice as quiet as

possible. "Puck, please tell me what happened to Jack. He can't be dead." It was more of a plea than a statement. She needed it to be true.

"No, not dead," Puck replied, his voice a low rumble, and he glanced at Tom from the corner of his eye. "But Oberon has locked him away for his failure. He may not have betrayed you to Titania, but neither did he bring you safely to the king. He'll never see the light again. And that, for a forest creature . . ." Puck lowered his gaze and kept walking. "That is death indeed."

"But he's not dead," she said. "He's still alive."

Puck turned sharply, his eyes narrowed to slits. "You don't understand. He might as well be. Jack isn't human, Jenny."

Her temper flared then, and she turned around slowly, glaring at all of them in turn, all the gnomes and sprites, the Foletti and the Dames Vertes, all the fairy-tale creatures who had been proved real to her. "And who among you is?" she asked. "I won't give him up, Puck. I won't let him be a sacrifice for me. I won't let him die in my place." That was Titania's way. Not hers. It would never be hers.

The forest path fell hushed. They stared at her as if she had just uttered something earth-shattering. And perhaps she had, for the unexpected words that had just come from her mouth had indeed come from her heart.

Puck's voice broke the silence.

"Will you be Queen o' the May, Jenny Wren?" His eyes

shone in the dark. "With all that it entails? The tithe is not the only sacrifice in the Realm, you know. The May Queen too. She must give up all in the end. She must die, to reign."

"This is madness," Tom interrupted. "You said you'd get her out, Robin. What's this talk of sacrifice now?"

Puck's lips quirked up at the corners. "Ah, but here we are."

And they were. The trees before them were the ones she knew from Branley Copse. Old bags and wrappers tangled in the briars still shrouded in morning shadow. Beyond, the morning sunlight streamed onto the top of the mound, casting shadows of trees in long lines across the sports field. The sound of traffic on Guildford Road hummed in the distance, a murmuring, and on the air a smell that made her nostrils flare. Tart and chemical. The tang of iron. The modern world. Her world.

Without hesitating, Tom stepped forward, through the trees, over the Edge, and into the scattered sunlight. He turned around with his arms stretched wide and laughed, a sound that spoke as music as much as anything he might play on his flute. *This* was her brother. The rumpled hair, the smile that turned up one cheek. His clothes transformed to a simple T-shirt and jeans, not so terribly different from those in which he had vanished, though larger to suit the body of a man instead of a boy. The flute was tucked into a leather belt at his waist, still with him. Always with him. He tilted back his head so the sunlight fell full on his face.

He was back in their own world and free of the Realm. All she had to do was follow and she would finally have her dream of so many years. She had brought her brother home.

Just step through. And it would all be over. All the nightmares, all the lies. Just a step.

"Go," said Puck, and he gave her a little push.

Jenny didn't move. She stood between worlds, right on the Edge.

"Jenny," Tom said, reaching out his hand in the sunlight, joy making his face look young again. "You did it. Come on. You can go home."

chapter twenty-four

J enny didn't move. Her feet felt rooted to the spot, though she longed to follow her brother.

"Is Tom safe?" she whispered to Puck.

"Aye, lass. Safe as houses."

"He can't come back. You made sure?"

"I've sealed it to him, just as you asked. And she can't touch him now that he's out there. Not without great sacrifice, which isn't worth her while. And you?"

She smiled, wishing with all her heart to step out of the woods, into the sun, into the newborn morning, to join her brother and go home. Oh God, almost all she wanted was just to go home.

But it wasn't to be. Not yet.

Tom seemed to realize. He stood there, staring back through the trees, the sunlight gilding the top of his head, his mouth open, eyes wide. "Jenny?"

"I—" She cleared her throat and turned to face her brother. "I have to stay," she called to him, and even to her own ears her voice was forlorn. "I have to find Jack, Tom. I owe him . . . that much at least."

"Owe him?" Tom exclaimed. "He sold you to the queen, Jenny! Are you insane?"

The word made her bristle, made the fire lick up inside her and strengthen her resolve. Insane. No. Definitely not.

"If he sold me, he never got paid," she said with a calm that belied her rage. She wasn't angry at her brother, no. She was angry that everything had gotten so twisted around that he couldn't see who was worth saving. She knew the feeling. Or had, at least. "He was duped as well. I have to stay, Tom. I have to help him."

"So be it," said Puck. "Then turn away. Come back with us, Jenny, for you're to be Queen o' the May. What is your wish, Highness?"

Jenny squirmed at the word. But a wish—her breath caught in her throat. She still had a wish. The wish for her heart's desire that the Leczi had promised her. She fumbled in the deep pockets of the apron, trying to find it.

She tore the apron off and tried to shake it out, catching the jack as it fell.

Puck and Tom looked at her, so very different from each other but wearing matching bewildered expressions.

"Don't you understand? I could wish for Jack. I could get him back with the stone!"

"Ah, Jenny Wren," Puck sighed and sank down to the mossy earth. "It's not that easy. It's never that easy."

With a soft chink, the stone fell to the ground, bright green, shining in the light.

Jenny snatched it up, scraped back the dirt, and buried it, patting the soil over it feverishly. "Jack, I wish for Jack. I want him back. I want . . . I love him . . ." She closed her eyes and pressed her hands down on the pile of earth. "Please . . ."

The ground beneath her rippled, as if deep inside the earth a tremor tore rocks apart, but nothing else happened.

Nothing happened at all. She stared at the spot where she'd buried the stone and then cursed loudly, words she shouldn't know, not caring who heard her anymore. She wanted to scream, to pound the earth.

Nothing happened.

Another trick, another lie, another betrayal in this wretched place that thrived on such things. Why would the Leczi be any different? Why had she even dared to hope?

She opened her eyes to see Puck shaking his head. Her dirty hands trembled and she couldn't bear the look of pity in his eyes.

"It's the long road, lass," he told her. "It has to be. Leczi stones work when the time is right, when they want to, and not a moment before."

No, nothing was ever easy, she thought. But just once—

just one miserable time in her life—it would have been good to have something go her way. She looked at Tom, standing there, waiting for her. He looked young. A boy. And she felt suddenly so much older than him. The expression on his face broke her heart.

"Go home, Tom," she said to him. "They've missed you so much. Just—just go home. I'll come as soon as I can."

"Jenny, you can't be serious. You can't go back in there and face Oberon. If you thought Titania was bad . . . You can't!"

She didn't move. Everything in her wanted to go with him. Everything. She laid her arms across the spot where she'd buried the stone and briefly rested her forehead on them. Everything except her heart.

"I've got to," she told him.

"What?" Tom called from beyond the trees.

She sat up and turned to him. "I've got to," she repeated, louder.

He started forward, heading for the trees to grab her and pull her out with him, but stopped at the Edge like he'd run into a wall of air.

"Damn it, Puck," he yelled. "Let her go. I know you and who you serve. He's Oberon's through and through, Jenny. He's worse than Jack. He serves the king. Don't trust him. Not even for a moment."

"I won't," she said softly, and turned away, looking down at Puck. "I really won't."

❧ ❧ ❧

Walking through the forest seemed different this time, less rescue and more . . . procession. She could hear no sound of the hunt, and if the queen still pursued them, the forest hid them far away from her. The faerie folk sang as they wove a garland of white flowers and settled them on her head as a crown. Flowering hawthorn twisted together—a May crown for the May Queen, but this time the thorns didn't hurt her. The petals brushed gently against her forehead.

As they passed beneath the trees, pale blossoms rained down on them. The gray servant's dress melted to white, as if the petals falling about her blended into the fabric. Strips of silver-birch bark wound themselves around her. They twisted together to make a shimmering material in elegant strips of iridescent white that clung lightly to her body. Tiny flowers of Queen Anne's lace and dandelion seeds, and fronds of Old Man's Beard, knotted in a delicate web like the finest filigree lace around her bodice, sweeping down to the skirts. Threads of gossamer wound about her waist, and gleamed as they caught the light. It was the dress from her vision, the dreamlike creation she had worn to the ball, but this time woven by the forest, from the forest, and far more beautiful for that. She turned slowly, admiring it, and yet fearing this magic. Fearing what it might mean. But she had agreed to be Queen of the May. Behind her, the gown's train swept through the forest, an abundance of flowers leaping up from the rich earth—lily of the valley, snowdrops, wood anemone, wild strawberries, daisies, and a hundred others, all pale and perfect. Sunlight followed her path, picking out the flowers like jewels.

"You're old, right?" she asked Puck.

"Old as the hills, old as the dales."

"And when you said the May Queen was a sacrifice?"

"I meant just that. She was a sacrifice, brought to the forest, brought to the king, and down through the centuries she became a myth. May is the month of rebirth, Jenny Wren. And to bring about a rebirth—"

"All right, all right. I get it. Something has to die first. So you're taking me to Oberon?"

"Of course."

"And you've no choice in the matter. I mean, you'd help me, if you could. Right?"

He glanced up at her. "I would. But . . . I'm bound. As bound as Jack was. I serve the king. You have a heart like no other, Jenny, and we respect that. All of us. And you might just be strong enough."

"What does he want from me?"

"He wants a willing queen. Then his power will be complete."

"And if I don't want that?"

"He'll ask a riddle, most like. Or a test. Or offer you a choice. You can never tell. It'll be a trick, though. He's never without his tricks, and he doesn't lose his wagers."

"And Jack? I can free him?"

"What's a Jack?" Puck asked. Jenny scowled down at him. What game was it this time?

"You tell me," she replied coolly.

"Jack the lad, Jackanapes, Jack Frost, Jack Tar, Jack O'Lantern . . . there are so many. Which one, sweetling?"

"Just Jack." She buried her hands in the folds of the skirt, where flowers became fabric. The gown had no weight at all. She twisted the material around her fingers. It was soft and smooth as silk. "You're the riddler, Puck. I get that. You're the trickster and you serve the king, but I thought . . . I thought you were my friend too. And his friend. Tell me what you know."

Puck's eyes darkened. He loved Jack too, she could see that, could recognize it as clearly as she knew it in herself. "He's everyman, and no one. He's the guardian of the Edge of Faerie, once the mightiest of the forest folk, as near to a king as we've ever had among the lesser fae, now the lowest of the court. Oberon stole him from us."

"To be his servant?"

"Yes. And no. He's a knight, the knight of the Edge."

"Titania seemed to hate him."

Puck laughed then, a bitter twist of his face. "*Despise* is nearer the mark. Yet she still wants him. Always will. He serves only Oberon, though the queen has power over him as well. He could have been hers. Titania doesn't care about holding the line against your world. If anything, she wants to bring the barriers down. She just wants to experience what you have, all of it, for good or ill. So Jack stands against her, but sometimes, doing that means conceding to her. Your brother was a case in point. But it isn't Jack's fault. He's the knight of the Edge, holding the barriers from both sides. Jack rejected her long ago, and again for you. He gave her up or failed her, she would say. He lost to Oberon and she can't ever forgive him that. It's a tale of something darker than love turned to hate. Jack is *his* knight. His, mine, and yours." Puck made a sound, something primal deep in his throat. "Don't you see it yet, Jenny Wren? On every border between the mortal and the Faerie Realm—in the earth, on the sea, on every front—there's a Jack, a guardian. And here, in the forest, he's Jack o' the Forest, Jack in Green. He's the knight, like in that game of yours—chess or cards or . . ."

"Every game has its Jacks," she said, the sadness of it pulling down the elation of sudden understanding. "The thing that acts as a wild card. It can't be counted on or predicted. A weapon, even. But he's in other places too, isn't he? And do you know what else a Jack is, Puck?"

He eyed her suspiciously, rubbing his neck.

Jenny smiled. "I do." And she closed her hand around the tiny spike of iron in her palm.

chapter twenty-five

The sun rose high in the sky as they walked through the forest, that curious procession of faerie folk accompanying Jenny. The white gown didn't hinder her, and she barely noticed the crown of flowers on her head. But the iron jack was heavy in her hand. Still, she clung to it. One piece of her world in all this madness. One thing to hold on to. Eventually the faerie folk fell away, until only Puck remained with her and they stood at the mouth of a cave, a dark hole in a cliff face. Endless dark amid the life of the forest.

It was dark as a pit, a deep and ancient, fetid darkness that spoke of hidden monsters. Jenny forced herself forward. Every muscle protested, every nerve warned, but she made herself step into the shadows.

"Be careful, Jenny," Puck whispered.

"You aren't coming?"

She didn't need to look at him for an answer. Some things had to be faced alone. She understood that now. And if she ever wanted to see Jack again, she had no choice.

"I've brought you here, fulfilled my part to both you and the king. You're here and you're here willingly. Be careful. Keep your wits about you. I'll be right here. I'll wait and, if the Elders will it, I'll see you out of the Realm again. With or without him."

She smiled and then bent to kiss his cheek. Puck inhaled sharply, but she didn't care. "Thank you. But I won't be coming back without him."

"I know," he agreed. "But I'll still wait. I meant it, about your heart. And my folk both know and appreciate that. We kept watch for Jack by the riverside. We'll be here for you."

She nodded, and walked into the darkness.

🌿 🌿 🌿

The path wound down into the earth, deep and endless. She followed it for what seemed like hours without being able to see it, using one hand on the strangely smooth walls to guide her on her way, the other clenched tightly around the jack. Once her eyes adjusted to the complete darkness, she thought she saw a glow coming from the depths, the hint of a fire in the distance. Hellfire, she thought briefly and dismissed it. That was an old confusion. Oberon was not the devil. He was just tied to ancient traditions that suggested it.

Traditions like sacrificing a maiden to him on May Day.

May Day, m'aider, help me . . . Words tangled together in her mind, twisted into one another with panic and fear.

Jenny took a breath and forced herself onward. The light bloomed, and up ahead, she saw the tunnel open out into a chamber.

"Jenny Wren," said a molten voice. It shivered through her body, touching something deep, making her legs weaken and her stomach knot. Her lips warmed as if she could still feel Jack's lips pressed against them. She drew in a breath and opened eyes she hadn't realized were closed to find the vast darkness falling away with firelight.

"Brave, Jenny Wren. But not ready for me yet, not quite." There was amusement in the voice, but it went beyond simple pleasure. A modicum of malice, perhaps, the hint of a threat, and the promise of things Jenny didn't understand yet. Things that called to her, tempting, taunting. "So what brings you here? I take it this is no social call." Oberon laughed, and Jenny felt a powerful urge to turn and run. She knew him now. The magic of the May Queen filled in the gaps in her meager knowledge. Oberon had so many names. Alberich, king of the elves, Amadán, the trickster, Cernunnos. Ancient memories whispered in the back of her mind, memories she didn't know she had, names that chimed with power. The horned god. And the mask he wore now was Oberon. Charming, elegant, terrible.

A man stepped from the shadows of the cave, the king from her vision, swathed in a cloak of leaves much like Jack's. But these leaves were spiked and glossy, holly leaves.

Clumps of red berries stood out against the cloak like drops of blood. Through the black curls of his hair, she was sure she could make out horns, a crown of antlers. He was handsome too, devilishly handsome.

He's not the devil, she warned herself, though that was the image that immediately sprang back into her mind. *No more than Mab is.* But it felt like he was. The devil of the old stories Grams used to tell—the suave, silver-tongued persuader in black at the back door at midnight. The one who charmed every member of the household before destroying them with their own greed. Oberon was the one who seduced the chambermaid and left her with a bastard child, or the one who spirited away a baby, leaving a changeling in its place. He was the card shark who stole their last penny and then offered to play for their souls with his marked cards in a game they could never win.

And when he smiled at her, something in her treacherous heart wanted to see that smile forever.

The king. Her mind filled with the litany of his names, a sea of echoes across time and cultures. She felt her knees go slack. If he touched her now, she'd be lost; she knew that. He was the king from her dream. The one who had put her on the hawthorn throne and commanded it to build the cage around her so she could not flee.

The one for whom she had worn this very gown. Or something like it.

The one who controlled Jack.

Jenny had but one protection. She closed her hand into a fist so tight, the iron jack jabbed into her skin, opening the cut again with its sharp points. Blood and iron . . . the strongest magic of all. Blood and iron mixed and the pain was a burr, bringing her back to her senses. Oberon stood less than a foot from her, so close that she could feel the warmth that rolled from his body, could smell the tang of salt-sweat. His hand, long-fingered and elegant, hovered just above her cheek, and even as she watched, his head dipped toward her.

Jenny shied back before he could kiss her, and Oberon paused, a question stirring his endless eyes. If she leaned in to him now, she'd never want for anything again. Oberon would keep her safe and keep her out of Mab's clutches. He would protect the Edge so that Tom would always be safe. He would fill her days with joys and pleasures that would be beyond anything she would otherwise know. He wanted her to come to him. He could force her, no doubt, enchant her or beguile her, but he didn't. The May Queen had to be willing or the magic wouldn't work. It was her choice. He could offer her anything, and deliver it.

But there was something he couldn't give her.

The ghost of Jack's kiss played on her lips. She remembered his body enfolding her, bringing her out of the dark cold of the river, back to the light and warmth of the forest.

She couldn't leave Jack like this, lost in the darkness. He needed the sun, he needed the trees.

Oberon moved toward her, the bulk of his body dwarfing her own.

Their lips met, but she felt nothing. His heart was as cold and empty as the winter wind.

Oberon caught her shoulders and thrust her back from him, studying her at arm's length.

"You've the kiss of an innocent, Jenny Wren." His liquid voice rumbled through her. "It's almost as if you're kissing another. Whatever are you doing here? And why do you not react to my kiss, *Gwenhyfer?*"

"I—I came looking for—for Jack."

"Jack o' the Forest? And what do you offer me in return?"

She stretched out her hand and uncurled her fingers. Oberon recoiled, his eyes widening, the pupils pooling to fill them with blackness. His upper lip drew back in a snarl.

"You threaten me?"

She couldn't show fear. Whatever she did, she had to hold firm. "No. But Jack is my friend. He rescued me. He took my necklace and gave me this in exchange. This is all I have left, but I'll trade it for him. An iron jack for a forest Jack. My brother may be safe from Titania, but I can't forsake Jack."

A slow smile spread over Oberon's face, bringing his handsomeness forward once more. His eyes flushed green for an instant before resolving back to their endless black.

"You snatched your brother from Titania? And you'd give me iron as a gift." He laughed and turned away from her. "Iron is poison to our kind. Most metals are unless they are pure, like gold and silver. Even then, they must be given freely. And yet you come and offer me *poison* for my most prized knight." He glanced over his shoulder. "It shows bravery, I suppose, or stupidity. And the iron explains your resistance to my will. But no matter. I want no payment for him. He isn't going anywhere. He's mine. And will remain so." He turned and walked away from her.

"No!" Jenny exclaimed, marching after him. "This is all I have. You can't turn it down."

He twisted back to face her abruptly, brutal in his speed and agility. "Not so, Jenny Wren. Jack calls you the May Queen. If that's true, you have much indeed to offer. So here is my bargain—a wager." He smiled knowingly, a smile that made her stomach tighten. "Enter into a wager with me, Jenny Wren, and if you win, you can leave here with your Jack."

"And . . . and if I lose . . ."

His fingers slid down the side of her cheek, too intimate, a caress that seemed intent only on claiming her. "Then no one goes anywhere."

❧ ❧ ❧

The cavern unfolded before her, a vast, dark space lit by sparks of light in the gloom. Here and there, fires burned, vast jumbles of wood and flames that belched forth a thick and pungent smoke. The air itself seemed red around them, but farther on, all was darkness. She remembered her vision of the ball. This then was where it had been. She tilted her head back and stared upward. Roots of great trees twisted together and then spread out, like the ribs of a vast cathedral ceiling far above her. They merged again, twisting their way in and out of the rocks and earth, to form pillars all around the chamber. She was far beneath the forest. In the stony heart of the Realm itself.

Oberon's cold hand pressed into the small of her back, pushing her forward. As her eyes adjusted to the light, she could just make them out, skirting the edges of the cavern, figures, hundreds of figures. Their eyes made those points of brightness she had seen. But they didn't show their faces. She didn't want them to.

"What . . . what is this place?" she asked, ashamed of the hesitation in her voice. She glanced back at the King of Faerie.

He grinned, his teeth very white in the darkness. "A waiting room," he chuckled. "You asked me for Jack. It was a very polite request and one I'll respect, if you can win him, but nothing's free, nor without risk."

"This is part of your wager?"

His hand moved to the curve of her neck and she flinched away. He laughed outright, and in that sound she truly heard the Amadán, the Trickster, the King of Fools. It sliced her nerves like a blade through paper.

"This is my wager. All you have to do is find him, little one. Call his name and see if he can answer. Just find him and all the happily-ever-afters can be yours. Well, as many as you can expect with a Kobold. That's not going to change."

"That's all?"

"Of course." He gently wound a strand of her hair around his fingers. "But if you don't find him, or can't . . . or won't . . ." His tone was possessive. "Then you'll stay here, Jenny Wren. May Queen. You'll be mine for eternity. My queen. You'll accept that, accept me, and submit to my will."

She pulled herself free and faced him, a protest rising in her throat.

"Those are my terms, *Gwenhyfer*. And you're already here. I don't even have to give you this much."

He used the oldest form of her name, ancient Welsh, the name that had become Guinevere, another lost queen. It meant the fair, white, and pure, all the things associated with the May Queen. Even her name, he seemed to say, marked her out as his.

"Then why?" she asked between clenched teeth.

He spread his arms wide. "To prove to you that I am a gracious lord. And a kind and generous master. Ask your friends. Ask Puck." He laughed again, that dark and frightening laugh. "Ask your Jack."

He turned and walked away from her, the leafy cloak billowing out behind him.

Jenny waited until the echoes of his laughter had died away, waited for her eyes to adjust more fully to this place of lies and fire-thrown shadows.

One of the figures moved. She watched the familiar, fluid motions, the animal ease with which he slid into the light. Jack stepped toward her warily and she felt her whole self leap at the sight of him. But before she could move, another figure resolved out of the shadows, another Jack, so closely matched to the first that one of them could have been a reflection. And from the shadows another emerged, and another.

Jenny backed up as more and more images of her Jack appeared. Her back met the gnarled surface of a door, rough and knotted like old tree bark. Everywhere she looked, she saw Jack, and each one gazed at her with his eyes like shining marbles, one blue, one green.

"Jenny Wren," said the nearest, fondly, and each of them repeated it, a hundred times over, the echoes taking up the sound in mockery. A heat burned behind her eyes, tingled in the bridge of her nose. Her throat tightened as if an invisible hand closed around it, choking the life from her.

"Jack?" She slid down to the ground, the door's rough surface tugging at her dress, scratching her back through the light fabric of flowers.

"Trust your heart," he'd said. But her heart was thundering wildly against her ribs. And each of these Jacks wanted to

trick her, wanted to serve their master and so enslave her as well.

"Jenny, listen to me," said the nearest. He crouched down before her and shook his dark hair from his face, smiling his crooked smile. "Jenny, it's not so bad, sweetling. Really. You just need to relax." His hand touched her arm, but his touch was cold and hard as polished wood, not at all like Jack's. She recoiled, scrambling to her feet.

Not so bad? To be a servant without free will, to be a puppet, even to a lord who said he loved you . . . She gripped the tree-bark door behind her, digging her nails into the surface.

Puck had said Jack was a tree spirit, a child of the wood, but he was trapped when his tree was felled. Oberon had carved a figure from the timber, a servant, a Kobold.

"No," she whispered as realization blossomed in her mind.

A Kobold was a slave, kept in a case only to be let out to do his master's bidding. And Oberon was his master, from the moment she had met him, now and always. Jack had no choice but to serve him.

"What did you do, Jack? Did you do what he told you to? Is that why you changed your mind and helped me?"

The ersatz Jacks gazed at her and murmured without comprehension, so many images of him, none of whom could know the real answer, none of whom would help her.

"Did Oberon tell you to help me?" Tears rolled down her

cheeks, salty on her mouth. "Or was it her? Did you bring me to Titania as Tom said only to have her betray you in return? Did she promise to set you free? Because you're not free. Was this what you meant when you said they'd hidden your heart? Oh Jack, where did they hide your heart?"

"Locked away," he had said. Locked. Locket . . .

She stumbled to her feet, her legs wobbly.

A Kobold was locked away and the children were taught never to go near its cage. Their parents made toys, brightly colored, loud, terrifying—Jenny took a step forward, peering between the Jacks. Then another, pushing them aside so she could see better. And then another and another. She was running through the hall now, pushing Jacks out of her way, seeking desperately through the shadows at its edge.

"Jack!" She yelled his name until her voice was hoarse. "Jack, where are you?"

She fought her way through the crowd of imitations, their confused murmurs like the wind through leaves, over oceans, through mountains. Oberon must have summoned them all, pulled them out of every patrol, every duty, to be here, to deceive her, to trap her. He cared nothing for his borders, nothing for the Realm or its people. All that mattered was that he win.

That he win her.

The Jacks did nothing to hinder her. In fact, they suddenly seemed eager to get out of her way, to get away from the insane girl who was throwing herself into the darkness. Let them stand there, openmouthed. Let them stare. She was used to people staring. She didn't care anymore. At the far end of the hall, she found what she was looking for and the very thing she had been dreading. Boxes were scattered haphazardly around the edge of the chamber, a hundred or more boxes, for a hundred or more Jacks. Garish colors splattered over each one and there was no way to tell them apart. She skidded to a halt, her frustration a nearly palpable fire in her chest that turned in a moment to ashes.

"No," she cried, and dropped to her knees. "No. Jack, help me. You have to help me. Please."

She remembered the feeling of the slim gold chain on her neck, the solid weight of the gold heart against her sternum, the rapid series of clicks it made as she ran it along the links when she was nervous. She remembered her only treasure. The place to keep her secrets.

And the boy she had given it to.

From the darkness she heard the ghost of Oberon's laughter. It was the only answer. Jack was silent. Jenny closed her eyes against her tears.

Jack slept without dreaming. Wood didn't dream and dead wood even less so. When Oberon had shut him up in his prison, all thoughts and feelings had seeped away. Winter claimed him and he slept, his limbs hard and lifeless. He didn't feel Jenny's necklace clutched in his hand, but the metal chain entwined his fingers. He had held it close as he felt the change steal his life, his memories, his consciousness. The tiny heart pressed into his palm and the skin had molded around it in the moments before he could feel no more.

Winter was all, winter that buried the smallest spark of life deep inside him, winter that made him hard and cold. He waited, hidden in his wooden heart, the box made of his heartwood. Like all seasons, winter had its time, and in that time it ruled all.

But also like all seasons, it was subject to time. Winter had to end with the coming of spring. It had to yield, just as Jack had yielded to winter. Winter yielded to the coming of spring's herald, the Wren, the May Queen.

And from the first touch of spring, the oak burgeoned to new life, ready for summer, ready to be king and protector.

The pendent heart warmed in his grip, the first touch of spring's sun. The sap was rising, warming his body, returning life where life had fled.

"*Jack.*" He could hear her voice like the distant fall of rain, the rain that like the sunshine fed the heartwood and brought forth new life. "Help me. You have to help me. I can't find you."

His arm jolted, muscles spasming, the tendons snapping to rigidity. His fist slammed into the roof of his prison but did not break through. His eyes opened and he dragged in a desperate breath.

"Jenny," he tried to call, but his voice was too weak, no more than the scratching of twigs at a windowpane. "Jenny," he tried again, to no greater effect. Gritting his teeth, he clenched his fingers around the locket and slammed his fist into the wooden wall. "Jenny," he cried as the fleeting newborn strength began to fade and he felt Oberon's will reassert its hold. He was a prisoner, after all, a slave and subject to laws as old as the Realm of Faerie.

"Jenny," he breathed in defeat as the darkness of winter rose around him again, like fresh snowfall blanketing all sensations.

❧ ❧ ❧

Jenny. The voice was faint as a breeze through leaves. It could have been any of the other Jacks, hovering behind her, intent on and bewildered by her display. But as her body jerked to alertness, she knew it wasn't. The thud sounded a second time, from the left, and she scrambled forward on all fours, unable to waste her time getting up. His voice came again, distant and in pain. Jenny froze, like a hunting cat, poised to track a sound, a scent. There was another thud, another anguished cry. She could picture his frantic eyes in the darkness.

"Jack?" she called. "Jack, I can hear you. Once more, please—help me."

Self-disgust clawed at her. It was all she ever asked of him. *Help me, Jack. Guide me. Save me.*

Now it was her turn to save him. She wasn't going to fail.

Jack hadn't let her down. He'd done just as she had asked.

"Did he never let you down?" said an insidious voice. She glanced around to see one of the Jacks kneeling behind her, his eyes like twin gas flames. "He let Titania capture you. She promised to free him, you know. When she didn't, your Jack brought you here, to our master, as per his instructions."

"Jenny," Jack whispered from one of the brightly colored boxes, his voice stretched with despair, with guilt. He believed them, even if she did not.

"No. I asked him to bring me to the palace. He tried to fight Titania, to warn me. And he didn't bring me here, I came myself."

"If he wasn't here, would you have come? No, I don't think so. He was always going to bring you here, whether he wanted to or not. That was his mission."

"You're lying. You'd say anything right now."

The other Jack laughed the Amadán's laugh. It spread through the hall, ricocheting off the walls in waves. And Jenny heard the thud again, saw the slight vibration of a colored box buried among many. She stumbled over and threw herself on it before anyone could stop her. Taking it in her hands, she wrenched the lid open.

chapter twenty-six

Jack burst from the box, gasping for air. He pulled her into his arms, a brief and perfunctory embrace. But he was warm and vital, and his unmistakable scent surrounded her. It was him, really him. He drew the Jester's sword, putting himself between her and the other Jacks.

"Did they hurt you? Did he touch you?"

No question as to who the "he" was. "No. I'm fine. We have to go."

"Just like that?"

"I made a wager. If I found you, we could go."

"By the Elders, Jenny." He turned toward her and his eyes glinted metallic with shock. "What if you *hadn't*?"

"Then we would have both stayed here."

"You still might," said Oberon. The fires flared, bathing the chamber in their infernal light as he walked forward. "No one ever claimed I kept my word."

Jenny went cold. She should have guessed, should have thought . . .

But Jack didn't move. "Not so, my lord. You're bound by your word. You always have been."

The king laughed, a hollow sound, and ignored Jack. Instead he smiled at Jenny with a calculating expression. "It could have been a perfect marriage, *Gwenhyfer*. It still could be."

"The May Queen chooses her king," Jack interrupted.

"Then let her choose, Jack." Oberon spread his arms wide, palms up. "Jenny saw how Titania treats her people. She could change that, be the May Queen they deserve."

"I've seen many of her people," Jenny said. "Maybe they have the queen they deserve."

But she didn't mean that. She knew she didn't. Stepping around Jack, ignoring his grunted protests, she faced the king, his knights lined up on either side of him. Every one of them looked like the boy she loved. And yet they didn't. Couldn't. Not one of them was really like him. They lacked so much. Her Jack alone was special. She had always known that.

"Oberon, you're the king. If you chose to, *you* could stop it. Stop her. Set free those she has enslaved. If you only took responsibility for your actions instead of simply trying to find another queen . . ."

Oberon stared at her. "You would lecture me, *Gwenhyfer*?"

She set her jaw. "My name is Jenny. And I'm not your May Queen. I will never be. Your May Queen was Titania, but you let Mab engulf her, overpower her. Or perhaps it was Mab as well, long ago, and you let her become that bitter and twisted thing. If you don't choose to love her, then how on earth could I believe that you would love me?"

Oberon lifted his lip in a sneer. "You disappoint me. You're just a girl. A child with a head full of fancies. Get out, and take him with you. Freedom from this place is all I offer him. Curses still stand, promises cannot be unmade. Take your Kobold with you. He has not defeated me. I could have protected you, Jenny. Now I will not. I release you both to the forest, where my queen is hunting."

The world wavered, shifted, and re-formed. Stones and fire became leaves and trees, and the light of the setting sun. Jack grabbed Jenny's hand, pulled her back against his chest. She turned into his arms, lifted her face, and his lips captured hers in a slow kiss that reached deep inside her. The breeze lifted her hair, and the scents of the forest wrapped around them.

The distant sound of a hunting horn pulled them back. Jack's eyes widened, the pupils dilating to pools of darkness inside a ring of vibrant color. He glanced at the sky. "We have to run. We have to get to the Edge."

He took off, pulling her after him, fleet and surefooted in his forest. They sprinted through the trees, and the forest seemed to fold itself out of their way to speed them along, just as it had when Puck had brought her to the Edge.

"Puck," Jenny called to Jack. "Puck promised to help us. If we made it out."

"I wouldn't count on it. Puck is Oberon's creature."

"But he—"

The hounds bounded into the clearing ahead of them, white as albinos in the dimness, with burning red eyes. The points of their ears and muzzles were scarlet, as if dipped in blood. Jack cursed and pulled her back, bringing the sword up in an arc of light.

"Stay behind me, Jenny."

The nearest hound snarled, baring razor-sharp teeth. Its muscles bunched, but it moved too fast for her to see it leap. It was just a ghostly blur in the fading light. Jack's sword took it from the air, with a ribbon of bright blood trailing after it. Another attacked, and another, but he moved even faster than they did, his blade mightier than their teeth and claws.

The remaining dogs barked and snarled, but finally turned tail and ran.

"They're off to get the hunt, to lead them to us," Jack said. "There isn't much time. Hurry."

But someone else stood at the edge of the narrow clearing now, a small brown body with goats' legs and horns. Puck.

"You didn't think I'd lie to her, did you, Jack? I gave you

my promise too. Her brother is safely home. There's just Jenny to get out of the Realm now."

Jack turned on him. There was a wildness in his eyes. "It's almost time, Puck. Can I trust you? Can you get her out?"

"I'm not going anywhere without you," Jenny said. "Not now."

"The hunt is coming, Jenny, and night is coming with them. I can't . . ."

"Yes you can, because I'm not going anywhere without you."

"I can't, Jenny. I just . . ." Panic entered his eyes now and he glanced from her to Puck and back again. He caught her wrist. "We must get you to the Edge. And quickly."

But even as they raced onward, the sound of hooves grew louder, the shouts and whistles, the cries and the baying of the hounds.

The light changed as they sped onward, redder, darker, staining the leaves and the branches gold and scarlet, like looking at the world through stained-glass windows. Jenny stumbled as she ran, but Jack's grip, strong and unyielding as a tree root, kept her upright, kept her going. Though her heart hammered in her chest, and the base of her throat ached as if it might tear apart, she ran, with Puck leading the way, heading for the Edge and freedom.

The ground shook and trembled as the hunt thundered behind them, around them, encircling them and bringing them to a halt, just yards from their goal. Beyond the trees, cut by brambles and bushes, Jenny could see the hill, the flickering lights of evening, the way home. It was blocked.

Horses danced on the spot, reined in by their riders while the remaining dogs milled around them, snarling and snapping at Jack and Puck. But Titania's mare stood like a sculpture, with the queen just as still. She wore a gown of lavender and silver that trailed almost to the ground at the side, and strands of silver wound through her golden hair, contrasting with its sheen. Her eyes pierced the growing twilight and she smiled.

"Too late, Jack o' the Forest. Too late. Night is falling and you didn't run fast enough with your Wren. Now she's going to be our sacrifice and I will take your heartwood from my husband just to watch it burn."

But Jack stood firm, pulling Jenny to his side, Wayland's sword their only defense now. His hand shook, the vibration traveling up the blade to the tip, and he stared at it in alarm. His knuckles turned bone-white against the grip, his tendons and bones starkly visible through his skin.

"Take it," Jack whispered. Jenny's hand closed around the hilt and she took the weight of the blade. She wrapped her other arm around Jack's neck, bracing herself against its weight.

"What's wrong?" she asked.

"Trust me. Please trust me."

And with those words, the change took him. His back arched, his limbs stiffening in agony as his skin transformed to wood and briar, to bark and thorn. Leaves erupted from his hair, vines tumbled down his back, and his eyes became like polished knots as hard as any stone. His mouth opened in a silent scream and the tendons in his neck stood out like wires. His grip on her loosened but she held on to him, refusing to let go.

"And now you see what he is?" asked Titania. "A creature, not man nor beast, but wild, as wild and untameable as the forest itself. For he is the forest. And the heart he forsook is made of wood. Our poor defeated Oak King. He couldn't love me enough. And he cannot love you. He never will."

Jenny's hand slipped on the hilt, then tightened as she saw the locket, the golden heart she had given Jack, looped around his neck. All Titania's words were lies. Jack had a heart after all. And yet, they were true as well. It was Titania's strength—twisting truth to lies and back again.

"Look at him, Jennifer," Titania growled. "Look and see what he is, what he really is, this *thing* you claim to love."

Spikes ripped their way down Jack's side. Jenny cried out, trying in vain to avoid them, but she held on to him nonetheless. If she let go, every instinct screamed she would lose him. A long briar lashed out, encircling her waist and tearing the gown, but she clung to him more tightly than ever. If she let him go, she knew with all her heart that she would never see him again, that they would both be lost.

"I was wrong," Jack hissed in a voice made of the rasp of bark and the crack of branches. "Let go. Let me go!"

His fingers fumbled with her hands, trying to tear her from him, to set her free, even if it meant losing himself forever. But she held on. Even as the transformation continued, and the pain grew worse, so much worse. Thorns and bark, briars and spikes couldn't hurt her as much as the agony that blazed in his eyes.

Trust me, he'd asked her, without really thinking what he was asking. *Please trust me.* And she did. He tried to shake her off, twisting and turning. His gaze pleaded with her through the anger, through the wildness. Blood made her hands slick and tears blinded her, but she dug her fingers into his wooden body, clinging to him as she would to her life.

With a roar like the breaking of the greatest tree in the forest, Jack threw back his head. His mouth distended as he screamed, a howl of pain that went on and on, echoing through the twilight. Titania stretched out her hand, drawing out the process, Jenny realized, making him suffer even more. Jenny screamed his name and held on. Blood covered him. The same blood that blossomed like roses on the pristine white of her gown. Her blood.

"Hurts," Titania snarled. "Doesn't it, Jenny? Can you see how it hurts him? Putting him out of his misery would be a kindness. He's not even an animal. Certainly not human. So what is he?"

"He's Jack." Jenny's voice was harsh in her throat. "And I will not let him go."

Jack's head turned toward her. His eyes burned with the same wild light as the Jacks in Oberon's cave. Feral eyes, one blue, one green, like fireflies before her.

And sentient. Dear God, he was still in there somewhere, though he might not realize it himself, or remember it in the morning. He was there. Jack. Her Jack.

"I will not let him go," she insisted again and dug her fingers into the bark covering him, finding a curious calm deep inside her. And from inside his body, pressed against hers, she felt a deep slow sound, a rhythmic drumbeat, his heart.

Before she could make sense of it, Jack's grip on her loosened. The wooden exterior melted away and beneath it, she saw his face. Her Jack. He tried to smile, but when he saw the damage he had done to her, his features crumpled, and shame and grief filled his face.

"Kill them," snarled Titania to her hunting party, her face twisting. "Kill them both."

Huntsmen and hounds moved forward and Jack took the sword from Jenny, his jaw tightening, his body tensing for attack. But they were too many, all those fluid and dangerously beautiful Sidhe warriors. They drew weapons that gleamed and glinted in the growing moonlight, like water, like death.

Jenny sucked in a breath, ready to shout, but before she could, the forest became absolutely still and another voice spoke instead.

"I don't think that will happen," said Puck. "No. Not likely at all."

The forest silenced all around them, every bird, every leaf, every creak and rustle.

From the undergrowth and the upper canopy, from holes in the ground and from the trunks of the trees themselves figures appeared. They slid out of the bark, bearing its patterns on their skin. They descended from the upper branches, their hair dappled with light and shade. Dames Vertes slipped between saplings and gnomes pushed their way out into the air. Rocks unfolded into misshapen goblins and leaves unfurled to reveal pixies. Even the Foletti appeared in blurs of rainbow colors.

Puck stood firm at the forefront of them, glaring at the queen with an ancient antagonism. The Sidhe stopped in their tracks, staring at the creatures all around them as if some ancient, slumbering cur they'd never paid any mind had suddenly risen from its place by the fire and snarled at them.

"What is the meaning of this?" Titania found her voice first, her face ugly in a sneer. "You have no place here, Goodfellow. You serve the king."

The forest fae far outnumbered the Sidhe. More appeared every second. Each of them bore a similar expression—one of cold and implacable hatred.

"Who is the King of the Forest?" asked Puck.

"The Oak," they cried, in a thousand creaking voices. "The Oak is King of the Forest."

Puck took a single step forward, and all the forest fae followed him. Just one step. The Sidhe fought not to recoil. Most of them failed.

"Who is the King of the Forest?" Puck repeated.

"The Oak!" The sound roared through the trees, rumbled through the ground.

"Puck," Jack groaned. "What are you doing?"

Puck paid him no mind. He kept his eyes fixed on Titania. "The Oak is King of the Forest. Our king has been freed, made our king once again." He turned to Jenny and bowed, as graceful and stately a bow as she had ever seen. "The May Queen chooses her king. Her blood is on him. Her sacrifice given. I serve the king, Titania," Puck said solemnly. "I always have."

The Sidhe retreated, trying to move without appearing to do so. But the forest was having none of that, tripping them and toppling them to the ground. Only Titania stood firm, her horse still poised like a statue beneath her, held by her will.

All around Jenny, the forest fae bowed. She held on to Jack, feeling the beat of his heart. The heart Oberon had stolen. The heart they had won back.

"The old queen has no place here," said Puck to Titania. "You are no longer welcome in the forest. It rejects you. It rejects all your kind."

A branch lashed out toward Titania and for a moment it seemed likely to knock her from her saddle. The queen raised a dismissive hand and the branch burst into flames. The sound of shrieking wood rang out for a moment and the forest fae hissed in raw hatred. Leaves, mulch, and living things smothered the flames, and the forest fell silent again, terrible in its absolute unnatural quiet. Titania gazed down on them. She was still powerful, more powerful than any single one of them. But together, they presented a threat even to her.

"You may have your new queen," she said. "Aye, and your old king. But it cannot last. She won't stay. He can't go. The Realm will not allow it. He can't pass the Edge. And the old magic doesn't just require blood, as well you know, Puck. It calls for a death. Like the tithe. Like all the old magic."

She tightened the reins and the spell on her horse finally cracked. It whinnied and paced back, trying to retreat from this hostile place.

"Go then," said Titania. "Go and relish your victory. It won't last long. Nothing does. Nothing in this world or your own." She turned the horse's head toward her home. Her shoulders sagged, her head hung forward.

Jenny let her breath out softly. Everything ached, from her feet to her fingertips. For a moment, just a moment, the tension in her began to uncoil and Jack, sensing it perhaps, let her go.

Titania spun around, twisting in her saddle. One hand lashed out, twisted like a claw, and a sheet of flames sprang up between them, cutting Jenny off from the others. The heat drove her back with its intensity, the flames licking into the night.

The old queen leaped down from the bucking horse, which fled, whinnying with terror, bells jangling in a cacophony. Titania crouched low, moving so slowly, like a spider advancing along her web. In her face, in the black depths of her endless eyes, Jenny saw nothing of the austere beauty from before. Hardly a trace of Titania remained. The twisted smile, the deviant glint in her eyes, it was Mab. The beauty drained away to leave something else behind, something shriveled, corpselike, ancient.

An obsidian knife rang against its jeweled scabbard as Mab drew it forth. The firelight turned the blade a deep crimson, the color of old blood. Jenny stumbled back, fell, but continued to scramble away until she'd backed up against a tree and there was nowhere else to go. She tried to push herself upright, but as Mab advanced, fear robbed her of the strength to move. She could only stare in horror.

The flames caught the leaves and branches above them, devoured the undergrowth, spreading through Jack's precious forest like a living thing consuming all in its path. The forest fought back, but all Jenny could see was the spider-like figure advancing on her.

Mab crept forward, her head tilting this way and that as if expecting Jenny to run, daring her to do so. She spread her arms wide, the knife making intricate patterns in the air.

"Mine now." Her voice cracked, the silken purr discarded. Or else Titania was no more. "Mine to have and hold. Mine to taste. Mine to consume."

Less than a foot away now. Less than that. Inexorable, relentless. Jenny scrambled back, but there was nowhere to go.

Mab reached out, one gnarled hand stroking the length of Jenny's hair, as if she was testing the texture of fabric. She smiled—or at least bared her teeth, yellow and broken from age—and her hand closed around Jenny's throat. The fine sleeve of her gown hung loose around a wrist skeletal rather than elegant. She stank of the grave, of blood and sacrifice.

"What did you think the May Queen was, little girl?" She lifted the knife and pressed the point against the underside of Jenny's left breast.

Images flickered through Jenny's mind—girls in white, crowned with flowers, paraded through villages, fêted and celebrated and brought to the edge of the forest.

Oberon only asked for her heart in the figurative sense. Mab was actually going to take it. Just as she had taken all the others. All of them. Those who won and those who lost, through conquest or deceit. Mab always won.

The obsidian knife-tip dug into Jenny's skin through the gown, and she closed her eyes. Mab's hand felt like desiccated leather on her skin, tightening until she couldn't breathe.

"Ancient magic calls for blood, for sacrifice, so the earth can be made new. You've given your heart to the trees, and now you must give it to me, so the earth will be made new. And when this fire purges the deadwood, we'll make the forest anew as well. We'll make it better. You'll see. Jack will love us and he will be king. And we will be queen again. Oh yes."

Mab leaned in, her stench engulfing Jenny, her lips rasping against Jenny's cheek.

"Ready yourself, child. This is your moment of sacrifice. It's a little price to pay and now you'll live forever in me. And I in you."

Jenny's hands scrabbled against her own body, seeking something, anything that might help her. It couldn't end like this. She didn't want to die. And she didn't want to be reborn as that *thing*.

Jack burst through the sheet of flames, sword in hand, his body smoldering, fire catching on his arms and legs. "Leave her be!"

At the same time, Jenny thrust her hands into her pocket, and closed her grasping hand on something.

Something hard and spiky and cold, so cold.

Mab turned, distracted by the arrival. When she saw Jack, she grinned again, gloating. Her mouth opened wide as she cackled.

With all the strength in her, Jenny thrust the iron jack into Mab's mouth. For a moment the queen froze. Jenny shoved her back and Mab choked. The knife tumbled from her fingers, which now grasped at her own throat. She thrashed, clawing at her leathery skin, tearing at her neck. A sound came from her, something between a scream and a clogged drain.

Jenny pulled Jack toward her and he wrapped his arms around her, even as Mab's body thrashed, arched, her muscles ratcheted in agony. Finally, she fell still.

The flames dwindled to smoke, to patches of black, and the forest reasserted itself, tumbling back over the scars.

"Are you hurt?" Jack asked, breathless, his eyes flicking over her, not trusting her to tell him the truth, so intent was his examination.

Beneath them the earth moved. Like a great beast rolling

under their feet, the ground itself shook and reared up with a howl of loss and dismay.

Oberon burst from the soil, rocks and roots torn up around them. Jenny and Jack were thrown backward in a tangle of limbs amid the scattering forest fae. Seeing his fallen queen, Oberon threw back his head and roared like the breaking of a mountainside.

"Who has done this?" He gathered her up, a frail and tiny body in his massive arms, her hair a swathe of gold again. Her limbs dangled from his embrace like a broken doll. Mab and all her vile traces were gone. All that remained now was Titania, beautiful as dawn.

"Who has done this?" the king repeated, and the words stretched out with grief. His head swung around, a wounded animal seeking the source of its torment. His maddened gaze fixed on Jack and Jenny, and the pain turned to malice.

"You!" he snarled, spittle flecking the air before him. "Oath-breakers. Murderers!" He cradled his queen's limp figure against his chest and slammed one fist into the quaking earth. "I let you go, and this is how you repay me? You killed her! My queen!"

Jenny froze, horrified as the monstrous king bore down on them, driven out of his mind with anguish. He'd loved her. Even after all that had happened, he'd loved Titania. And now losing her had made him mad.

I'm sorry, she wanted to say. *I didn't mean . . . I didn't think . . .*

All lies. She'd known, even as she did it. She had fought for her life, done the only thing she could.

Jack's body tensed, ready to do something. What, she didn't know. To run, perhaps. Or fight. She risked a glance at his face, recognized that expression. He held the sword in a firm grip. He meant to fight.

"No, Jack," Oberon roared. "Not this time. She killed the queen. She's forfeit. She's mine. My May Queen, bound by the blood she has spilled, by the death she has wrought. Would you fight me again? Would you give up this freedom once more? You aren't strong enough yet, boy. You never will be. I'll break you as I broke you before."

"She goes back," replied Jack, in a voice just as powerful. "She isn't yours or mine. She's going home."

"*Mine!*" Oberon's voice barely sounded human anymore. It was the sound of the rock-fall, the thunderclap, the roar of the mountain. His features froze like petrified wood, hard and implacable.

Jack dipped his head so his lips passed close to her ear. She could feel his breath against her skin, moving strands of her hair. His words shivered against her. "Forgive me."

He seized her, flinging her over his shoulder, and he ran for the Edge.

The forest around them shrieked. Stones and earth bucked beneath them. The trees and branches twisted to stop him. Not for Oberon's sake, Jenny knew, for her own mind screamed the same warning. They had to stop him. Because if Jack—the old forest king made new again, creature of wild magic, the Oak—crossed into the mundane world of mankind, if Jack carried her over the Edge—

"No!" She struggled, trying to break free, to topple him before— "You have to stop, Jack! You have to—" She fought against his arms, tried to throw herself out of their grasp. She wasn't strong enough. But neither was his magic. Not to cross the Edge. Not to cross it and survive.

Jack tore his way across the Edge, carrying her to safety and himself to his destruction.

The broken cry that came from his mouth took them over the Edge, and into her world. The mortal world.

He collapsed as his feet passed over the threshold, momentum carrying them on, out into the thin and meager moonlight. Earth, trees, and briars moved like the blades of some terrible machine on the far side of the Edge. Trying to stop him, to save him from himself. But they failed and then fell still. Too still.

Jenny's eyes dragged their way back to Jack, to the transformation that was even now gripping him, tormenting him like a seizure. He stretched out on the grass, his body arching, jerking as if electrocuted. The change swept over him far too quickly, his legs already no more than ancient wood, his hands reaching for her mottled with bark and lichen.

"No!" She grasped at him. "No. Stay with me!"

"Would," he gasped, and his eyes leaked sap-like tears. "With all my heart, I would. But I can't. Your world. Not mine. Wish . . . wish . . . I . . ."

She grabbed his hand but found herself touching only wood instead of flesh.

"Why did you do it? Why cross? You knew this would happen! You were free. You were king. If you had just stayed—"

His eyes were all that remained, still bright. His crooked smile was melded on a face that looked like the rough bark of the oldest tree. "Nothing in the world . . ." His whisper was the sound of a tree creaking in the high wind, strange and familiar to her. Horrifying. ". . . worth so much as you . . . my Jenny Wren . . ."

And with that he became tree and leaf, moss-covered and silent, lost to her.

"No," Jenny whispered. "Please no."

Her locket still hung around his neck. She reached for it just as the earth unfolded and rose up to swallow it, and what remained of Jack, whole.

Someone had to die. She looked up to find them behind the trees, watching from between branches, all the forest fae, their elation gone, mourning him for a third time, their lost king.

"It's what he wanted," Puck murmured. "To save you. To get you home, to safety. All he ever wanted." The hobgoblin flopped into the long grass right at the Edge, while still remaining on the far side. Safe. He tried to reach for the mound that had been Jack, but he couldn't. Tears covered his face, dripped off his nose and chin, and he rubbed his eyes with clenched fists. "I warned him. I swear I warned him. No forest child can cross the Edge, not without powerful protection. Not even our king, not until they're old and strong as Oberon, not without that sort of power. This second time he had only his love. It wasn't strong enough, not for this. Both journeys were for you, Jenny."

Jenny pressed her hands into the grass and her tears fell between them. The grass drank them down.

Sirens cut the night behind her. She heard shouts, people calling her name and the beams of flashlights searched the darkness. Tom's voice, her mother's, her father's, their neighbors'. But she didn't answer, couldn't listen. All she could hear was the echo of Jack, all she wanted was Jack.

The forest had taken him back, the earth itself growing over him, grass and roots and dirt, flowing over him, reclaiming him at last. Not as a monster, nor a man, but as part of itself. One of its own.

"Here," said Puck, and stretched out his hand, offering something to her. Jenny barely recognized it through her tears. The Leczi's stone. He'd dug it up, brought it back to her. "Wishes may work quicker in my world, but they have more power in yours. Try again."

Snatching it from his hands, Jenny thrust her hand into the earth where Jack had lain, digging down and dropping the stone into the hole. Nothing happened.

"I want him back," she cried. "I want Jack. I love him. Please."

Her words fell around her in the darkness. She looked up and Puck was gone too. The forest stretched dark and silent before her, no longer the forest of the Realm. Just Branley Copse, an isolated piece of ancient woodland that had once been so much more. Her cry burst from her mouth and she raised her face to the trees.

"Jenny!" Tom yelled. He seized her by the shoulders, pulling her to her feet and into the arms of her family.

chapter twenty-seven

Jenny looked up from her book as the professor entered the room. The usual pre-class bustle died down and was replaced with the rustle of papers, click of computer keys, muted laughter, the sounds of people rummaging in bags and folders.

"Okay, settle down, please," the lecturer said. "These tutorials are meant to deepen your knowledge of the mainstream of your lectures and fine-tune your reading lists. So what did you make of your first week? Anyone have any additions to the articles and chapters assigned?"

Silence settled over the classroom. And then someone spoke.

"O'Kelly's *Forest Folklore* and Kennedy's *Green Man?*"

"Good examples, eh . . ." The tutor checked his list of names. "Mr. Woodhouse."

A few offhand remarks, jokes, and chatter followed, and a brief discussion of what had been said. But Jenny wasn't listening, not anymore. She looked up at the student sitting at the table opposite her. He was smiling, a smile that lifted familiar lips and sparkled in mismatched eyes. Jenny's mouth went dry, and the thunder of her heart was so loud she was sure everyone in the room could hear it. But Jack just leaned his chin on his fist and continued to smile without noticing her, his attention on the professor.

Jenny sat in silence through the lesson, listening to them talk about things she'd experienced as though they were just myths, fairy tales, dark tales to frighten children.

And all the time, Jack sat there, and he didn't know her.

Every other moment she thought, no, she'd been mistaken, but then he'd smile, or frown, and it was him. Could only be him. Sometimes his face looked different from the corner of her eye, but when she looked at him, really looked at him, it was Jack.

In the general rush to leave, Jenny lost sight of him. In truth, she could barely bring herself to move. It had been months, and perhaps . . . God, perhaps she was imagining things now. It was possible, wasn't it? They'd watched her after her escape, her parents, overjoyed at the return of their son, but horrified at the so-called attack on their daughter. It had taken her the summer to persuade them to still let her go away to university, though a large part of her had wanted to stay near her brother. She and Tom—they had seven years' worth of time to make up for. Counseling and psychiatrists hadn't really helped, of course. *"What really happened?"* they asked again and again. But Jenny knew better now. She kept most of it to herself. What could she tell them without ending up in an asylum? Tom took the same line, feigned amnesia, and if no one was fooled there, the sheer relief that he was home quelled the questions.

She had kept the faith, secretly, silently, with only Tom to rely on. But even so, her old friend doubt gnawed away at the edges of her mind. And she couldn't help but wonder.

It had to have been real. Hadn't it? That was *Jack*.

There was no sign of him in the corridor when she left the room. Nor on the stairs, or the corridor beneath. Mr. Woodhouse, or whoever he was—the name made her smile—had vanished.

The desolation returned, the smile slipped from her face. Head down, she walked back through the quadrangle, to the lawns beyond. Better this way, without false hope. Better than enduring such a crushing disappointment again.

"Excuse me?" someone called from behind her.

Every cell in her body shuddered. She turned to see him sitting under a tree. An oak tree. She stared at him. It was. It was her Jack.

And at the same time not. Just a boy in jeans and a T-shirt, with a backpack slung over one shoulder. But his eyes . . . his expression, his smile . . .

"You're in my folklore class. Jenny, isn't it?"

"Yes," she managed.

He laughed then, and blushed, getting to his feet with fluid movements. He shook his dark hair out of his eyes. "I'm sorry." He offered his hand. "I can't get over the feeling that I . . . I've met you before . . . I'm Jack," he said.

Jenny let her hand close around his, felt his fingers wrap around hers. The warmth of his skin, the sensations of his touch were real, and just as they had been. It couldn't be a mistake. But how? Her breath hitched her chest as she struggled to stay still. Her eyes snagged on a flash of gold at his neck and she saw it, recognized it.

Her locket.

She stared too long at it and his other hand rose to close over it protectively. His hands, so familiar, long elegant fingers that had entwined with hers once upon a time. His other hand held on to hers and his grip tightened ever so slightly. She could feel the calluses on his palm and fingers. She knew every one.

She dragged her gaze back to his face and found his color high, his eyes bright with embarrassment.

"Jack," she said slowly, aware that her eyes were shining with tears. She must look like a crazy person. He didn't know her. Couldn't remember her. But he was here. He was truly here.

Jack stared at her, a confused smile playing over his lips, fading into something else. A distant recollection, the dawn of a remembered dream. He released her hand slowly and slid his fingers into his jeans pocket. She stepped back, uncertain.

He must have noticed.

"Wait a minute, please Jenny." He reached out, offering her something. A green stone. Polished and bright.

Jenny stared with wide eyes.

"It's yours. Isn't it? I don't know where it came from. I . . . I kind of found it, but it feels like—like it's yours." And he blushed more fiercely, flustered. He looked so very young in that moment with the shadows of the leaves playing over his face, like a lost boy.

She plucked the stone from his palm, closed her hand into a fist around it, and wished. She wished with all her heart.

Jack watched her and slowly, something else trickled into his expression. His eyes widened, as if he were seeing her for the first time. He made a sound like he was trying to breathe and speak at once.

He reached out again and she didn't pull away. Memories flooded his eyes, making their blue and green glisten. His pupils dilated and she saw herself reflected in them, herself and so much more. Jack stepped back, stumbled and caught himself, still staring at her. Then strong arms wrapped her up, lifted her, and she slipped her arms around his neck, holding him close. "Jenny." He murmured her name into her hair, and spun her around in a dizzying circle.

He finally set her down again and took a step back, his hands grabbing hers, his eyes taking her in. "My Jenny Wren. I've missed you." Earnest, true, words she knew she could believe, from the boy she could trust. He touched her nose and smiled. "Freckles."

Jenny threw back her head and laughed, laughter that rang out through the leaves of the oak tree above them. Jack pulled her to him, to kiss her and whisper her name again. And the oak tree above them whispered back, of love and sacrifice, of a king and a queen, and a future made anew.

acknowledgments

There are many people I'd like to thank for their help on this novel and the great fear is always there that I'll leave someone out. So to everyone who has read, guided, critiqued, and made suggestions over the years, thank you.

I'd like to send special thanks to the ever-wonderful Gnats of Ooh Shiny, best writers' support group of all time: Dayna, Lee, Crystal, Kate, Patti, and Lori. Just remember that for every . . . Ooh! Shiny!

Thanks also to Ciara Franck, reader extraordinaire, a bright girl with a very bright future ahead of her. And to the lovely Stacia Kane for giving me a healthy shove in the right direction.

More thanks than I can ever give to my agent that was, the fabulous Colleen Lindsay, my agent that is, the fantastic Suzie Townsend, and my wonderful editor at Dial, Jessica Garrison. The invaluable input, knowledge, and advice you've given has helped to shape this book into something more than I'd dreamed. I'm also deeply grateful to Danielle Delaney for the beautiful jacket design, which takes my breath away each time I see it.

I'd like to thank Jeff Goddard of The Friends of the Ridgeway and Jennifer Delaney for answering many questions on the Ridgeway and Wayland's Smithy. Any mistakes are my own.

Last but by no means least I'd like to thank my family, especially my husband and kids, who hike up hillsides and scramble through passage tombs, who replace the mugs of cold tea with hot ones, and who put up with an awful lot.

You're the best.